WHISPERING MURDERS

DEEPANJANA G. M.

To my husband, Sisir

and son, Sankhya

for inspiring me to take challenges and supporting my dreams

Contents

Acknowledgements   *vii*

1. The Beginning   1

2. Haunting Of The Shadows   3

3. The Plan   9

4. The Party   15

5. After The Party   24

6. The Past - 1994   29

7. Jhimli   37

8. Patravali   42

9. Jhimli And Patravali   47

10. Jhimli's Love Story   51

11. The Writer Mayurakshi Bose   59

12. Vicious Whispers   65

13. Death Of The Koel   70

14. Dead Bodies   79

15. Spotlight On The Previous Year   90

16. Tezz The Car Rental Company   99

17. Patravali's Letter   103

18. The Dark Labyrinth Of Lies   108

19. The Train Journey   114

20. The Favourite Window   120

21. Visiting Senjuti   128

22. Whiff Of A Trail   135

23. Lump And Else Together   142

24. Witness   150

25. The Withered Rose   160

Contents

26. Bring To Light   167

27. Needle In A Haystack   175

28. Skeletons In The Cupboard   183

29. Silver Bullet   192

30. An Evening Of Rememberance   200

31. An Evening Of Stories   212

Acknowledgements

This book would not have happened without my mother's unwavering attention to my made-up ghost stories and murder mysteries. She was the most dedicated audience to my stories. Thank you, Ma, for all those lovely afternoons of storytelling, which made me super innovative and creative with my imagination.

I am forever grateful to my husband and son for being my inspiration, support system, love and motivation. Thank you, Sisir, for being my rock. Thank you, Sankhya, for your excitement and ready feedback.

CHAPTER I

The Beginning

28 May 2022

Despite their age difference, Timir Chatterjee and his wife Patravali made a lovely couple. They owned the magnificent, lucrative property called Senjuti, nested in the picturesque town of Simlipur. It was pretty late in the night, and the melodic tune of a ghazal filled the spacious living room of Senjuti. The glass lamps glowed with mellow yellow lights, creating the perfect romantic atmosphere. Timir Chatterjee looked at his wife Patravali with love and pride. She was humming the ghazal with a promise of a smile playing on her lips. She looked happy and content with her eyes closed.

Timir and Patravali often read together or listened to music after dinner.

Suddenly, the ringtone of the mobile disrupted the heaven-like peacefulness. Timir's phone was ringing. A frown appeared on his forehead when he saw the number. He walked away from the room to avoid disturbing Patravali.

"...*zid na karo...aj jaane ki...*" She was humming along and was wholly immersed in the mood of the ghazal.

THUD! The loud sound came from the room where Timir had gone to take his call.

"What happened?!" Patravali awoke from her blissful state with a jolt.

She ran to the adjoining room and found Timir lying on the floor. His body was writhing as if he was in pain. His face was distorted with pain, and he had difficulty breathing. But he was trying to say something. He looked frightened and had a terrible shock. Patravali realised that he was having a heart attack. Patravali shouted for help and then ran to summon help. She did not see that his phone had fallen from his hands and was lying under the sofa.

The call had been from a family member. At the time, she did not realise that the phone call had been the source of his shock.

The next few desperate hours were spent trying to save Timir Chatterjee. Doctor Dilip Dutta and his associates were in the ICU. Patravali sat outside the ICU on the bench with the live-in maid Bindi.

She looked like a statue; her lips trembled a little as she prayed incessantly.

Around midnight, she was called into the ICU. Timir was lying on the hospital bed. Electrodes were still attached to his chest, and the monitor showed a flat line.

"I am sorry, dear Patravali... I am sorry. Timir is beyond any help," Doctor Dutta said tearfully. He, too, had lost his best friend.

"Did he say anything?" Patravali asked in a stunned manner.

Doctor Dutta hesitated. He did not know the meaning of his last spoken words. He wondered whether he should tell Patravali what he had heard.

"Nir... Nirma... Nam..." Patravali said softly.

Doctor Dutta looked surprised because those were the last comprehensible words spoken by Timir Chatterjee.

CHAPTER II

Haunting of the shadows

22 February 2023

It was very late at night. The world around Senjuti was sleeping, creating silence like a funeral. Senjuti, the expansive, beautifully maintained property's owner, Mrs Patravali Chatterjee, was seated at her favourite study desk. She was busy writing in her journal.

Sunday, 22 February, 2023; 00:30 a.m.

Senjuti

Deceits and lies become the magic poison when whispered repeatedly in soft tones. It works slowly and replaces the truth with a web of lies. Sometimes, I glimpse their actual faces hidden behind their friendly smiles.

Should I try to convince them that no one can replace my Timir and I miss him terribly? But why should I bother? People see what they want to see.

They want a scandal. They cannot forget that once, I had no money and family. And then, Timir married me and made me feel exceptional. He always believed in me and my worth. I thought them to be friends. But they are biased and judgemental. Now, I realise that gossip and scandal are their only entertainment. One day, I hope to be able to laugh at these ridiculous insinuations of a love affair between me and the friendly Professor. He is good company, but I do not need a shoulder to lean on. Although I am not prejudiced or biased against any religion, my narrow-minded neighbours and friends would find it entertaining and scandalous to gossip and spread rumours of a love affair between me, a Brahmin widow and the good Professor, a Muslim gentleman. Sometimes, I doubt his friendship with Timir, but he knows of Timir's actual incidents when he lived another life with Rimjhim.

At times, I feel something dangerous about his charms. But this feeling is ridiculous because he is genuinely a lovely gentleman. I am sure Professor Ahmed feels my reluctance and neutral attitude towards him. He is careful and never says anything to displease me, but his eyes, body language and affectionate behaviour speak for his interest in me. My silence is not my consent, but I do not wish to give undue credence by making protests and unnecessary comments. Neither am I playing with his emotions because my heart is filled with Timir's love.

Mr Raha and Indu made another offer for our beloved Senjuti, but I will not part with it. I must protect it for the child.

Now, I know that Timir had the shock of his life. That phone call had been the cause of the fatal heart attack. And Timir died. What had he meant by Nirma or Nam... I am still trying to find out about the phone call. What did she say that gave him the fatal attack?

Now, I fear the invisible eyes that keep vigil on me continuously...

I feel their cold, menacing stares. Are they planning something evil? Why are Ayah, Bindi, and Dhaniram acting so strangely? Are they working for someone who wants something from me? Who can be that person? Jhimli cannot be involved in all these. She is too proud to play ghost. Then who is orchestrating these? Can I trust Mrs. Mitra? She has no reason to lie. Where is Jhimli's grandmother at present? Is she alright?

Mr. Raha and Indu are interested in Senjuti. But they have an established business and would not be involved in anything illegal or fraud. I cannot imagine either of them dressing up as Rimjhim's ghost to scare me. But can they hire someone?

Suddenly, Patravali heard a soft tapping coming from the back door at the end of the long corridor. She stopped writing in her journal and listened intently. The gentle tapping sound was evident in the silence of the night. It was repeated a few times. Bindi, the housemaid and Ayah used the backdoor to enter the house. They had their keys. They returned to their quarters around half past ten and were not expected to come until tomorrow morning or until summoned. Patravali's heartbeat escalated with fear at the tapping. Slowly, she tiptoed to the back door. She switched on all the lights on her way to the back door. But the tapping stopped as abruptly as it had begun when she reached the back door. She went to the kitchen to see the backyard from the kitchen window, but there was no one. Patravali returned to the corridor connecting all the rooms on the ground floor. She stood alone in the corridor. She was alone in the house. A tingling sensation of terror overwhelmed her. She knew that Rimjhim's ghost would be seen now. This has been happening for a week now. She returned to her study and switched off the lights save for the Murano glass table lamp. She stood at the window in the semidarkness. Patravali's muscles gradually relaxed, and her pounding heart resumed usually.

Patravali was lost in deep thoughts when she suddenly sensed a movement in the garden. She felt the fine hair stand on her nape. It was nearly one in the night, and this was the seventh consecutive day that she had perceived the presence in the garden. Few low-power solar lights in the garden's winding path created more shadows than brightness. The lady in a long red dress appeared in the play of darkness, tinged with a slight halo of light. Her waist-length wavy hair looked darker and wild. Her fair skin was too delicate, like she had no blood in her veins. Patravali looked on, fascinated with terror and curiosity. How could this be true and happening? After all, she had been dead for twenty-eight years. Patravali pinched herself hard and flinched. Yes, she was wide awake. This was no dream. The lady in red was the ghost of Rimjhim Chatterjee—the first wife of Timir Chatterjee and mother of Jhimli.

The woman in red, or Rimjhim's ghost, seemed to be moving without moving her legs. Patravali could see the ghostly apparition moving slowly on the winding cemented path leading to the flame trees where, many seasons ago, Rimjhim had committed suicide. Patravali took out her binoculars to see better. As she adjusted the lenses, the woman went behind the shadow of a flame tree and did not appear again. Patravali was determined to find out more about the ghostly lady in red.

She returned to her study table and started writing again, knowing that the ghostly apparition would not return tonight.

'Every night, the soft tapping sound starts after midnight. The sound stops when I go to the corridor and switch the lights. I can see

no one from the kitchen window. I also switch on the lights in the living room and the dining room. Ayah and Bindi have their keys to the back door, but I have not called them, nor are they expected to come at this late hour. Dhaniram is drinking a lot more. I wonder where he is getting the money to drink and gamble, as I do not pay him any cash. I have caught Ayah looking at me strangely as if waiting for something to happen. Sometimes, I have glimpsed contempt flicker for me in Ayah's eyes, but then she hides it well. Are they keeping a watch over me? If so, then why? I have always been a generous employer and treated them fairly. But why do I feel this subtle change in their attitude towards me? It is hard to pinpoint the exact change. They refer to Rimjhim and her daughter, Jhimli, more often. Their silent, contemptful stares worry me. Bindi once told me that she used to be terrified of Rimjhim, yet she remained loyal to her. And Ayah was like Jhimli's mother. Why are Ayah and Bindi influenced by someone who has been dead for twenty-eight years? What do they know that I do not? When I came unexpectedly to the study this morning, I found Bindi trying to open the locked drawer. She looked guilty when I caught her in the act, but she managed well. I let her go because I need to find the link to the ghost, the knockings, and the constant vigil on me. I am terrified. I feel threatened. Should I tell the good professor? Doctor Dutta needs rest. I shall not confide my troubles to him. What did Timir mean by Nirma? Nam... Nirma...'

Patravali covered her face with her palms and let out a deep sigh. She will fight till she finds the source of all that is happening. Mentally, she noted all her resources, friends, and people she could trust. There weren't many whom she could trust. She needed to keep her wits about her.

Patravali had many questions, but nothing seemed to fit the jigsaw puzzle. Long ago, it was rumoured that Rimjhim's ghost haunted the flame trees. And then Timir had married Patravali. Gradually, Patravali fashioned Senjuti according to her taste and personality. Every corner and nook of Senjuti reflected Patravali's artistic creativity. She had found happiness and love with Timir. But she had become lonely after Timir's sudden death and felt vulnerable by an unknown gripping terror. *'Why does Rimjhim's ghost appear every night?'* Patravali reasoned that she had taken nothing from the dead woman, and they had never met while Rimjhim was living her life. Everything that Timir had given Patravali had been his to give. He had made a fortune from mining mica, supplying raw road construction materials. He had been a successful businessman.

It was nearly two in the morning when Patravali went to her bedroom on the first floor. She peeked at the servant's quarters as she climbed up the stairs. All the windows were dark. She sighed in relief.

It had started raining. The sound of trickling water on the window panes in her bedroom created soothing music. Patravali fell asleep peacefully. But her peaceful sleep became a nightmare. She dreamt that a lady with waist-length dark wavy hair was stooping low, over her, close to her face, watching her breathe. She couldn't see her features clearly, but Patravali sensed that the lady resembled Rimjhim. Patravali's senses heightened, and she felt strange, half-awakened. Suddenly, a cold, silky hand touched Patravali's face. A soft, gentle touch made her breathless, yet she couldn't open her eyes. Gradually, the cold touch changed its pattern and deepened on her throat. She felt suffocated, and Patravali screamed soundlessly. She struggled to free herself of the dangerous touch and threw her arms in the air. She heard a low laugh, menacing and devilish. Patravali woke in a cold sweat in her bedroom. She was all alone, and no one was around. But her bedroom door was ajar, and the water jug at her bedside table had toppled over, spilling the water. Her side pillow lay on the floor beside the bed, and her silken coverlet lay crumpled at her feet. She forced herself to get out of bed and peek into the corridor opening in front of her bedroom. There was no one. Patravali did not look into any of the adjoining rooms. She returned to her crumpled bed and lay there staring at the ceiling.

"It's a dream only", she tried to convince herself. But was it a dream? She touched her throat and felt a little pain. "Surely, I am imagining. No one can enter without making noise." Patravali tried to reason. "Are the servants involved in this?" the thought made her cringe with fear. It was nearly four in the morning. It was still very dark, and she seemed to be the only one awake. She was too agitated to go back to sleep again. "I must act soon. I will start tomorrow for the preservation. I must be as sharp as a nail and quick as lightning.

CHAPTER III

The Plan

25 February 2023

Patravali's secret life began after the dinner ended and the domestic help had retired. She was still working in the study. She has been working till late at night for the past few days. It was a quarter past midnight, yet there was no tapping sound. She thought, "Everything would depend on Mayurakshi's ability to decipher if something goes wrong. I feel like I am walking on a thin sheet of ice. But I shall not be dominated by fear. I can trust Mayurakshi to read my letter properly if anything goes wrong…"

She had spent the last two days organising and notarising legal documents. Patravali had checked thoroughly and looked for hidden cameras in her study. She found nothing. She sat in her study and thought about her day. There was only one glitch that irritated her. It was the failure to communicate with Mayurakshi. Patravali had tried to call her using a public telephone, but the phone was switched off. She felt irritated at her friend's aversion to mobile phones. Patravali didn't take any risk of calling from her home on her mobile for fear of eavesdropping by one of the staff. Patravali tried to compose her jittering nerves and concentrate on the letter. She started writing the most critical letter addressed to Mayurakshi Bose. She had taken precautions by switching off her mobile and laptop before composing the letter. She feared the tapping of her phone and her laptop.

For an hour, she worked hard on the letter, and finally, when satisfied, she sealed it in an envelope. It was way past one, yet there was no sound on the back door. Patravali was ready with a movie camera and was waiting for the ghostly appearance. She opened her journal and started writing.

Patravali's Journal Entry:

'25 February 2023

Senjuti.

The lines are becoming so blurry. What is the truth, and who is lying? All are wearing masks of friendship.

Does the pain of a lost love fade with time? Many years ago, Ashok Trivedi and Rimjhim were the talk of the town. They were in love. Ashok Trivedi loved her with all his feelings, but did Rimjhim love him back? She went to Kolkata for another love but was shunned and took her own life. How could Rimjhim forget about the little one? Her daughter Jhimli. Why couldn't the love of her child stop her from running away?

I don't blame Jhimli for hating me. Her whole world was her father. Timir did everything possible to keep her happy, and he had every right to find love again. He saved me from the shameful, sorry life that I was living. Now, it seems like another life. I tried my best to make friends with Jhimli. But her hate was stronger. Was it hate for me or her ego or something more...? Shall I ever know what made her alienated from her father? She was just fifteen and very stubborn. I hope what I have heard is not valid. But I am not taking any chances. I shall go to Kolkata again and lodge a missing person's report. Mayurakshi is coming home in a week, and I will take her along to dig out the past. As of now, I do not have any hard evidence to prove what Mrs. Mitra said. But then, she is also not so sure. Jhimli's grandmother's phone is switched off. Jhimli has no social media accounts, which I find very unusual. Jhimli's grandmother's Facebook page has no information.

What happens when two acquaintances meet after eighteen years of separation? Of course, I cannot expect to find Jhimli as she was when I last saw her eighteen years ago. She was too proud and too stubborn. But then, she was just a child. In eighteen years, people change their ways and look.

I wish I could confide in Doctor Dutta, but it has only been a month since he suffered a stroke. He needs to recuperate first.

I cannot confide in the friendly Professor Ahmed, too. Sometimes, I feel suspicious of his perfectness. He seems to have stepped out of a storybook. He is too good to be true. Perhaps I am being paranoid unnecessarily. He came here in the first week of January after I returned from Kolkata. He introduced himself as Timir's friend. Then I went to our mica mines and the factory. By that time, he had already established himself at the Club. I know that he is in love with me. He believes in showing off his affection for me. The funny part is that when I am with him, I forget all the suspicions and enjoy his company. Like Timir, he too respects women, which I find very alluring. How silly of me to write so much about him.

On the home front, I caught Ayah red-handed while she was going through my diaries lying on the table. She gave me a flimsy excuse for cleaning, but I am sure she was looking for something else. I caught her trying to see the caller ID when Ms Angana Deb called. Bindi was also trying to understand if I made any will. My house staff are working for somebody else. Why are they trying to deceive me? I feel threatened. Who will gain if something happened to me?'

Patravali stopped writing in her journal. It was quarter to two, and she was tired. Patravali thought, "I think that Rimjhim's ghost is resting today. She will not visit me. They became cautious when I asked about the tappings on the back door and the ghostly appearance. Now, I am sure that my staff are involved. They must have informed the lady in red and her associates. All my preparations will go in vain if she doesn't appear. But I cannot wait here for the rest of the night. I have to bid you goodnight, Rimjhim's ghost."

Patravali switched off the table lamp in the study and sat for a moment in the semi-darkness. She went to the window and stood hidden by the heavy curtains. She looked at the garden through the half-drawn blinds. The garden looked dark and mysterious, with the low solar lights casting huge shadows. The sky looked ominous with dark clouds. Patravali sighed and was about to turn away when suddenly she perceived a movement among the bushes. 'Oh, my camera... here she is coming...' Patravali took out her movie camera and started filming the dark garden. She didn't have to wait long as the red lady appeared suddenly. She walked on the same cemented path where she had been seen walking since the first night. Patravali looked on, fascinated. The lady in red was still far from the house, yet Patravali could make out the woman's whiteness. She had a deathly pallor. Her whiteness was tinged with an unhealthy sheen. Patravali shivered at the appearance and put her camera into action. She stood filming the lady walking effortlessly on the winding path leading to the flame trees. She had the same long, curly black hair and was tall and slender like Rimjhim. Patravali could not make out the features clearly as the lady in red had her head averted to the other side, but there seemed to be a solid resemblance to Rimjhim as she looked in her photographs. Suddenly, the lady in red stopped in her tracks and stood very still. She was still far from the house. Patravali looked on mesmerised. The ghostly lady seemed to be looking at the study window, where Patravali stood hidden by the curtains. 'Does she know I am standing here watching her every move?' Patravali looked closely and thought the resemblance ended with the height, hair and slenderness. The face was not the same as the photograph of Rimjhim. The lady again started her slow walk towards the trees. A dark cloud engulfed everything at that moment, and it started raining. The lady vanished in the dark shadows of the flame trees, where many moons ago, Rimjhim's ghost was rumoured to be lurking.

Patravali was unable to sleep that night. She was tensed about the work that lay ahead. The ominous-looking clouds did not rain much, and it remained dry.

Patravali went out to her Rose Arbour when the sky began to lighten. She was going to execute her plan. She looked around, and as expected, nobody was around. There was no sign of life in the servants' quarters also.

Usually, Patravali worked at her Rose Arbour in the morning every day. She had designed a portion of land in the sprawling open area of Senjuti and lovingly named it The Rose Arbour. She had created a beautiful garden with a gazebo and rose trellis laden with white, red, pink and yellow creeping roses at the Rose Arbour. A wide zig-zag patterned path of thick granite slabs led to the Gazebo at the top of The Rose Arbour. She had been creating miniature lily ponds in big concrete tubs, placed at every convenient flat step that led to the elevated land where the gazebo was built. Patravali was inspired by Claude Monet's famous waterlily paintings series. Patravali sighed sadly as she remembered all the poetry, musical little private parties, and happy moments she had shared with Timir.

She reminded herself to work fast and complete her mission before the household woke. It was the usual routine for Patravali to carry her gardening stuff, books and writing accessories to the gazebo. And today was no different. She looked around and ensured she was alone before starting her work according to her plan. There was no sign of life near the servants' quarters yet. She worked quickly and deftly with concentration.

She finished her secret work sooner than expected and looked around. To her relief, she was still alone in the vast garden. In the far distance, at the other end, she could see the particular flame tree where the ghostly lady disappeared each night. A slight shiver of apprehension ran through her as she realised her plan was set in motion. Now, she must wait for further developments.

Patravali meditated about all the written evidence in her journal and sighed in respite. She thought of Rimjhim, Timir and their daughter Jhimli. Around six thirty, the sun shone through floating light clouds. The morning looked promising, and Patravali relaxed. Patravali sat thoughtfully in the pavilion with a book when Bindi came with the tea and breakfast. Bindi knew Patravali was always happy to work in her garden and became thoughtful while reading. She didn't find anything unusual.

"Bindi, I will not have lunch at home." Patravali smiled as Bindi greeted her while setting her tea and breakfast.

"Bahuji, will you go to the club?" asked Bindi.

"I might, or perhaps I will visit our Doctor Dutta ... why do you ask Bindi?" Patravali sounded casual and not interested.

"What shall I tell if Professor Ahmed comes?" Bindi lingered.

"You need not worry, Bindi. By the way, Dhaniram is drinking too much. You should be concerned. Have you forgotten the days when he drank too much? Are you not controlling the purse anymore?" Patravali asked in a casual tone.

"H-he is, I mean, he is his own master. Now, he is getting money from our son also... I cannot control him anymore. But I promise that he will not disturb you, Bahuji." Bindi sounded agitated.

Patravali sensed that Bindi was lying. Their son had his child to care for, and his wife was expecting again. Bindi's son has always asked for money from his parents. He had taken small loans from Timir several times, which he never paid back. Their son was not to be trusted regarding money matters.

"Is Dhaniram working somewhere else too?" Patravali looked straight at Bindi.

"W-What are you saying? We belong to Senjuti. I cannot forget the old days. Bahuji, we are not rich, but we are loyal and trustworthy," Bindi said emphatically.

Patravali nodded in agreement, and Bindi left her in peace. Patravali remembered that some years back, Dhaniram developed alcoholism, and Timir had spent much money to rehabilitate him. Bindi had the sole control of their money since then. Patravali remembered seeing new gold earrings that Bindi wore now. 'There is another source of income. Definitely,' thought Patravali. "I have done the right thing; my plan is in motion now," Patravali felt assured.

She sipped her tea and smiled as she ticked off the things she would do for the day according to her plan.

CHAPTER IV

The Party

28 February 2023

Patravali studied her reflection on the mirror. She looked lovely in a coral peach-coloured soft silk saree, complementing her peach-like complexion. Her petite, slender figure looked graceful and elegant as always. Her face was framed by loose shoulder-length hair, and her dark almond-shaped eyes looked darker with a hint of kohl. Patravali took out her favourite gold necklace with matching earrings. The gold pendant was shaped like a rose with tiny diamonds in the centre, and the matching earrings dangled with thin gold strings. It was the first gift that Timir had given her after their marriage. Patravali walked from her bedroom to the study to check her desk and the drawers. As she entered, Ayah came and stood at the door.

"Aren't you going to the marriage anniversary party?" asked Ayah in smooth tones.

Patravali nodded affirmatively.

"Why do you need the notebook and the pen?" Ayah asked bluntly.

Patravali was a little surprised at Ayah's impertinence and ignored her. Patravali put the tiny Moleskine dairy and her favourite Mont Blanc pen in her bag. She always carried a small notebook and a pen. Patravali checked the locks of her study desk and walked out of the study.

"Shall I wait for you, Bahuji?" Ayah sounded polite, but she looked at Patravali rather curiously.

Patravali shook her head negatively and went out.

She drove her white Tata Tiago to the club. The party was in full motion when she entered the hall, and a little stage was set for a performance. The hosts, Mr. and Mrs. Raha, came forward with warm, welcoming smiles. Mrs. Indu Raha was a friend and neighbour. She smiled mischievously and whispered, "He is already here and waiting for you, dear. This is what friends are for." Patravali understood that Indu was referring to the Professor. She blushed as she remembered the evening when Indu had invited him to her anniversary party. The Professor was visiting her at Senjuti when Indu came to ask her to the anniversary party. She had also extended her invitation to the Professor. Indu had smiled knowingly, which was irritating. And now she was pretending that she had invited him for her sake. Patravali had expected to see him, yet now, she felt ill at ease. She had hoped for a pleasant social evening with friends and acquaintances, but if Indu wanted entertainment at her discomfort, then she would have to leave as early as possible. She promised herself to be as inconspicuous as possible.

Patravali blended in with other guests and saw Doctor Dilip Dutta sitting in a corner with a coffee mug. They smiled. Mrs Sharma came forward and started babbling. Patravali could not evade Mrs Sharma without being rude and had to listen to her anecdotes regarding buying a gift. Doctor Dutta had risen from his seat and came forward to speak to Patravali, and at the same time, Professor Faisal Ahmed also came forward. He looked impeccable in a classic charcoal grey suit. His shoulder-length curly hair framed his handsome face. He sported a well-groomed moustache and French beard. The expensive-looking retro horn-rimmed glasses suited his wheatish complexion. There was a touch of grey near his temple. He had full cheeks, which did not mar his good looks. He was in great shape at fifty-two. Patravali had noticed that he was appreciated by women who came in contact with him. Patravali introduced him to Doctor Dutta, and they talked pleasantly. Professor Ahmed was a gifted speaker and had seen many places in India. He and Doctor Dutta shared many common interests, and they started a conversation. Doctor Dutta looked at Patravali rather quizzically as if asking her decision regarding her relationship with the professor. He seemed to like him. Soon, Mr and Mrs Singh confiscated Doctor Dutta to share private family issues.

The evening was pleasant. Professor Ahmed was good company and very attentive towards Patravali. But, soon, this made Patravali ill at ease because many guests were staring at them. She knew that before the end of the evening, the rumours of her alleged relationship and affair with the professor would be confirmed by many. And Indu Raha would be delighted to be proven correct. Mr Ashok Trivedi was eating and observing others from another hall corner. He waved his hand towards Patravali and gestured for her to come. Patravali obliged, which seemed like an opportunity to evade the Professor's attention.

"Hello, Patravali! I can see your professor is here, too." Smiled Mr. Trivedi.

"Mr Trivedi, where have you hidden your charming wife?" asked Patravali in a stilted tone.

"She does not like parties; besides, she is visiting her family in Banaras. Didn't you want to make a new will? I still have the ground floor office at my home. When can I expect you? Or shall I visit you in the morning one of these days?" Mr. Trivedi asked in his best professional tone.

Patravali was slightly surprised that Mr Trivedi knew about her wish to make a new will. She replied in a normal conversational tone, "I will let you know when I am ready. At present, I am happy with Timir's wishes."

Mr Trivedi was a successful lawyer, and almost all the residents of Simlipur consulted him. He also looked after the legalities of the Club. Many years ago, Timir and Ashok Trivedi had been friends. Then Rimjhim ruined the friendship. Patravali was about to excuse herself when Mr and Mrs Mehta summoned Patravali. They were talking to Professor Ahmed, and as soon as Patravali joined the little group, Mrs Mehta hugged her and smiled at Patravali all knowingly. They had been talking about weddings and love at first sight. At this point, Indu and two other couples also joined them. Suddenly, the professor hinted at his experience of finding love, which irritated Patravali. Everyone looked happy and congratulated the professor, who suddenly seemed to blush and was tongue-tied. Indu made lurid jokes and showered meaningful looks on Patravali. Indu was loud and had too many drinks already. Mrs Mehta, Indu, Professor Ahmed, and Mr Mehta discussed the advantages of finding love later in life. They hinted at the relationship between Patravali and Professor Ahmed.

Patravali decided to take refuge in the garden to cut short everyone's amusement. Some guests were sauntering with wine glasses in the garden, and a couple approached Patravali. They were Mr and Mrs Singhania. She was well known as a straight talker and said without any frills, "I congratulate you, dear Patravali. You should celebrate each day. Life follows death, and staying alone in your big house is a crime. You were very good to Timir Babu. You gave him happiness, but now, he is no more. You are too young and pretty to waste your life in anguish." Mrs Singhania meant well, but Patravali didn't enjoy the implications. She thought, "Am I showing too much affection for The Professor? Why are they reading more into the relationship when there is nothing more than cordial liking and mutual respect? I should be more careful with the Professor. He is excellent company, but..."

"Are you hiding or running away from all the attention? Shall I, too, congratulate you? I saw the Professor pouring his heart out to you... well done, Patravali. He is an excellent choice." Mr. Ashok Trivedi's soft voice jolted her from personal musings. Patravali excused herself rather embarrassedly and saw the Professor through one of the long windows. He was busy refilling his glass. He was alone. After filling his wine glass, the professor seemed to be looking for her. Patravali didn't want to meet him again so soon and sneaked quietly to the first floor to visit the restroom.

Patravali took the lift to the first floor and remained in the deserted restroom for many minutes. She looked at her mobile while waiting, but there was no signal. She killed the time staring at the mirror and thinking about her odd situation. She felt angry at Indu for spreading the rumours of her alleged love affair. Patravali was angry at herself for showing friendship to the Professor.

After her tumultuous thoughts were bridled, she slowly and silently walked through the deserted corridor. The first floor was completely deserted. All the rooms were closed, and the lights switched off. It felt a little eerie to walk down the lonely corridor. Unmindfully, her eyes scanned the camera installed in the corridor, and to her surprise, there was no blinking light in it, which meant it was not working. She wondered about the quality of maintenance of the Club. The club's first floor housed the library, the billiards room, the table tennis hall, the squash room, the cards and carrom room, and a small conference room. The restrooms were at the end of the corridor, and the lift and stairs were at the other end. As she walked past the billiards room, she heard some voices. Someone spoke in very low tones as if taking care not to be heard, but the sound travelled in the hollowness of the big billiards room. Patravali would have ignored and walked away, but she had to stop as she heard a familiar name mentioned. "Did I hear Senjuti?" Patravali took care to remain silent and hid herself behind the thick curtains at the door. She peeked inside. The room was dimly lit, with only one low-powered light at the farthest corner. It wasn't easy to see with certainty in the semi-darkness. Three men were standing closely. Patravali could only see a heavily built man properly. He was speaking and looking from one to the other. The other two men were back towards the door, and Patravali couldn't see their faces. Both the men were wearing white shirts and dark trousers. Patravali tried to catch the words. She heard bits of words and started recording on her mobile. She could catch fragments, 'garage... I told... Senjuti... under control... Jaipal... Jaipal... shot... under control... Senjuti... Chatterjee..."

Patravali's heart almost leapt out with terror. She was puzzled and thought, "What are these men doing or planning? Why are they discussing Senjuti? Who is Chatterjee? Do they mean me?"

"...police... not on the body, I checked... not yet dead... yes,...I checked...not dead, yet... not in his possession..." the man continued in low tone.

"Body! Does he mean a dead body?" Patravali's thoughts were disrupted as another man spoke louder, "I have everything under control. I did my part, and I am still working on it. She doesn't suspect anything... Senjuti is still..."

"Control...," the third man's deep voice cautioned.

Patravali did not wait there any longer. She had heard enough to know that she was the target of these men for some reason. She reasoned that Senjuti was a lucrative property, and these men wanted it for business. But she doubted the nature of their business.

She was frightened and shaken by the secret she overheard. She decided to leave and started walking towards the lift when suddenly she heard a phone call ringing in the billiards room. One of them started talking loudly, and his footsteps were heard coming.

Suddenly, she had an idea and tiptoed towards one of the dark, empty rooms on the first floor. After executing her thought, she waited for a second and crept out stealthily. She went back to the party. The singer and his band were already performing, and many guests were dancing. Patravali blended in with the other guests. Suddenly, someone tapped her shoulder. She almost jumped and turned to see the smiling face of the Professor. "Where have you been hiding? I was looking for you, and so was Mrs Raha," He asked in a friendly manner, but his bright eyes looked at Patravali curiously. The intensity of his curious eyes made her very uncomfortable. He was bending close to her as he spoke, and she noticed Mrs Mishra watching them with a satisfied look.

When she found the professor smiling at her, his eyes were curious behind his smile. She saw that Mrs. Singh and Mrs. Mishra were watching them with a satisfied look.

"Is something wrong, Patravali? You look worried and a little lost." Professor Ahmed stooped closer to her ears and almost whispered.

"N-No. Why do you ask?" Patravali sounded frightened and tried to control her shaking nerves.

He was tall, and their bodies were touching. He was too near for her comfort. She knew they were fuelling the gossip mongers, which irritated her. By this time, Indu had seen them talking, standing close to each other, and she came forward with a wide smile.

"Is something the matter, dear? I hope you approve of the songs. Or are you having a lover's tiff?" Indu said in a loud voice, her speech slurred.

"No, I am having a terrible headache. I have been outside. Thought it would clear my head, but it didn't help." Patravali told in a stilted manner.

"I must take you home, dear Patravali," said Professor Ahmed most concernedly. Indu laughed and declared in a slurred speech that soon there would be a wedding. The guests, standing close by, clapped and congratulated the couple. Patravali was mortified.

She didn't enjoy being the centre of attention.

Patravali walked away from the hall. On her way to the garden, she remembered that she needed to tell someone the secret before the night's end. She has to go home and do as she meant to do to protect the incriminating video. She was suddenly frightened as she comprehended the task before her.

Patravali looked around her, but no one was following her. She was alone in the well-lit corridor leading to the garden. She was away from the curious eyes and ears, and while walking to the garden, she took out her phone and called Mayurakshi. It was about four in the evening in Copenhagen. But before the ring could be completed, Mrs. Mishra and Indu came out looking for her. Professor Ahmed followed them.

"Shall I take you home? How are you feeling? Come, I will drive you home." Professor Ahmed sounded too invested in her wellbeing.

"I just want to breathe some fresh air. I will join you all in a moment." Patravali said tiredly.

"Yes, dear, we shall leave you in the care of Professor Ahmed". The ladies laughed and went back.

Professor Ahmed stood with Patravali without speaking anything. Her mind was in turmoil when she saw Doctor Dutta sitting near the French window. He looked a little tired.

"I need a glass of water," said Patravali. "I think you should eat something more solid. Your headache will get better when you've eaten. Let me bring something for you." Insisted Professor Ahmed and Patravali sighed in relief.

Professor Ahmed went inside to get some food for her while she went to Doctor Dutta.

"I have read about Queen Nefertiti. Doctor, please remember that I read about the most beautiful Egyptian Queen Nefertiti. It is most important for you to remember and tell Mayurakshi that I have read about Queen Nefertiti." Patravali babbled but looked most sincere.

Doctor Dutta was stunned at her incoherent speech. He looked genuinely concerned.

"Patravali, I thought that you never drink!"

"I have told you an important secret. Take it seriously, doctor Dutta." Patravali looked earnestly.

At that moment, Professor Ahmed came in with a plate full of food. He looked at them curiously. The singer was singing a slow number, and many were swaying with the music.

"Something important going on? You look very tensed," Professor Ahmed asked her.

"Headache... I was talking about my headache. I don't think that you have been introduced." Patravali introduced them.

The Doctor recovered quickly from his shock and said in mild tones, "I think she needs to rest. I know that you suffer from migraine."

Patravali nodded and smiled gratefully at the doctor. He was looking at her intently, and she nodded in agreement. She asked the Professor to remain and enjoy the party and left hurriedly.

She wanted to be seen leaving alone and put a break on the gossip mills.

Patravali's hands shook a little from the party's experience, but she managed to take her car out of the parking. She chalked out a plan while driving carefully. She kept her wits about her and ensured she was not being followed. She remembered that the cameras on the first floor at the club looked black, with no power light blinking. She relaxed a bit.

CHAPTER V

After the Party

28 February 2023

Patravali drove through the lonely avenue and reached home by thirty minutes past ten. The sky rumbled loudly. It was going to rain soon. She looked at the servants' quarters, but there was no light, and she remembered that Bindi was visiting her son and his family. Ayah was over seventy years of age and usually retired by ten. She needed to rest. Patravali's agitated nerves became calmer as minutes went by. She was always happy and peaceful at Senjuti, but tonight, she was tense as she had an important task.

Patravali walked to her favourite Rose Arbour to do her most important work at hand. Her heart beat wildly as she went up the wide zigzag steps of the Rose Arbour. At a distance, her house stood bathed in semi-darkness. Her hands shook a little as she started doing the job at hand. She was afraid of being watched, but tonight, she was alone. She felt thankful that Dhaniram was drinking again and was in no condition to spy at forty minutes past ten.

She returned to her favourite study after accomplishing her mission to calm her jittered nerves. Patravali thought about the party and realised that a lot was happening on the social front. She remembered the secret meeting she had witnessed at the billiards room, and a cold wave passed through her. "What did they mean by 'not on the body'? What do I not know? Why do they need Senjuti? For business purposes only?"

Suddenly, she couldn't bear it anymore and wanted to hear a human voice. She called her gardener cum all-handyman Dhaniram by the intercom. He mumbled something indecipherable when he finally answered after many rings. Patravali took out her mobile and called Mayurakshi, but she cut it off before the call could be placed. "No, I can't call using my mobile. This phone might be tapped... I must have patience... in the morning, I shall go..."

Suddenly, the mobile came alive with the Professor's call. Patravali was grateful for the call. Although a few minutes earlier she had promised herself to maintain a distance from the professor socially, tonight she felt thankful for his friendly chat.

"Hello Professor."

"Wow! This is the first time that you answered my call so promptly. It seems that you are okay after today's party," The Professor said in his usual deep throaty voice.

Patravali wanted to tell him about her fears, but instead, she said in a friendly tone, "I didn't expect all the guests to read so much more when we have no future together. I feel bad that you were dragged into all this."

"Dear Patravali, they are not mistaken. I am sorry my feelings for you were too transparent for them to read. I will wait for you forever because I have fallen in love." The Professor sounded happy.

"Please do not talk of love now but friendship, yes. I..." Patravali didn't finish her thoughts.

"Hmm... you are feeling lonely. The house is big, and the night is thunderous. Soon it will start raining too. Do you need a friendly voice and a friendly ear? I have no plans of going to bed anytime soon and would be very happy to be useful to you." It was as if the Professor could read her thoughts.

Patravali was still very agitated and thought about the robust and well-built professor and his charming presence, which would be very assuring.

"You are hesitating. That means I have a chance of meeting you tonight. Let's have a deal. I will visit you now, and we can chat more well over steaming coffee or chocolate mugs. I will stay there until all the guests from the party have returned to their abode, and we can keep this meeting a secret. So, no social pressure. I will not mention my feelings. And I will remain in my seat and be as gentlemanly as ever. Promise."

Patravali smiled at the offer but remained silent for a few seconds.

"Did I hear you say, 'Professor Ahmed, you may come now'?" The Professor said laughingly.

Patravali accepted his offer. She scolded herself for being a coward, but now the deed was done, and the Professor was on his way to Senjuti. She went upstairs to her room and changed into a comfortable salwar kameez. The front doorbell rang as she was coming downstairs.

She opened the door and found the Professor standing at her door, looking very thoughtful. She ushered him to her study. "You are looking rather thoughtful...," Patravali commented.

"Tell me, do you believe in ghosts?" Asked the Professor.

"What!?" suddenly, Patravali knew why he asked.

"I don't want to scare you, but there is someone in your garden... she looks a little ghostly. I have never been scared before... do you know who is she? The Professor asked hesitatingly.

Patravali knew the identity of the referred ghostly woman very well, but she feigned ignorance. It was a surprise that he, too, could see Rimjhim's ghost. Her staff had denied knowledge of Rimjhim's ghost. It proved that she was right in her mind and not imagining things.

He said, "If you have never seen her before, then tonight you would. Come to the window. Stay hidden behind the curtains and watch..." They both went to the window and saw Rimjhim's ghost walking in the garden. She was walking on the same path she was seen walking every night. Patravali shivered a little and asked in a shaky voice, "You can also see her. What is she wearing?"

"A floor-sweeping red dress. She is rather beautiful in a horrid way and has a shapely body. Who is she?" The Professor sounded curious and alert.

"She is Timir's first wife. She committed suicide about twenty-eight years ago. Every night, she comes to visit me. My staff denied any knowledge of her. You are the first person after me to see her." Patravali narrated the story of her death.

Suddenly, there was a thunder. It seemed to be very near. They looked back at the garden, but the apparition was gone. Professor

Ahmed sat thoughtfully with Patravali for some time.

"Is the ghost reason for you to be afraid? I know that you are afraid tonight. So don't deny, Patravali."

Patravali didn't answer. The Professor kept his word and remained on his sofa for a long time. They said many things other than the ghost or any incidents related to the club.

It was past midnight when the Professor asked for her leave. She was reluctant to say that she was still afraid of staying alone. Patravali became thoughtful and contemplated confiding in him. She looked at the assuring calm presence of the Professor. Something in her made her blurt out, "I know that Senjuti is the target for some bad purpose. I feel I am in danger, too."

The Professor was very surprised and had nothing to say for a few minutes. He sat down on the sofa again and became thoughtful. He said unexpectedly, after what seemed like ages, "I think someone is trying to scare you. Maybe they are doing it out of jealousy. What made you say that you are in danger, too?"

Patravali told him part of the secret meeting that she had overheard. She did not say to him about the video. Nor did she narrate word for word.

The Professor looked a little stunned at the news. He hesitated, "Are you sure they did not see you?

Patravali nodded in agreement and became thoughtful.

The Professor said cautiously, "Aren't you taking a huge risk? What if they had cameras installed in secret places? I think you should go into hiding for a few days. Why don't you relax somewhere else for a few days?"

"You mean that I should run away? Do I seem to be like the running away type? I don't think running away would solve the problem." Patravali sounded firm.

"Don't run away because running away from problems has seldom been the solution. I am suggesting you take a back seat for a while. Here, the residents talk so much about us that it irritates you. I will remain here while you go on a short trip. Or, if you want, I can escort you safely to someplace where no one will bother you for a few days. Then you can come back and resume your life." Suggested the Professor.

"How will it work? Rather, I will go to Kolkata tomorrow morning and talk to Detective Dipto Bhanu. I am sure he would help me." Said Patravali.

"Great idea! Why don't we start tonight? I mean, I am a very reliable driver, and if we start now, we can reach Kolkata by morning. You know that the early bird catches the worm." The Professor said enthusiastically.

"Now? In this horrible weather?" Patravali was surprised.

"Why not? I am very deft in driving through bad weather. I guarantee your safety, Madam Patravali. besides, even if the members of the secret meeting decide to visit you tonight, they would find the nest empty." The Professor's gusto made her smile, and she consented.

After half an hour, the Professor was seen carrying a big bag. It must have been heavy as he was bending with its weight.

When it started raining, Dhaniram had been sleeping in a drunken stupor under one of the trees. He woke up just in time to see the Professor carrying a heavy luggage. Dhaniram saw him put it in the back seat. Then Patravali came out and got in the passenger seat. She was still wearing the same sari she wore to the party. Dhaniram tried to walk, but his unsteady footsteps led him to the side of the path on the muddy ground. He tried to climb back on the path, but the car was already starting. He shouted from where he stood, "Bahuji!"

His voice sounded muffled, drowned in the pitter-patter of rain.

Patravali turned her face for a second to the source of the sound. Maybe she had sensed the sound. Dhaniram saw the Patravali's face for a split second before she turned away from his side. The Professor was sitting in the driver's seat.

Dhaniram smiled slyly. Patravali's car sped past him carrying the alleged lovers.

CHAPTER VI

The Past – 1994

RimJhim Chatterjee and the Flame Trees

There is always more to a story than what can be seen. Simlipur is a small town where the residents lead a peaceful, serene life. The British established the small picturesque town of Simlipur, and the colonial flavour still lingered among the residents. Many of the old houses were once owned by the British people living in India, and the houses built later were also designed harmoniously with the older houses. Senjuti was one of the old houses with expansive grounds and a large garden. Mr Timir Chatterjee and his wife Rimjhim Chatterjee were the owners of Senjuti. They had a little girl named Jhimli. She was five years old. The Chatterjee family looked like a picture-perfect happy family. But there are always undercurrents that flow along the daily life.

Rimjhim Chatterjee created undercurrents in her family, and the dark clouds of betrayal and deception hovered over the Chatterjee family. Rimjhim was always a hot topic at the Club. The Club was established when the British ruled our country. The members took pride in maintaining the same standard as before. The club members were the elite of Simlipur.

It was the night of 31 December 1994. The New Year's party was in full swing at the Club of Simlipur. Ladies were adorned in fancy silk sarees, and their husbands wore their finest suits. The band was playing happy tunes. Many were dancing on the dance floor. Some of the members were still to come. The Chatterjee couple were also late. The thirty-three-year-old, young, promising lawyer, Mr Ashok Trivedi, was sitting in a corner watching all the couples. He looked very anxious and gloomy. He was waiting for Rimjhim Chatterjee. He looked at his watch for the tenth time in ten minutes and nodded in frustration. Ashok Trivedi drank too many glasses of water while waiting for Rimjhim and now needed to go to the toilet. He cursed himself and went. Rimjhim Chatterjee was talking to a couple when he returned a few minutes later. Rimjhim was looking stunning in a figure-hugging, floor-sweeping red silk dress. She looked like a model on a fancy magazine cover.

Rimjhim was like a magnet, and men and women were attracted to her. She was a natural charmer, gorgeous, sexy, intelligent, and confident. Men fell in love with her charms, and women became jealous of her popularity amongst men. There were always rumours of her alleged love affairs. Ashok Trivedi had heard of her recent love interest in Kolkata.

Timir Chatterjee came with his wife Rimjhim but sat alone at the table some minutes later. Doctor Dilip Dutta and his newly wedded wife Sujata joined him.

"Where is Rimjhim?" Asked Sujata.

Timir shrugged his ignorance and said without malice, "I am afraid that I cannot tell about her... engagements for the evening. She is her own master and has her own social life."

Sujata looked a little surprised. She was still new in Simlipur and hadn't heard of Rimjhim's reputation. Doctor Dutta changed the topic and asked about Jhimli. Timir's face lit up at the mention of his daughter Jhimli. They chatted pleasantly while eating the delicious food. Timir scanned the hall casually and couldn't see his wife anywhere. Ashok Trivedi was also not in his place. Timir knew that their friendship was more intimate than the social norm.

The band started playing the most popular tune of the time, and Sujata called her husband on the dance floor. Timir sat alone in his place. He went in search of Rimjhim in another part of the Club, which was now deserted. Timir looked into the rooms and found Ashok and Rimjhim in one of the corner rooms.

"Rimjhim, please,... Rimjhim, say the word, and I will leave everything behind, and we can go. Please, Rimjhim, say it." Ashok Trivedi looked like a puppy asking for a treat. Rimjhim pushed him away gently and smiled. "Please Rimjhim..."

"Ashok, it is over. Whatever happened or was happening between us is now over. There is no future for us. Go back to your wife and leave me alone. Let us part as friends. No bitterness... please. We both enjoyed our time, but now... it is truly over." Rimjhim said in placid tones.

"Who is your new love interest? What does he look like? Does he stay here in Simlipur?" Ashok Trivedi sounded angry.

"Ashok! Please stop it. You should hear yourself. I am Rimjhim, which means the sound of the falling raindrops. Like the raindrops, I, too, cannot be controlled or owned. I trickled and fell all over you. We both enjoyed the ride, but now we have no tomorrow. Please let me go..." Rimjhim's voice shook as she spoke the last words.

Ashok Trivedi looked at her closely and became concerned. He said very softly, "You are crying! Why?"

"I lost Timir's love and esteem. I lost my chances of happiness with my little daughter." Rimjhim said between her tears.

Timir did not wait any longer but went back to the party. The band played a disco tune, and almost all the guests were on the dance floor. The light had dimmed, and the big clock displayed the time. Then, the countdown began for the new year.

"Ten, nine, eight, seven, six, five, four, three, two, one... Happy New Year!" Everyone shouted happily. They all embraced each other. Timir stood in a corner looking dejected. He still loved his wife despite all her affairs and infidelities. Rimjhim was still his wife. She was the mother of their child.

But Rimjhim liked to play with the emotions of men who were well-established and confident in their careers. She enjoyed playing with them and then flung them over when she got them under her control.

After the party, on their way to Senjuti, Rimjhim said unexpectedly, "Tomorrow, I shall leave for Kolkata. I will stay there for a month. Maybe a few days more than a month. Will you be here, or must you be away too?"

"For a month! And what about Jhimli? She is just five years old. don't you understand that she needs her mother?" Timir asked angrily.

Rimjhim laughed without humour and said, "You always put Jhimli as an excuse. She has two parents, and you can be a wonderful doting father. Besides, she has a dutiful and devoted Ayah. Why can't I leave your prison occasionally? Besides, having her was your idea. You loved the little accident. Having a child was your idea of the ideal family, happiness, and fulfilment. Don't include me in your ideals."

Timir Chatterjee was angry now, and his tone matched his mood. He said, "Why keep reminding me that you didn't want her? How many days have you stayed here in the last six months, Rimjhim? You have been visiting like a guest once every month for a few days. You treat Senjuti as a hotel. This cannot go on forever. Either you stay here as my daughter's mother or else..."

Rimjhim said seriously, "Are you threatening me, Timir? I don't need your money, neither your adoration nor your devotion. You can be a happy father without me, for you can have Jhimli. After all, she was your idea of a complete home, blissful family. I don't want any part in your ideas. Soon, I shall meet a lawyer and end my misery. I thought motherhood would change my views, but I feel suffocated and want my freedom back."

The couple reached home in a sour mood. Fortunately, Jhimli was fast asleep and did not see her parents in their present state. Rimjhim went to her room and closed the door with a bang.

Bindi and Ayah came running to assist her in getting dressed for the night. They were dismissed as soon as they entered. They looked scared. Rimjhim was in one of her famous foul moods.

The next day morning, Rimjhim was seated at the table for breakfast. Jhimli looked at her mother with awe and love. She loved her mother, but she felt too shy to talk freely in front of her. Ayah had brought up Jhimli, and she found Ayah more accessible than her mother. Timir came and joined them for breakfast.

"Jhimli, promise me that you will be a good girl. I am going to Kolkata, and you will stay with your Baba. Okay?" Rimjhim said sweetly to her daughter when Timir joined them.

"Mumma, are you going to Nanu's house? I want to go too. See my new dress." Jhimli said shyly and slowly.

Rimjhim looked at her and smiled. She said, "You are looking like an angel, Jhimli. Your dress is so pretty. And you can visit your Nanu in the summer break or when your Baba will take you there."

Timir looked at Rimjhim angrily. He wanted something permanent for Jhimli. The child always craved Rimjhim's attention and love. But for Rimjhim, the child was like shackles tying her to the simple domestic life. Rimjhim hated the simple domesticity.

Rimjhim noticed Timir's accusing eyes and blurted out angrily, "You don't own me, Mr. Timir Chatterjee. And you knew that I was not keen to settle down here for the rest of my life. This place is like the little stale pond. I shall go as I please and return on my terms."

Timir was very angry, but he controlled his tongue and temper. He asked Ayah to take Jhimli away to her room. The idea of a loving family breakfast on the first day of New Year was broken forever.

Rimjhim went to Kolkata that very day as promised and did not return for three months.

It was April, and Simlipur was dressed as a bride, with all the Simul trees laden with red flowers.

Jhimli was playing ball games with her Ayah on the big lawn. Ayah was devoted to Jhimli as she had raised her like a daughter since birth. Rimjhim had not returned since the first day of January. The household worked like a well-oiled machine with the help of Bindi, Ayah and Dhaniram.

Mr Chatterjee went to the garden, and Jhimli ran happily towards him.

"Baba! Can we go out because I want an ice cream?" said Jhimli.

"Yes, we can go to the Club." Said Timir Chatterjee.

"When will Mumma come back?" asked little Jhimli shyly.

"Are you missing her? Did you talk to your Nanu?" Timir asked.

"Nanu doesn't know when she will come. I think she loves to be in Kolkata. But you and I can have strawberry, chocolate, and butterscotch ice cream."

Timir's heart bled at Jhimli's awareness of her mother's irritation regarding her. Sometimes, Rimjhim would behave lovingly towards Jhimli when she was in a motherly mood. But that was rare. Now, Rimjhim wanted to be free of every responsibility. She basked in the adoration of young men in high places and felt it essential to be the talk of the town. Rimjhim flirted openly with Timir's friends and acquaintances. She loved to embarrass him. Once, she had tried her charms on Doctor Dutta also. But fortunately, he proved to be a better friend.

The father and the daughter were returning home after having the promised ice cream when Jhimli asked, "Baba, will you play Holi with me and Priya and Rahul?"

"Of course, Jhimli," Timir remembered that Holi, the festival of colours, was just a few days away.

On the day of the Holi, Jhimli played with colours with her friends and Timir under the flame trees at Senjuti. The orange-red, flame-coloured flowers bejewelled the flame trees stood in a row at Senjuti. Timir took Jhimli to Doctor Dutta's place that evening for a friendly dinner. They had a pleasant evening. It started raining on their way back home. They found Rimjhim home when they returned. She was sitting all alone in the darkened living room. Timir had never seen his wife anything like that evening. He switched on the lights in the living room and saw Rimjhim tremble hysterically.

She looked far different than her usual diva avatar. Her beautiful eyes had a sunken look, and her hair looked unkempt. She was very quiet, and something seemed to have died within her. Her blank stare was frightening.

Seeing Rimjhim in that awful state, Timir felt his anger and defeat melting away. His hatred was turned into compassion for his unfaithful wife. Slowly, he embraced her to offer her comfort and assurance that he was there for her.

"Don't touch me again, Timir. Yes, I am at last defeated and scorned and rejected. I lost the love of my life, but I can certainly live without your honourable love and pity. You cannot insult me with your compassion. We cannot start where there is no love. I cannot love anyone now." Shouted Rimjhim and pushed Timir away before running to her bedroom.

Timir tossed and turned in bed that night as he could not sleep. Rimjhim's demeanour had shocked him. Timir was more disturbed than usual, for Jhimli had witnessed his defeat. Jhimli had heard everything that Rimjhim said. Little Jhimli had been too shocked and frightened.

Gradually, as the hours slipped by, Timir's humiliation and pain subsided into a painful slumber filled with nightmares.

Suddenly, he was awakened by a lot of commotion. It was Bindi and Ayah howling and beating on his bedroom door.

Timir was fully awake in a moment and leapt out of bed. He had barely opened his door when Bindi and Ayah ran towards the garden without any explanation. He, too, ran after them. Dhaniram was kneeling on the wet ground in the garden under one of the flowering flame trees.

Then Timir saw her. Under the flame tree, Rimjhim was lying down on the cold, bare, wet earth. Timir ran to her and knelt beside her. Rimjhim's hands were stone cold. Her dead, unseeing eyes stared blankly at the flame tree branches laden with beautiful flowers. A little white foam had dried around her full lips. Rimjhim had committed suicide under her favourite flame tree.

After a while, the rumours started. The rumours of the mourning, the mysterious whispers and the ghost of Rimjhim walking around the garden at Senjuti.

Many local workmen and maids claimed to have seen the beautiful, unhappy ghost of Rimjhim dressed in her favourite floor-sweeping red dress. Some believed she visited Jhimli, and others said she repented wasting her life. The workers, hired temporarily, refused to work near the flame trees after sunset. They said that the flame trees whispered eerily after sunset, which sounded like Rimjhim lamenting and whispering. The flame trees of Senjuti became the talk of the town, where Rimjhim had breathed her last. People said that Rimjhim could never be free now. She will always haunt the Flame Trees at Senjuti.

CHAPTER VII

Jhimli

The Summer of 2005

Jhimli woke up with a start. Her body was bathed in sweat, and her throat felt dry. She was again having the same nightmare. Her mother was lying under the flame trees, and she was running to her mother to wake her up. The ground was still soggy from the rain. Her mother, Rimjhim, slowly sat up as Jhimli reached. "Mumma, Mum...," Jhimli cried and hugged her mother. Rimjhim did not hug her daughter. Suddenly, Rimjhim's limp body fell backwards on the ground, taking Jhimli with the force of falling. She was clinging to her mother and realised that her mother was dead. She looked at her mother's face, and the dead eyes stared back at her lovelessly.

She was merely five years old when Rimjhim committed suicide. No one had noticed the little girl, who had awakened by the chaotic noises in the house. The little girl was Jhimli and had seen her mother's dead body. Jhimli had always wanted affection and love from her mother, but she had been very busy with her social life.

It was dark outside, and Jhimli sat on her shared bunk bed. The other girls were still sleeping peacefully. She was in a residential school and was now fifteen years old. She was going home with her father tomorrow, and the thought comforted her.

The summer holidays were always exceptional for Jhimli. Her father made it more special by taking her to beautiful places. She chose the locations and planned the trips with her father. Timir had sent her to the residential school when she was eight years old, and since then, the summer holidays had been their time together.

Jhimli sat on the narrow bed in her school hostel room and looked at her parents' photograph by her bed. Her mother looked stunning in a beautiful red dress, and her handsome father looked happy beside her. They were a gorgeous couple, but Jhimli knew it was an illusion. They were never happy together. She witnessed many of their fights and often saw her mother with other gentlemen.

Jhimli had always yearned for her mother's attention and love, but her mother remained unattainable. She had never been able to please her mother. The feeling of rejection had moulded her personality. She suffered from low self-esteem and blamed herself for things beyond her control. But she portrayed herself as an arrogant and confident person. It was her mechanism for protection against criticism. Her inner self always craved love and attention.

Jhimli's father doted on her and tried to fill the gorge created by her mother's rejection. Jhimli loved her father because he was the most loving and caring person.

Jhimli finished packing and waited eagerly for the hour of departure. This year, she was expecting a visit to the Garhwal Himalayas. Every year, her father surprised her with a planned getaway. It was almost ten o'clock when the clerk came to take her to the visitor's room. Jhimli had been ready to move since eight in the morning, and she almost ran to meet her father. The smile on her lips died when she entered the big waiting room decorated with plush sofas and modern furniture. The man waiting for her was not her father. She was surprised to see her maternal grandfather waiting for her.

"Dadu, what happened to Baba? Why is he not here?" asked Jhimli.

"Your father had to attend a crucial meeting, and he is not expected to be back before a week." Replied her grandfather.

"A week! Must I stay home doing nothing? What about the vacation in the Garhwal Himalayas that Baba promised?" Jhimli asked.

"Jhimli, you are going to Kolkata, and your Nanu has planned the most wonderful parties. I promise you will enjoy your holidays, and we will make this holiday memorable for you." Answered Jhimli's grandfather.

Jhimli's mother's family lived in Kolkata. They were pretty wealthy. Her grandparents gave her freedom and tried to keep her entertained. But Jhimli was unhappy with the situation as she had hoped to spend another memorable summer with her father.

"Dadu, why didn't Baba call me? I want to talk with him now." Jhimli persisted.

"N-now? Why don't you call him after reaching Kolkata? It will be more private." Her grandfather said thoughtfully.

Jhimli insisted on calling her father, and in the end, she called. After several rings, her father answered casually, "Hello, Jhimli."

"Baba, you did not come to receive me. Now you want me to go with Dadu and stay there. What about our trip?" Jhimli sounded angry.

"I have some important business to take care of. I am truly sorry, my child. I promise to make up for the lost trip." Her father said unapologetically.

Jhimli couldn't believe her father could have anything more important than her. She was angry and obstinate and even pleaded with her father to cancel whatever he was busy doing, but she didn't win.

Jhimli was disappointed but had no other option and went silently with her grandfather, hating every moment of the journey. This was the first time in ten years that her father had broken his promise. This was the first time since her mother's death that she would spend her vacation without her father. She began to bite her nails and hated going to Kolkata with her grandfather.

Jhimli went shopping, saw movies, and ate at restaurants while she stayed with her grandparents. Ten days passed, but her father did not come to Kolkata to see her. He called her several times and chatted with her, but was vague and did not clarify his reasons for not coming. Jhimli felt hurt and neglected. The mother's rejection of her had made her doubtful of every relation, and she blamed herself for her father's absence.

She counted the days left for the summer vacation to end. She wanted to return to her abode in the school hostel and remain lost amongst all the girls.

She had almost given up her hopes of seeing her father that summer when her father surprised her by coming to take her home to Simlipur. He was very reflective and seemed anxious. Jhimli had to repeat herself to receive half a response from her father, which made her feel insignificant and dismissed. Jhimli had never seen her father so distracted, which hurt her.

The train was running two hours late at the railway station, and her father took her to a pizza joint while waiting for the train. She was happy to devour her favourite pizza and ice cream but noticed her father's anxiousness.

"Baba, what has happened? You can tell me because now I am fifteen and can understand. Are you all right?"

"Hmm... I have something to tell you, Jhimli."

"W-What?"

"Jhimli, I have married."

"Married!" Shouted Jhimli in her mind.

But she could only stare at him blankly. She felt betrayed and abandoned again. This time, the sense of abandonment was too much for her because it came from her father. Her father! She trusted and believed him never to give her the feeling of rejection.

Yet, she knew that her father must have been lonely, and he had every right to marry again. Her grandparents must have known, but they also kept her in the dark.

She blamed the new Mrs Chatterjee for breaking the trust in her father. She had faith that her father would never reject her as her mother had done. Her mother had left such bitter memories and gave her nothing but rejection.

Jhimli's rumination was interrupted as her father said, "I have married Patravali."

Timir continued talking about Patravali, his new bride. It was evident that Jhimli's father had fallen in love again and cared greatly for his new wife. He told her he couldn't take her on the promised trip because he had to cover certain legalities.

She interpreted 'certain legalities' as the honeymoon with the new wife.

Suddenly, Jhimli realised that by marriage, Patravali had taken over Jhimli's father's love, time, and money. Now, she also owned her Senjuti.

Jhimli vowed silently never to like the new Mrs. Patravali Chatterjee."

CHAPTER VIII

Patravali

The Monsoon of 2003

It was a hot and humid day during the monsoon in July 2003. Patravali had washed all the clothes and had hung them to dry on the rooftop. She had some time to herself, and she relaxed. This was one of the rare opportunities she did not want to waste. Her uncle was in the living room waiting for a guest, and her aunt was finishing the carefully prepared lunch. The guest was Mr. Timir Chatterjee, a wealthy businessman with whom her uncle wanted to do some business. Patravali's aunt had given her strict instructions to remain in her room while the guest remained in the house. It had become standard practice for Patravali to remain invisible to the guests. It was an open secret to the neighbours that her aunt treated her like a labour, but the secret must not be revealed in front of Mr Timir Chatterjee.

Patravali's windowless, tiny room was on the corner of the spacious roof. It had been a storeroom for broken things and old newspapers before it was assigned as her living quarter. She had created a small garden on the rooftop, where she hung the wet clothes for drying. Patravali was reading a book discarded by her cousin when suddenly it became very windy. The sky rumbled, and dark clouds promised heavy rainfall. Patravali rushed to collect the clothes from the clothesline, and one of the clothes flew away before she could catch it. To her dismay, the flying garment landed on the face of Mr Timir Chatterjee, who was entering the courtyard at that moment. Patravali looked at Mr Chatterjee with apprehension because the incident would initiate her aunt's wrath. Mr Chatterjee took the garment from his face and looked at the terrified young girl, leaning from the second-floor rooftop. For a few seconds, their eyes remained locked, and it started raining. In a moment, the rain became heavier, drenching them. Patravali's uncle came out with an open umbrella for Mr Chatterjee, and they went inside quickly.

Patravali moved in slow motion. The moment of their mutual stare was replayed in her mind repeatedly. She collected the dripping clothes and entered her room in a dazed state. She was afraid of her aunt, and at the same time, she thought of the handsome stranger. He looked to be in his late thirties. In her dull, monotonous life, the little incident caused a big ripple in her young heart. She weaved romantic episodes in her mind resembling the romantic novels that her cousin read. It was a fantasy of a twenty-year-old woman who had little means of entertainment or freedom. Patravali savoured the sweet moments in her little private world as she had nowhere to go and had no reason to hurry because she was supposed to remain hidden in her tiny room.

The rain stopped as suddenly as it had started. There was a cool breeze, and an ominous dark sky loomed over. Patravali was walking in her rooftop garden, humming a song, when she felt a presence. She turned around, and to her delight, her eyes met with the handsome guest, Mr Chatterjee. Her uncle accompanied him. Mr Chatterjee said pleasantly, "I wanted to see the view from the rooftop..." He looked around the small garden and smiled in appreciation.

Mr Chatterjee looked quizzically at Patravali's uncle, who reluctantly introduced her to him. Patravali was his brother's daughter and an orphan. Her uncle and aunt never missed an opportunity to remind her about their kindness in giving her shelter after her parents died six years ago. They did not enlighten Mr Chatterjee about her status in the family. She was treated as a live-in maid. Her schooling had been stopped, and she was forbidden to pursue her interest in reading or writing. Patravali took her cousins' discarded books and notebooks and created her magic world when she was alone. Often, she sneaked unused books of her cousin's, and she was severely punished if caught. One such day, Mr Timir Chatterjee suddenly visited them and witnessed the true nature of her treatment by her uncle and aunt. They were furious as she was caught with her cousin's school book. Her aunt was beating her with a belt when Mr Chatterjee came. In one swift movement, her aunt threw the belt away and pushed Patravali out of the room, but Mr Chatterjee had seen and understood her plight in her uncle's house.

Since that day, he brought her presents consisting of books and stationery items. He placed them in front of her room unnoticeably. Sometimes, he would send her books by a man's hand, whom he sent with official papers for her uncle. The man knew the art of discretion and evaded the scrutiny of her aunt and uncle. The friendship between Patravali and Timir Chatterjee grew silently.

Patravali's young heart fluttered every time she saw Mr. Timir Chatterjee. He was the epitome of a gentleman in her eyes. He often visited their house as her uncle started a business with Mr Chatterjee, and Patravali stealthily looked at him. But he was always aware of her presence and made her feel special by smiling at her. Patravali knew they had no future, yet she loved him more as the months passed. His compassion made her love him, desire him. In her mind, she had become utterly devoted to Timir Chatterjee. He never made her conscious of her old, worn-out clothes or looks but always treated her fairly as an equal. Two years went by, and Patravali nourished her love for Timir secretly without any interference from her uncle or aunt. She dreamed of a life with him, of freedom, but that would never be true. Patravali's formal education had been stopped since class ten, and she had no financial freedom.

One summer day in 2005, Patravali was asked to wear a bright silk saree and put on some makeup. She became afraid when her aunt insisted she take some clothes in a bag. In the afternoon, her uncle and aunt took her to a shabby restaurant and waited in a cabin. Patravali asked her uncle and aunt's intentions, but they did not reveal a word but smiled slyly. She became suspicious, pretended to go to the bathroom, and hid behind the curtains. A few minutes later, a stout-looking man in tasteless, loud clothes joined her uncle and aunt. She overheard part of their conversation and saw her aunt assuring the man of Patravali's virginity.

Patravali did not waste another minute but ran to the nearest bus stop. She had no friends, money, formal education, or other relatives to depend on, but she remembered Timir Chatterjee. She asked for some money from the passengers waiting at the bus terminus. One kind lady gave her a few rupees, and she telephoned Timir.

The call was brief, and there were no romantic words. She asked him plainly if he would keep her in his household as a maid, for she did not expect him to commit to her. For her, being a maid or a mistress to Timir Chatterjee, the kind gentleman, was a better option than being sold at a brothel.

Mr. Timir Chatterjee hesitated because he understood the gravity of the situation. He could not ignore Patravali's plight and felt responsible for her. Two main obstacles needed to be considered. Firstly was his age, for he was twenty years her senior. She was twenty-two while he was forty-two, a widower. Secondly, his fifteen-year-old daughter Jhimli's attitude was also a factor. Jhimli's summer vacation was about to start in two days, and he had promised to take her to the Garhwal Himalayas.

He hesitated at the suddenness but recovered soon. He arranged to meet her in a nearby shop. He knew he loved Patravali and did not care for their age, social, financial, and academic differences. He came there as soon as his car took him.

She was standing among rows of sarees, looking a little lost. She looked vulnerable and innocent. His heart bled at seeing her standing all alone amongst the strangers. There was no time for romance or loving words. He knew what he had to do.

When she turned to him, he took hold of her hands and said plainly, "You know that I am a widower and have a teenage daughter, and I am twenty years your senior. I may not be suitable for you as a husband."

She smiled shyly and replied firmly that she did not care about their age difference and wanted to be a part of Timir's life.

The next few days were spent collecting proof of Patravali's age, registering the marriage, informing Rimjhim's parents and arranging for Jhimli's summer vacation. Timir had to deal with Patravali's uncle and aunt's wrath. They threatened to go to the police with abduction charges against Timir Chatterjee, which didn't happen as Timir sought help from the local political leader. A short wedding was arranged at the registrar's small office. Few of his factory staff were witnesses to the small wedding.

Patravali was exhilarated as she looked around her new home, Senjuti. Yet, the uncertainty of her stepdaughter Jhimli's acceptance of her as Timir's wife made her nervous and apprehensive. Patravali wanted to make Timir very happy. She loved Timir and was loved, cared for, and desired by him. Patravali felt content and blissful. She adored her newly married status and her home. Here, she was secure and felt a lot more confident than she had ever felt.

Patravali did not mind being the second wife. Instead, she felt grateful that Timir had married her. She dreamt that she would become essential to her husband just as he was to her.

Patravali remembered that day when she first felt love stirring in her heart on a wet day in July. She believed in love at first sight. In her case, it proved to be true.

CHAPTER IX

Jhimli and Patravali

The Summer of 2005

Patravali looked at the clock for the tenth time. She had already checked all the arrangements made for welcoming Jhimli. Patravali had personally taken care of the little details like keeping fresh pink and yellow roses in Jhimli's room, making the chocolate pudding with little chocolate chips, preparing chicken pakora and the white sauce, homemade coconut sweets, all the things that were Jhimli's favourites. Everything was done with love and perfection. Patravali sighed in relief as the arrangements were perfect, but her heart beat with apprehension.

Bindi talked about Jhimli's temperament since morning, which made Patravali more nervous. Now, she came and stood by Patravali in Jhimli's room.

Bindi began without context, "Jhimli's mother was wonderful, but she did not know how to love. Our master loved her, but she loved being loved by other men. She was like a brilliant diamond with a splendid shine but cold within. She owned everything: jewels, houses, and other material things, but she loved playing with people, including the master and treated him like her pet puppy. Jhimli is much like her mother, but our Master does not see the truth. One day, Jhimli will be a stunning lady like her mother. Ayah is devoted to Jhimli as she has been mothering her since birth. She can see no one beyond Jhimli when she is around."

Patravali felt a cold shiver run through her with all the voluntary information.

"Bindi, have you checked the swing? Timir told me that Jhimli loves to spend her time under the mango tree." Patravali's young voice was polite and firm as she changed the subject.

Bindi answered eagerly, "Yes, I have checked everything, Bahuji. My husband, Dhaniram, is very efficient in all these. But, Bahuji,

Jhimli will not be the loving daughter you are hoping for. You have taken away her father from her... I mean that she will consider you her enemy. Do you know that once Jhimli had seen her mother's ghost walking in the garden wearing her favourite red dress? Many hired workers claim to have seen her ghost. They swear that the whispers of the flame tree are her spirit anguishing for her broken heart. Our Master never goes there anymore, but Jhimli goes there often. Maybe she misses her mother. She is the apple of the master's eye. He thinks the world of her; according to him, she can do nothing wrong."

At that moment, there was a little commotion in the garden. Dhaniram, the gardener cum all-handyman, and Ayah were heard welcoming Jhimli. Timir was home with his daughter. Patravali went outside to receive Jhimli. She had a plate with a lamp and other auspicious things for welcoming Jhimli, but her smile died on her lips as she faced Jhimli's displeased, sulky countenance. Jhimli brushed past her into the house rudely.

In the next few days, Patravali tried several ways to make a bond with Jhimli. But she remained unaffected. She blamed Patravali for everything, like her father's secrecy and breaking of trust, her missed trip to the Garhwal Himalayas, and her heartbreak at her father's failure to communicate the marriage news earlier. Jhimli did not appear for any social visits by Doctor Dilip Dutta and his family, Mr Trivedi and his family, Mr Bidyut Bose and his wife, Mayurakshi Bose. Jhimli could not be reconciled to the fact of her father's second marriage.

Timir threw a small party in honour of Patravali. She was dressed in a pretty silk saree and wore some simple jewellery. Patravali had never been so happy or so appealing. Timir was glad to see her excitement. Jhimli became angrier and more frustrated as her father paid attention to his new wife. She didn't want any celebration in Patravali's honour.

Jhimli called Patravali to her room before the guests arrived and said, "Do not try to mother me, Patravali. You are just seven years my senior, and I know why you married my father, who is twenty years your senior. He was very much in love with my mother, and now he married you because he cannot go to the street women to satisfy his manly needs. And he is quite wealthy and a good human being. I know an opportunist like you must have planned to squeeze his money. Maybe you have dreams of replacing my mother's place, but you are no match for her. I suppose you know that you are nothing but a bed partner. Soon, he will be bored with your uneducated, unsophisticated stupidness. Women like you know how to play the damsel in distress card. You were successful in catching him in your web of lies. But, do not even dream of making my sympathetic father your stepping stone for hunting other victims. I shall tell everyone about your background; your true nature will not be hidden for long. I shall ensure that Bindi, Ayah and Dhaniram also know about you. You are no better than a gold digger."

Patravali whitened with shock at the young girl's hatred. There was nothing more that she could do to win Jhimli's heart. As Patravali stood shaking, Jhimli smiled cruelly and walked out just when Timir came searching for Patravali.

The guests were already coming in. He saw Patravali standing rooted to the spot. She looked ill. It was not difficult for Timir to understand the situation. The party had meant much to Patravali before Jhimli had shaken her confidence, trust or dreams. Patravali went through the party like a doll with a smile pasted. Timir blamed himself for not being able to convince Jhimli that he was in love with Patravali.

Jhimli did not come home to Senjuti after that bitter summer vacation of 2005. Ayah became sad and blamed Patravali for driving away Jhimli, whom she loved like her daughter. But with time, she adjusted to the arrangement.

In defiance of Jhimli's feelings about the marriage, Patravali and Timir found happiness, solace, and friendship in each other. By nature, Patravali was just the opposite of Rimjhim. She did not crave attention or want to be in the limelight at parties. She became happy with little things like gardening and reading. Everyone admired her insight and understanding of the little things that matter most in life.

At first, she was a little shy, but with Timir's tenderness, she blossomed like a rose. She became more confident and loved pursuing her interests. Timir and Patravali made a lovely couple. Patravali passionately landscaped the Rose Arbour and the garden in front of the house. Patravali's passion and affection shined in every corner and nook of Senjuti. She never saw the famed ghost of Rimjhim nor heard any whispers. The servants and the neighbours said Senjuti had finally found its true mistress, and Timir had found a real wife.

CHAPTER X

Jhimli's Love Story

August 2009

College for Jhimli was fun. She was never short of pocket money or friends who enjoyed partying like her. She tried her best to hide the feeling of incompetence that seemed to overwhelm her sometimes. She smiled a lot and always tried hard to please those who avoided or looked down on her.

Ritabhari Ganguly was the envy of most students. She was called Ritu by her fellow mates and could balance between studies and fun. She was an achiever in all her activities, and her parties were glamorous. Many students wanted to be included in Ritu's group, but she was choosy. Jhimli also wanted to be included in her group, but Ritu thought she was immature. Ritu had a string of admirers, and it was difficult to pin her on a particular boy, while Jhimli had a steady boyfriend. He was Rakesh Gupta, an undergraduate student in the same college as Jhimli. It was the summer of 2009. The new semester she had not begun. Students were enjoying and having parties.

Jhimli was arguing with her boyfriend, Rakesh, whom she called Ricki. He was a year senior and was in love with Jhimli. They were quarrelling like a pair of parrots. Jhimli growled, "You are jealous and too possessive. Why shouldn't I go to Ritu's party? She did invite me to her Birthday Party at her farmhouse."

Rakesh replied similarly angrily, "I saw the whole episode. Jhimli, you were practically begging her to invite you to her party. Why do you always need to be in everyone's good book? Ritu has been ignoring you for six months, but you have to win her friendship. Why? What is so special about her? Why you cannot feel special on your own?"

Jhimli became quiet from the outside but said in her mind, "I have to win every goddamn person who ignores me. If Mother were alive now, then I would have won her too. I have to prove that I am adorable and good... it doesn't matter if the other person is ignoring me, but once they see the real me, they cannot overlook my charms. I make sure that they know how resourceful I can be..."

Rakesh became exasperated at Jhimli's silence and grunted, "You have nothing to say! You are tongue-tied because I said the truth. You are one admiration-hungry narcissist." Rakesh walked away.

"Ricki! Going to one of Ritu's parties is important because I think her parties will give me the right kind of people to befriend. Besides, I always wanted to go to one of her famous parties. Ricki..." Jhimli pleaded and ran after Rakesh. She knew that she needed him as an escort to the party.

Ritabhari invited only a few students to her parties, and those few invited were envied and revered by all. It was a social achievement for the young ones to be invited to Ritu's parties. Jhimli couldn't ignore the allure of the upscale sophistication. She tried various tactics with Rakesh and ultimately convinced him to attend the party. He was in love with her and could not resist her charms.

Rakesh and Jhimli went to the party on his motorcycle. Many guests had arrived when they reached the farmhouse. Jhimli had not expected to see many cars lined up at the gate. As soon as she entered the farmhouse, she knew she had never seen anything like this. The light arrangement, the serving maids, the food, the music, and the drinks. It all looked like a film setup. Many of the guests wore designer clothes and took drinks freely. Jhimli stood awkwardly as Rakesh went to the drinks corner and helped himself.

"Feeling lonely, beautiful?" Suddenly, a deep Baritone voice whispered in her ears.

Jhimli turned round and met a pair of dark, scrutinising eyes. He was handsome, like a Greek god. Tall and lithe-bodied, he looked like one of the heroes out of her Mills and Boon pages. Before she knew what was happening, he pulled her to the dance floor. She could visualise herself and her enigmatic partner dancing gracefully. Jhimli saw their bodies mingling sensuously in her mind, creating a fascinating image. The handsome stranger must have noticed something in Jhimli, and he lowered his mouth to her ears and asked her name. She was mesmerised by their closeness, his sensual touch at her back, his manly after-shave perfume, and his firm, lithe body. She trembled in his embrace as she felt him getting hot.

"Hey, you are ignoring me, Neel! After all, I am the birthday girl. Are you trying to make me jealous, Neel?" Ritu came between them and claimed the fascinating young man from Jhimli. He laughed throatily and took Ritu in his arms, instantly forgetting Jhimli.

Jhimli stood in a corner, watching Ritu on the dance floor with her enthralling partner. They made a beautiful couple while dancing. Jhimli felt jealous and, at the same time, sad. She was not sophisticated or worldly-wise like Ritu. She knew there could never be anything between her and that fascinating man. But she wanted him.

"Jhimli, are you forgetting that you are with me? Keep away from that man called Neelesh Dutt. He eats little girls like you in his breakfast." Slurred Rakesh.

"Ricki, why are you drinking? Who will drive now? You know very well how you handle drinks!" Jhimli spat out her frustration.

"So, now I am your driver? And you mean that I will disgrace myself again! Wow, Jhimli. This is not what you said before I agreed to come with you... hey, did Neelesh promise to keep you warm? But look at them, Neelesh and Ritu. They are dancing so intimately... he has forgotten all about you, Jhimli." Rakesh shouted suddenly.

"Ricki, keep quiet and let's leave." Jhimli's voice trembled.

"Keep quiet and leave? Why, the night is so young. Ritu has an ace up her sleeves. She always does. Don't you want to taste all that she has to offer? That fascinating Neelesh will not leave so early either... He may want more... don't you have something for him? Ritu is not serious about Neelesh. He is here for some fun with girls like you." Rakesh was drunk and couldn't control his voice or manner. He went back to the drinks corner. Jhimli stood in another corner, her eyes filled with humiliation. Ritu was dancing with another man. Jhimli looked for Neelesh. She found him dancing with another girl, who looked much older than the rest of the group.

"You should take your man to the toilet…" A voice shouted near Jhimli's ears. Jhimli looked around and faced Ritu. She looked displeased at Jhimli and repeated herself. Jhimli nodded and went towards Rakesh. He was sitting on the floor with his head turned to the bed. He was ready to vomit. Jhimli and a serviceman helped Rakesh to reach the bathroom.

Sometime later, Rakesh was lying in a heap on the bathroom floor. He had puked, and Jhimli couldn't make him get up from his place in the bathroom. She was unable to drag him either, for he was heavy. Her beautiful black dress was partly wet, and she smelt of alcohol, puke, and something disgusting. Tears of frustration fell from Jhimli's eyes. Rakesh had ruined the party most embarrassingly. The party was over for her, and she needed clean clothes to go home to her grandmother.

"What happened here?" Said the deep voice of an arriver. Jhimli turned and saw the hero-like man, Neelesh, enter the bathroom. He quickly surmised her situation and said, "Leave him there for the time. You can change your dress if you want. Ritu has her stuff in one of the bedrooms. I can help you find one dry, clean dress."

Jhimli nodded shyly in acquiescence and went with him to one of the bedrooms. He momentarily scrutinised her, then picked an outfit from the wardrobe.

"Wear this, and you may come with me."

Jhimli felt giddy with pleasure at Neelesh's attention. She went to an empty bathroom with the dress.

Jhimli was surprised at Neelesh's familiarity with Ritu's farmhouse, but then she realised they were more than friends. She had seen them dancing in an intimate style. Jhimli felt stupid yet jealous.

That night at the party, Jhimli saw Neelesh with many women but did not come anywhere near Jhimli once she had changed into dry clothes. The party was over for her, and she took a cab home.

A month after the party, Ritu went into her hibernation mode. She was preparing for admission to a medical college in the United States. But Jhimli had no such ambition. She wanted to win Neelesh's love and attention and be revered by him. She found out about Neelesh's hideouts and tried to be seen by him.

In a month, she was with Neelesh and his group more often. She ignored Rakesh and clarified to him that she was trying very hard to be Neelesh's girl.

Rakesh could only caution Jhimli to avoid Neelesh, but she had become completely obsessed with the handsome man.

"Do you have any idea about his background or his qualifications? What does he do when he is not taming girls or being creative in siphoning money from his rich friends? I know at least two secrets of his misdeeds that would land him in jail. Please stay away from him. He is a dangerous man."

"Why do you try to make Neelesh a dangerous villain? He is just a young man who recently graduated in Engineering." Jhimli asked him angrily.

"Why do you think he is not getting any job even after passing out as an engineer? I will tell you why. He stole a motorbike, but incidentally, that motorbike belonged to an influential fellow. The fellow has made sure that Neelesh never gets any job offer. And there was the incident of the stolen car." Ricki told her.

"He has told me of the incident. There was confusion regarding that motorbike, and Neelesh was mistaken. It is all sorted out. And the car you are referring to was stolen by some criminal. The police did not find the culprit. Why are you blaming all these incidents on Neelesh? Ricki, you are jealous of him." Jhimli was adamant about her notion.

"One day, you are going to regret your choice, Jhimli. He is a slippery, snake-like, vicious fellow. He will drain your resources, beauty, smile and your very life. He will enjoy your youth; afterwards, you will be thrown away like the other girls." Ricki spoke these words vehemently and went away.

Timir and Patravali came to Kolkata to celebrate Jhimli's nineteenth birthday in July 2009. Patravali insisted that she meet Jhimli to persuade her to go home.

Timir pleaded with Jhimli to make it up with Patravali, but she was moody and adamant. She refused to go to Simlipur and also to meet Patravali. Jhimli made it clear to her father that she did not want Patravali in her life. There was nothing that Timir could do to bring his daughter home or promote any relationship between his daughter and his present wife. Patravali felt guilty for being the reason for the rift between father and daughter. They returned to Simlipur in sadness and with beaten spirits. Timir and Patravali did not meet Neelesh. But Rakesh met them before they went back home.

All the news provided by Rakesh made Timir sadder. They returned to Simlipur discouraged and beaten.

After a few days of Jhimli's nineteenth birthday, it was raining heavily on a night in August. The hour was past midnight. Jhimli's grandparents had retired, and so had the live-in maid. Jhimli was alone in her bedroom on the house's first floor. She was watching a movie when suddenly she heard a soft knock. She looked at the clock and was surprised at the lateness of the hour. It was long past midnight. With a hammering heart, she went to the door and peeked through the glass. To her amazement, she saw Neelesh standing at her door. She hadn't seen him for a week and was overjoyed.

"How did you come up? Who opened the main door for you? Hey, you are dripping!" Jhimli was too excited to see Neelesh. She didn't care if someone heard her.

"I climbed the walls to enter your courtyard, and then climbing the spiral staircase was easy." Laughed Neelesh at her excitement and said in a low, husky tone, "If you shout like this, then your grandparents will have me thrown out. This is our secret rendezvous."

"Okay... I'll be as discreet as possible. But while climbing the wall, you have hurt yourself. Look at your shirt sleeves." Jhimli said in a lower tone and pointed to a reddish splatter smudged in rainwater.

"Oh! This is nothing. I can climb Mount Everest for you, Jhimli. You are so fresh and lovely. You are like the rainwater... " Neelesh flattered her.

Jhimli gave him towels and dry clothes from her grandfather's wardrobe. Within an hour, the clothes were forgotten and became useless. He spent the night with her. Neelesh made sure that their intimacy would be intoxicating to Jhimli. He knew that Jhimli had no prior experience with any man, and this was the first experience for Jhimli. Neelesh was a fantastic lover. He was knowledgeable and learned all the tricks of sex to control a girl. Jhimli was too naïve and too easy to conquer for Neelesh.

There was a police case of murder, and somehow, Neelesh was named as a suspect, but Jhimli gave evidence that on the same night of the murder, he was with her. She saved him, and in return, Neelesh proposed, and Jhimli accepted with joy. Neelesh said that he had no close relatives, and neither did he have parents, but that did not bother Jhimli. Instead, it made her happy that she was the only family he would have. She knew that he had studied engineering, but where he worked or what he did to earn his living was not clear to her. It did not matter, as she was hopelessly in love with Neelesh.

Timir opposed the match with her grandfather, but parents are seldom successful in preventing such unions. And when least expected, Jhimli eloped with her lover. She was just nineteen, and he was in his late twenties. She left a short note to her father stating, "Baba, I will be happy in my way. You need not bother. He is not a gold digger like your little young wife."

For Jhimli, the marriage was her delicious revenge and protest against her father's sudden marriage to the poor orphan Patravali. Neelesh was also an orphan like Patravali. Jhimli took her mother's jewellery worth fifty lakh rupees and had fixed deposits of twenty lakh rupees.

The new couple settled somewhere in Durgapur. They did not leave any forwarding address or any phone number. She detached all threads of relations with Senjuti.

The truth hit Timir very hard. He realised that his daughter was more like her mother, Rimjhim, in many ways. Jhimli was just as adamant and selfish. She also did not hesitate to cause agony like Rimjhim had inflicted pain nonchalantly. Like her mother, she too became a frequent topic of chitchat in the social life of Timir and his wife Patravali. With time, Rimjhim and Jhimli were lost in the recesses of the memory of the people of Simlipur.

CHAPTER XI

The Writer Mayurakshi Bose

Copenhagen, 28 February 2023

Mayurakshi Bose was looking for her spectacles in all the possible places. It was not on her writing desk, the dining table, or the coffee table. She frowned and tried remembering what she was doing the last time she wore her glasses.

"Bidyut, have you seen my glasses?" Mayurakshi asked her husband, Professor Bidyut Bose.

"No, but I have seen your mobile phone. Do you know its whereabouts?" Bidyut asked smilingly.

"I need my glasses... now... I think I was preparing breakfast... Bidyut, please help me find my glasses. Please. I need to finish the draft..." Mayurakshi was speaking while looking inside the kitchen cabinets.

"Mou, do you know where I found your mobile phone?" Bidyut said teasingly.

Mayurakshi muttered angrily and continued her search.

"What happened to the other glass that you keep in your handbag? You should use it and look for the lost one later. I can also..." His phone interrupted whatever Bidyut was about to say. He looked at the number and frowned.

"What happened, Frederick?" asked Bidyut.

After listening momentarily, he rose from his desk and dressed quickly. "Mou, I have to go to the lab. Frederick has made a mistake, and we must start the process from the beginning. By the way, if you need your mobile, find it on your desk. I found it in the garage. By the way, I think you should use your other glass..." Bidyut went out.

Mayurakshi flopped down on her study chair and took out her other glass from the handbag she always keeps ready by her study table. She was an eminent Bengali fiction writer and wrote psychological mysteries. She was supposed to send the synopsis of her next novel by the end of the previous week. Her publisher was pushing her, and she was losing things. That always happened when she was in the author mode. Mayurakshi looked at her dead phone but did not bother to charge it.

She focussed on the current matter that her protagonist was dealing with. She tried to sum up the protagonist's feelings as she stared at the blank screen of her laptop. In her mind, she could see the little cottage and the girl with the baby. Mayurakshi started typing intently. She lost count of the hours slipping by.

Bidyut returned in the evening. The house was blanketed in darkness. The only source of light was the table lamp on Mayurakshi's table. She was typing furiously between moments of staring at her laptop screen with unseeing eyes.

Bidyut stood at her room's door for a second, then switched on the light.

"Oh, when did you come?" Mayurakshi looked at her husband's scowl and asked falteringly, "What have I forgotten now?"

"You forgot to tell me you are going home to India on the 7th. When were you planning to tell me? Does Giti know about your trip?" Bidyut sounded very angry.

"Oh, yes, of course. I am leaving on Saturday, 7th March. Giti knows. And I thought you also paid attention when I discussed the dates and told you after buying the ticket. Bidyut, you are angry because you were busy with your new project and missed taking note of the information. It's nice to know that Mr. Perfectionist, too, can sometimes miss something important." Mayurakshi answered flippantly.

"Okay, agreed that I missed the information. How long are you planning to stay?" Bidyut asked in a more amiable tone.

"I don't know yet. I will stay at Suprabhat in Simlipur for at least a month until I have this story under control. Then I will visit my mother in Kalimpong... and lastly, I will visit your father in Delhi. This year, Giti wants to visit her grandparents in Delhi and Kalimpong. I remember to have discussed all these before." Mou stood up from her chair and went to the kitchen to make coffee.

"Mou, are you planning to stay there for over three months? I know that you always stay for at least a month in Simlipur. Kalimpong is equally important to you, and I don't think you will spend only a few days in Delhi. So, how long?" Bidyut sounded offended.

"You are a self-dependent man, and I trust you to care for yourself. Our daughter Gitisha is at her college dorm and doesn't need Mamma all the time. So, why are you being so grumpy, dear husband?" Mayurakshi asked playfully.

"You are always forgetting your stuff, and now you forgot to mention this trip. Don't you think that you've got to get serious? Did you do your exercises today? I know you didn't. Did you charge your mobile phone? No, madam, you didn't. What if your mother or anyone else needs to call you in an emergency? Mou, you need to be more careful..." Bidyut would have continued with the lecture, but Mayurakshi interrupted and said smilingly, "You are here to care for the little things... Now, let's discuss my trip."

Bidyut and Mayurakshi have been married for twenty years. They have known each other since they were in their early teens. Their families were close friends. She had always known that one day, she would marry Bidyut. "Bidyut, you need to relax. I am not the little girl anymore."

"Yes, I know you are forty-two years old and the mother of a nineteen-year-old daughter but you do forget things. I still remember that twenty-year-old woman who cried her heart out because I was going away to do research. I had to marry her...," Laughed Bidyut.

"Are you suggesting that you married me because I cried? But I also remember how you wanted to marry me before leaving for higher studies. So, we both wanted to be married." Mayurakshi said in mock anger.

"Yes, Madam, we conclude that we both wanted to marry each other. We were madly in love and we have been married happily. Now, let us discuss your visit to India. Tell me about your plans again. This time I will document it on my calendar." Bidyut was ready with his little diary.

"This year also I will be staying at Suprabhat during Holi. Perhaps I would stay there for a month until I finish the final draft. So, I will stay in Simlipur till the tenth of April and then one month in Kalimpong. And lastly I will visit your father and two prospective publishers in Delhi. Gitisha has plans to visit in May, and we may return together," Mayurakshi spoke in a friendly, cordial manner.

"I remember the discussion. But there was no mention of the dates. I will not be able to go anywhere soon. I have just started a project, and it is time-sensitive. Giti told me she would visit her Nana in Kalimpong and Dadu in Delhi during the Christmas break and not in May." Bidyut said reflectively.

"Okay, Giti will visit in December and I would return in the last week of May at the latest. By the way, why were you so obsessed with my mobile phone? You know I avoid it when I am in a tight situation and there is a deadline." Mayurakshi asked.

"Patravali had called you, but since your mobile was switched off, she called me instead. You should call her back. She sounded a little strange and she was using a public phone," Bidyut said while sipping the coffee.

"Public phone? How did she sound strange? What did she say? When did she call?" Mayurakshi was concerned.

"Strange means... she seemed to be in a hurry. She was very brief and just asked me about your plans for the visit. As I didn't know the date, and I couldn't confirm. She seemed to know that you would visit during the Holi. She also said that I must tell you that she has quite a lot of detective work for," Bidyut replied.

"Detective work!"

"I also asked her the meaning of detective work but she didn't elaborate. She said that once you reach Kolkata you have to call her and accordingly she will plan her moves."

Mayurakshi took Bidyut's mobile and called Patravali. The phone was switched off. She thoughtfully said, "Why do you think her phone is switched off?"

Bidyut calculated the time and said, "Now, it is almost 8 p.m., so the time in Simultala is 11:30 at night. She might have gone to bed."

"Only 11:30 p.m., and she has gone to bed? That seems unlikely... Oh, by the way, today is Indu Raha's marriage anniversary. She is throwing a big party. Patravali is also going. Maybe she is driving now... I have to call her tomorrow morning. Remind me to call her in the morning, Bidyut."

He smiled at her.

"It seems like yesterday when I first met Patravali. She was so shy and sensitive. We made a hit from the start. She had just been married, and I was in Simlipur with little Giti. You were still in the US doing your research. Then you surprised us with your visit, and we went to the little party thrown by Timir Babu... they were so much in love... like us." Mayurakshi remembered the time.

"You were always so romantic. I remember there was a girl, I mean daughter... Timir Babu had a teenage daughter, and Patravali was many years younger than him. He had been an unhappy man before he married Patravali. They made a nice couple. Do you remember anything about the first wife?" Bidyut asked.

"Not really... she hardly stayed in Simlipur. And we visited Simlipur during the summer holidays. I just remember that she committed suicide when the daughter was only four or five years old. There was so much scandal regarding the first wife. Patravali was a different story. She was so good with Timir Babu. And she is such a warm person. We shared so many common interests. She also liked writing letters. We both loved reading and shared the same interest in music. We shared so many beautiful moments. Their property, Senjuti, and my grandparents' property, Suprabhat, are adjacent. Giti loved visiting Senjuti from the back garden. There were swings arranged for Jhimli..." Mayurakshi frowned as she remembered something.

"Jhimli! Who?"

"Jhimli is Patravali's stepdaughter. I remember her only vaguely, as she was eight years my junior; we had nothing in common. She severed all ties with Timir Babu after he married Patravali. I heard that she, too, was fond of boys. She had married someone secretly. She ran away with the boy..." Mayurakshi would have said more, but she caught the funny look in her husband.

"What's so funny?"

"You listened to gossip! Unbelievable... I know that writers are a dangerous species. They can twist any plain thing into a mystery, and if the gossip were any good, you must have already used it. Correct?" Bidyut said smilingly.

Mayurakshi shook her shoulder mysteriously and smiled.

CHAPTER XII

Vicious Whispers

3 March 2023

Mayurakshi Bose was strolling by the lake in Copenhagen's botanical garden. She was not in a hurry, for she was thinking deeply of a relationship gone sour between her protagonist and another character of her next psychological thriller book. A well-known film director had bought the rights to her recently published book and wanted the upcoming one she was working on. A few of her stories have already been made into films and TV series.

Her reveries were disturbed abruptly by the ringing phone.

"H-- Hello." Answered Mayurakshi absentmindedly.

"Enjoying your honeymoon, dear?" Teased a female voice in her ears.

"What?!" Mayurakshi looked at the caller ID. It was her friend, Mrs Indu Raha from Simlipur. She could be very annoying sometimes.

"Dear Indu, I think that it is you who is itching for another sexy honeymoon. Belated Happy Anniversary, dear Indu. I hope you had the most wonderful party." Said Mayurakshi laughingly.

"No, I am not itching for anything, but you must be having a wonderful time with your hubby. Gitisha is now out of your hair... I mean, she is living away from home. So, it's nothing less than a honeymoon for you. By the way, did I interrupt anything sexy?" Laughed Indu Raha.

"Cut it short, Indu, come to the point." Mayurakshi was annoyed by her friend's talk.

"Oh! You have no romantic sense, or perhaps you are writing and busy as usual. By the way, do you know where your best friend is?" Indu asked seriously.

"So, this is about Patravali?"

"Yes, your Patravali is enjoying her honeymoon."

"Indu! Why are you saying such nonsense? After all, she is your friend too. What happened to your integrity? You know very well that Pats is still grieving Timir Babu's death. You should give her some quality time and your friendship." Retorted Mayurakshi.

"Yes, I know I should have been more accommodating and offered her companionship. But I think she is past grieving now. Or perhaps she was putting on an act of the sad widow. I am certain that I saw things and heard things that prove our Patravali is not so lonely anymore. She has found happiness in the arms of another widower. By the way, that charming person is not a Hindu. At first, I couldn't believe my eyes, but then I confirmed it from the horse's mouth. And I was proven true. Our dearest Pats has a taste for wealthy widowers." Goaded Indu Raha satisfyingly.

"Do you have any idea how you are sounding? And what do you mean by horse's mouth? Explain."

"Horse's mouth means the person with whom our Patravali is romantically engaged. Professor Ahmed told me about them. He is the one with whom our Patravali is having her second love life."

"Surely Patravali would tell me if she marries again. But if she wants it to be a secret, I will certainly not force her confidence." Thought Mayurakshi in her mind.

"Dear Angel, you have no questions?! Don't you want to know who the lucky guy is or when all this happened? But dear Mou, keeping your curiosity buried within yourself will make you sick. So, I shall tell you that Dr Faisal Ahmed is a Professor at Bhopal University. He is a linguist and poet, and our Honourable Hindu Brahmin widow, Madam Patravali, has escaped with the Professor." Said Indu.

"What do you mean by escaped? When did she meet Professor Faisal Ahmed? Who introduced Professor Ahmed to Patravali? What have you seen?" Mayurakshi's curiosity was piqued.

"Oh! Now, so many questions! On many occasions, I have witnessed Patravali's happiness in the company of Professor Ahmed. I have seen him going to Senjuti on more than three occasions. I saw them having lunch together at the club. And when

I went to invite Patravali, I saw him at her place and invited him as well. They were together at my anniversary party, which was quite exciting. He has set an example for all men in their early fifties. He was the most romantic and so very attentive. I think Patravali is smart to choose first Timir Babu and now this gentleman, Professor Ahmed. So, I am not spreading all lies... when there is smoke, you know there has to be fire. They have gone away together from Simlipur on Saturday, 28th February, and today is 3rd March. Yesterday, I spoke with Professor Ahmed on the phone, and he confirmed their relationship and the elopement." Gushed Indu.

"Did Patravali, herself, tell you the news of their elopement? Or did Professor Ahmed confirm their elopement with you?"

"Patravali had switched off her mobile phone. I tried to call her the day after my anniversary party, but her mobile was switched off. It is still switched off. So, I called the Professor, who told me the good news. Patravali tried to keep it a secret and not include me in her plans. You know how Patravali likes to keep things bottled up... so this elopement, too, was a secret. Maybe she was afraid of the wagging tongues. But she couldn't fool me. I saw them together... yes, he was in love with her, and she was with him." Indu gloated.

"Why did Professor Ahmed reveal their plan? When could he also have kept mum about it? There is something not fitting..." Thought Mayurakshi.

"You have become very thoughtful, dear Mou. I think this is shocking news for you," Indu said.

"Indu, I am not shocked but would request you to have a little discretion and tell no one yet of the elopement."

"Are you insinuating that I spread rumours?" Indu sounded angry.

"I am only suggesting that sometimes it is better to be quiet.Often, what seems real is nothing more than an illusion crafted with lies. Sometimes lies, when whispered with passionate conviction, can become honeyed poison. And it can become dangerous, too. Maybe Pats has her reasons to be secretive. Let's try to be discreet until she is ready to divulge her status."

"Mou, I know that you trust Patravali, and you share a creative friendship, and perhaps you share secrets. But now I feel that I do not know the real Patravali. Maybe she had married Timir Chatterjee for his money. After all, he was twenty years her senior, and she had no money or status. Maybe, now, she wants someone to warm her in bed and at the first opportunity, she secured the man who is closer to her in age and desires her. I am not a fool and would not be taken in by her sad act of grief of losing her husband," said Indu maliciously before hanging up.

Mayurakshi was disturbed because she thought she knew Patravali and had known her for eighteen years. They both had been young wives, and they were neighbours in Simlipur. Patravali was a very dear friend, and they had no secrets. Yet Mayurakshi could not recall any conversation mentioning Dr Ahmed. Mayurakshi knew about the pain and sadness of Patravali at her husband's sudden death in the previous year. Mayurakshi tried to recall the last time when she had spoken with Patravali. She had her phone with her, and the call log showed they had a small conversation on the 10th of February. Mayurakshi knew she had deliberately ignored the mobile from the fifteenth of February until yesterday when she finished her upcoming book's synopsis. They often wrote lengthy letters to each other, but it had been some time since they exchanged anything.

"Perhaps she has already written a letter to me... I think I told her about my ticket confirmation for Kolkata on 7th March. I will go to Simlipur the next day... that will be the 9th of March, as I will reach Kolkata on the 8th... it is difficult to imagine that Patravali found another man to love and start a new life, all in a short span of a month. What did she mean by detective work? Why did she call from a public phone? More surprising and disturbing is that after all these years of friendship, Indu now mentions Patravali's status as an orphan before her marriage to Timir. Patravali had worked hard to be educated and learn all the finesse of a cultured person. She is warm, spontaneous, and respected for her honesty and refined artistic taste. Suddenly, all her positivity seemed obscured to her friends and neighbours. Why is this happening? Indu talks a lot... how much truth is there in her information? Should I call Doctor Dutta? He suffered from a stroke ... is he okay now? Or should I call Umanath Ji, the priest of the Kali Temple? I cannot talk to them before talking to Patravali. That would betray her trust and slander Patravali's reputation, too. I shall not speak another word about Patravali until I go to Simlipur." Mayurakshi kept thinking deeply but reasoned that people do things beyond expectation and imagination.

Besides, it was not illegal for a forty-year-old widow to elope with a person belonging to a different religion and culture. Patravali was financially independent and had no liability. What surprised Mayurakshi more was that Patravali chose to elope when she could have married the person and stayed in the comfort of her beloved Senjuti. After all, Patravali was not a coward, and she was reasonable and level-headed enough.

Mayurakshi started counting the days left for her journey back home to India.

CHAPTER XIII

Death of the Koel

3 March 2023

It was another Saturday evening of the Bollywood Gala at the Durgapur Club. The members flaunted the Retro Bollywood fashion. It was exciting for the members as the Bollywood Night was specially arranged to lure new sponsors. The main attraction was the Bollywood singer and dancer Zinnia. She looked young and was quite attractive.

The hall was decorated with low lights, which displayed soft shadows. A platform was set for the band, and the musicians in coordinated costumes played a merry tune. The ladies' dresses and jewellery glittered softly in the low light, and their men were dressed in dark suits drinking expensive liquor. The guests spoke in hushed tones, afraid to display bad manners or taste.

Suddenly a spotlight became alive with the beautiful singer Zinnia wearing a long shimmering red dress, slit high with her shapely legs peeking out. She had red plumes draped across her sexy figure. Her skin looked flawless and glossy. She started swaying slowly and hummed a sensual tune. Gradually, she took centre stage and performed an old Bollywood song in a sexy style. Her performance was nearly erotic.

Zinnia performed one sensuous song after another. And they held the audience captive with her passionate performance. The bar was at the far end of the hall, where three men were drinking beers and concentrating on Zinnia's performance. They were Lawrence, Raghubir and Ricki.

Raghubir didn't look like a member. He did not look like any guest either. He wore flashy, loud clothes, which made him prominent in a negative way.

"Raghu, you have to spend your time in the playroom. Now leave before he comes." Said Ricki in a stern voice.

"N-now? Why? I, too, want to m-meet your guy, Handa. Last time, too, you did not let me stay. Did I not work hard to be included?" Raghubir did not sound confident.

"You are looking like a street urchin in flashy clothes." Lawrence supplied.

"I don't want any flashy-looking person to scare him away. Let us make the deal. You will also get the benefit." Ricki said patiently.

"Since when have my clothes bothered anyone? In our profession..." Raghubir was cut short with a kick beneath the table. He stood up looking furious but did not waste any other words and left the bar. He was the most hot-headed amongst the foursome. He was impulsive, too.

Zinnia was still singing. Ricki looked at the CCTV camera and frowned. Someone had turned the camera on despite his taking precautions. It was blinking in the corner.

Ricki looked at Lawrence pointedly. Lawrence was puzzled at first, but then he realised about the camera and left hurriedly to take care of it.

Ricki sipped his teaand looked at his watch. He was careful not to drink anything intoxicating while making a deal. It was time for Mr Handa to come, yet too many people were around the bar.

"Hello, Rakesh." The squeaky voice, sounding like a grasshopper, didn't match the big man sitting on the high stool.

Ricki swirled around to see Harman Handa smiling at him.

He ordered whiskey for the newcomer and took him to sit in a corner of the hall. Zinnia had gone, and the band was playing a merry tune. Five girls were dancing to the happy tune. The music was loud, and people were talking. There was a hum that made talking difficult.

"When will Jaipal come?" Squeaked Mr. Handa.

"He will be a little late." Replied Ricki.

"Simlipur is ready." Mr Handa spoke in Ricki's ears.

The two of them spoke confidentially. At this time Zinnia returned to the stage, and the girls moved to the side to give her the centre stage. Zinnia started singing and was slowly moved to the hall. Her swaying body touched some of the male guests deliberately, and she crooned sexily. She was moving around the entrance and progressing towards Ricki's corner. As she reached their table, Harman Handa smiled lasciviously at her. Zinnia played with his necktie and leaned on the table. Then, suddenly, she turned and glanced briefly at Ricki and nodded in understanding before moving away from the table. Her eyes shined, and she smiled with a secret knowledge. Ricki understood the threatening undercurrents and clenched his fists. His jaws tightened. He looked angry, but the other man didn't notice, for he was captivated by her sexy performance.

Zinnia finished her performance and went to her little dressing room at the back of the clubhouse. Many of the male guests had sent their phone numbers written on napkins while she was performing, which were lying on her dressing table. They had money, were habituated to getting what they wanted, and desired Zinnia's private dance show. Zinnia had stopped doing private shows since her engagement to Jaipal, but she was doing many club performances and hoped to save enough before it was time for her to be rejected by these clubs. She knew that she wouldn't be young and attractive forever. She stared at her reflection in the mirror and thought, "Yes, with makeup, I still look like twenty-something. My hair is still perfect and skin... soft, smooth...breasts... firm...the middle... okayish ...flat." The sudden buzzing of her phone brought her back to the confined dressing room. Zinnia looked at the caller ID and smiled.

"I am sorry to have missed your performance. But we can have some fun before the night ends." Laughed a deep male voice in her ears. It was her lover, Jaipal Bajwa.

"He was there with Ricki. Why didn't you come? Is he making a new deal without you?" Zinnia was concerned.

"You mean Handa, right?" Jaipal asked seriously.

"Yes, Handa was having a nice cosy chat with Ricki. I wouldn't say I like how Ricki sent you away to wash his dirty linen while he was sharing secrets with Handa. We have to be smarter." Zinnia sounded furious.

Jaipal became silent for a few seconds, then said, "If he tries to pin that murder on me, then I will use the little surprise to get even with Ricki. In the meantime, don't leak anything. Be your own happy, beautiful self. Let me handle the situation."

Zinnia became excited. She knew that Jaipal was wanted by the police of at least two states, yet he was indeed in love with her. She also loved him and trusted him. Sometimes, she wants to have a family with Jaipal in the future. She tensed at the thought of the 'little surprise'.

"Babe, you have become too thoughtful. Did anyone bother you during the performance or afterwards? Wait, is it Lawrence again?" Jaipal sounded anxious and angry.

Zinnia knew that he was the possessive and protective type of lover. He needed to be handled with love, and she was ready to shower him with her passion, money and everything else to keep him to her.

"I am a big girl and know how to deal with men like Lawrence." Stated Zinnia.

"Are you certain?" Jaipal hissed.

"I cannot see beyond you, Jaipal. Don't you trust me?" Zinnia said coquettishly and purred like a cat.

Suddenly, a loud knock interrupted their conversation, and Zinnia put Jaipal on hold to open the door. Vivek, the waiter, was standing outside. He looked apologetic and awkwardly, "Mr Handa is asking for you, Zinnia. Shall I tell him that you have left?"

"Yes... no, wait, tell him to wait in the bar." Zinnia said hesitantly before closing the door.

"Why did you agree to meet that man? He has a reputation." Jaipal sounded worried.

"Jai, don't you have any faith in me? I know about him and will handle him with kids' gloves. Don't worry about my meeting him, but worry about the deal."

"Okay, I will concentrate on getting control over Ricki. He doesn't know yet that we know the date and the names. Where have you hidden the video?" Jaipal sounded relaxed.

"In the same old place... you know." Zinnia whispered.

"Hmm. I think tonight would be wonderful. Ricki is planning something dangerous. His new love is waiting, and we can safely intimidate him. He will be careful not to displease us. From now on, we can be free, and I can control Ricki." Jaipal smiled with satisfaction.

"It is not wise to be euphoric before we are secured. We must be careful, Jai." Zinnia reminded him. She had a perfect plan to scare Ricki.

"My smart girl! No one must know of our plan and the video." Jaipal was cautious.

"Yes, my love, I know when and how to pull strings." giggled Zinnia.

"Naughty girl!" Laughed Jaipal.

She was ready to leave as she finished her conversation. Suddenly, there was a light knock on her door. She knew it was not Vivek again.

"Who is there?" she asked in a worried tone.

"It's me. I have an important message from Jaipal." Replied Lawrence.

Zinnia opened her door and saw Lawrence standing in the low light. He looked a little drunk and nervous. A waiter was passing through the corridor, and he smiled at them.

"I was talking to Jaipal only a few minutes ago. Why are you doing this, Lawrence? You know that we are engaged. We are going to get married soon. Don't mess with me. Jaipal's reputation as a brutal, violent person is not at all fake or exaggerated." Scoffed Zinnia.

"And I shall tell Jaipal something is happening between you and Ricki. Are you two having it?" Threatened Lawrence.

"Do your best, Lawrence. I don't care. Tonight, let Jaipal come. Then he will take care of you also. Why don't you find someone who is inclined to you?" Retorted Zinnia.

"You will regret Zinnia. I can make you very happy and keep you safe forever. I am not yet wanted... you know by whom. We can start afresh somewhere, far away." Lawrence insisted.

In one swift movement, he clasped her to his body. He was aroused. Zinnia pushed him away with her might, but he was unwilling to let go of her. At that moment, another waiter entered the narrow passage and stopped near Zinnia's room. He could hear muffled, struggling noises. The waiter smiled wickedly and moved away from Zinnia's dressing room.

A Few minutes later, Lawrence walked back to the bar. He was looking angry and frustrated.

Were you having fun with Zinnia? She sure knows how to make a man dance with her sexy ways." Laughed Ricki.

"Remember, you wanted the camera to be fixed. Vivek was busy somewhere, so I had to find him first. And I didn't go to her room." Lied Lawrence.

"Sure, I have not seen anything nor heard anything. Don't worry; Jaipal will not know about your little bouts with his girl. Not from me, at least. You are smart, Lawrence, but be careful with Jaipal's girl." Ricki cautioned him.

Lawrence didn't reply. He was angry at Ricki for his knowledge about his feelings. And also because Ricki met Harman Handa in his absence. Jaipal was also away, and Raghubir was sent on the pretext of misfit clothes, which was bullshit, in his opinion. He was having doubts about Ricki's intentions of including him in the new deal with Handa. He walked out to the cards room, where Raghubir was playing cards. He joined him at the cards table and lost track of time as they started winning, and the game became interesting.

Zinnia exited her tiny dressing room and went to the bar for a glass of wine while looking for Harman Handa. She was draped in a blue chiffon saree with sequins. She looked sophisticated, pretty, and worldly, like any other wealthy guest of the Club. Many of the members and the guests had already left. A few of the remaining guests were scattered around the club. Sam, the bartender, smiled at her and said, "You are in demand today. Mr Handa was waiting for you, but something came up, and he left. Then, another gentleman was enquiring about your whereabouts."

Zinnia smiled preoccupiedly and asked for a glass of red wine. As she was sipping her wine leisurely, Vivek Malakar came and slipped a note in Zinnia's hand when nobody was looking. She read the note and frowned.

"Who gave you this?" asked Zinnia.

"A gentleman, but I have never seen him before," Answered Vivek. He didn't look happy.

"How does he look?" Asked Zinnia.

"Oldish with thinning hair and thick glasses. He sported a healthy moustache. I don't remember his clothes. Maybe he was wearing a black tee shirt," Vivek said.

Zinnia reread the short note. It read, "I have been looking for a sexy dancer for an item song in my web series. Today, I found the correct candidate. You would look fabulous as Heera. If you are interested, then come to meet me in the garden. Vanraj Joshi of Doosri Awaz."

Zinnia looked around but couldn't find the note's writer. "Can this filmmaker Vanraj be the same Vanraj Joshi, the film director I always wanted to meet?" She thought to herself and breathed deeply.

"Vivek, are you sure the gentleman didn't give you his name?" Zinnia asked.

"W-well, he did say... his name... Vanraj Joshi. But think Zinnia, why should he come here? Don't you think that this is something fishy?" Vivek asked earnestly.

Zinnia smiled at him sweetly as she was elated with the offer and dreamt of being in the film industry. She thought about her opportunity to meet other film people. With a fluttering heart, she stepped out. Vivek looked on helplessly. He thought of the camera in the garden and tried to calm his frayed nerves. He didn't know why he was feeling so agitated. "Should I follow Zinnia... at least I can help her if..." Vivek looked outside through the glass windows.

The Club's spacious garden had lamps, but the night was dark and cast long deep shadows. Zinnia took a few steps and looked around. There was no one waiting for her. She contemplated returning when she saw the bench where a gentleman was smoking a cigarette. She tried to have a better look at Vanraj Joshi, but he was sitting directly underneath one of the lamps, which cast long shadows on his frame. Zinnia looked back at the club and hesitated for a moment. She saw Vivek standing framed in the doorway. She relaxed as the thought of being covered calmed her. Besides, the desire for stardom and fame pulled her towards the gentleman sitting on the bench. She waved at Vivek in recognition.

"Yes, I can manage him." She said to herself and walked confidently to the bench.

"Hello sir, I am Zinnia..." her introduction trailed off as she saw the man turn towards her.

She had never expected someone like him to be Vanraj Joshi. He looked different in the photos.

"I know, I look different in the photos. That's makeup, you know, showbiz. Today, I came here to meet a distant relative and saw your dance. I liked your moves and turns. I am looking for someone to play Heera. She is one of the main witnesses in the series. Before I leave, I wanted to take an audition of you. How about tomorrow morning?" Vanraj Joshi almost whispered the words.

Zinnia turned towards the doorframe to look for Vivek and felt glad he was still standing where she had seen him. Vanraj Joshi also looked in her direction and said smilingly, "You should have brought your young man along, and he would have seen that I don't bite... but I need to keep our meeting a secret. Can you please accompany me to that seat beneath the big tree?"

Zinnia was surprised at his request and hesitated but ultimately decided to cater to his whimsical wishes. She thought that creativity makes one whimsical and fanciful. She started walking to the big tree and turned back to see Vivek standing at the door still.

They reached the big tree, and Zinnia looked back at Vivek, but he couldn't be seen from that place. Suddenly, Vanraj Joshi took hold of her hand. His grip was firm like steel. Something about him alarmed Zinnia, and she tried to cry for help, but he put his other hand over her mouth. She tried to free herself. His steel-like grip tightened, and she was like a butterfly caught in the net. Vanraj Joshi had great strength and held her captivated in an odd position. Suddenly, he gripped her throat with one hand, and she felt faint, and his grip tightened. He was like a wild, hungry animal with easy prey within reach. Zinnia couldn't utter another sound. Her choking breathing stopped. The devil's smile was the last image she saw before everything became black. Her limp, lifeless body fell to the ground, and the man walked away without once looking back. It was evident that he was an expert in the art of killing.

CHAPTER XIV

Dead Bodies

5 March 2023, Kolkata

"You should have been more careful about Zinnia. Now, I am also in the same boat as you. You will pay dearly if anything happens to me for your stupid love. I promise I will not let you go," Raghubir growled like a caged lion. "I know it was Vivek who ratted us out. He has to pay for this. Leave Zinnia out of this mess," Lawrence muttered quietly, but it was more effective as Raghubir became silent. The small, dingy room smelled of stale food. The tiny openings on the walls were windows opening into a dark alley. Raghubir and Lawrence were arguing about Zinnia's death when Raghubir's phone rang. He put the phone on speaker and looked at Lawrence. The speaker was Ricki, their boss.

"We all know that Zinnia is dead. And Jaipal thinks that you both are responsible. Why did you mess with his girl? You know Jaipal, and now he's looking for you both. You should be careful."

The brief message was like a bomb. Raghubir and Lawrence paled and became very agitated. They both knew that someone else had killed Zinnia, but Jaipal was super possessive about Zinnia, and he could be an adamant bull. On many occasions, he had shown his ruthless killer instinct. Now that she was dead, it would be challenging to control Jaipal. But Lawrence and Raghubir suspected each other for Zinnia's murder. Jaipal suspected Raghubir and Lawrence to be responsible for Zinnia's death.

"I was playing cards after Zinnia's performance. I know I am not responsible for her death, and I also know that you went to meet her after her singing. Was it jealousy or frustration of rejection that made you lose your mind, Lawrence?" asked Raghubir. He had visibly changed his tactics.

"No, no, I didn't kill her. I liked her and wanted her, but I never wanted to hurt her. I know something was happening between

Ricki and Zinnia behind Jaipal's back. Can we trust Ricki? He was planning something with Harman Handa and playing a game with Zinnia. I saw them both looking at each other like hunters looking at targets. Maybe they started something, but now that Ricki has another girl, he doesn't want to complicate his love life." Lawrence stopped talking and became thoughtful.

"Maybe she was punished for getting greedy. We all know the rules. Ricki never tolerates prying into his business. Zinnia was becoming overconfident and curious. She asked too many questions. I think Jaipal also knew something, and he was supporting her. Sam told me that a film producer came to meet Zinnia. I wonder about this mysterious film producer." Mused Raghubir.

"Sam, the bartender, told you about the film producer? I think that whoever gave Jaipal the idea that we are responsible for her death is the murderer. We should ask the servers and other staff at the club about Zinnia's engagements for the evening. I am worried about Ricki's motive. He seems to be starting something new and doesn't want us." Lawrence pondered.

They both became pensive and started making a list of people who had been seen with Zinnia the previous night.

"Raghu, I think only Ricki would gain from our deaths. He wants to leave this whole mess and start a secure life. It was going great until the incident near Bhopal. Now the police are looking for us. They have learnt many of our secrets, too." Commented Lawrence.

"Do you mean the death of that university professor, the Poet? He was murdered in cold blood. His death was just a by-product," Raghubir remarked.

"And the other man, his associate, somebody Singh, was the witness, and so he too had to die. The Police are looking for the killers. I thought Jaipal was responsible for the murders and Ricki was the helper. But the work was not neat. The witness lived long enough to give his statement to the police. They are looking for Jaipal and Ricki. But they have no idea how they look, and we can help the Police. That's why Ricki and Jaipal are afraid we will make a deal with the Police. But I am not sure about the murders. I think Ricki murdered them because shooting someone from close is Ricki's speciality. Jaipal is good with his bare hands. And since they think that we can help the Police to identify them, they are after us. We must run before Ricki or Jaipal gets us." Observed Lawrence.

"Do you know about Detective Dipto Bhanu Chowdhury? He is taking an interest in Ricki's business. The other day, I slipped from their clutches by a fraction of a moment. Detective Bhanu Chowdhury is not for sale. He was asking a lot of people about Ricki. By the way, the police call him Raka. The detective is working with the Police of Bhopal and Durgapur. I would hate to be tortured by the Police. I will reveal all and become the state witness. Ricki has been cutting me out of many of his businesses. So, Ricki would hate if I get caught." Stated Raghubir.

"He is planning something big with Harman Handa. He kept me out of it, too. I know he is planning something in Simlipur. I surprised Ricki when he was talking to someone, Das, on the phone. He became so furious. And I have suspicions about Nirmala, too. Something was happening between Nirmala and Ricki just before they went to Mandarmani. I wonder how and why she drowned. Did she commit suicide? She had been Ricki's angel for a long time. Now, Ricki has Layla. She will die readily for him. I also know about his short fling with Zinnia. And like you, I would rather tell all than take the torture of the Police. So, I am also a threat to Ricki." Agreed Lawrence.

"Let's make a pact with Jaipal. I think he will be interested in knowing about Simlipur. He can find out more about the deals and Harman Handa. We would be safe from Jaipal, and three can take down Ricki." Raghubir smiled maliciously at his idea.

Police Detective Dipto Bhanu Chowdhury is well known among criminals and colleagues for his ruthless and uncompromising success at incarcerating felons. He was talking to Inspector Ramprasad Banik, the investigating officer in charge at the Durgapur Thana. Detective Dipto Bhanu said, "Inspector, I want to see the CCTV footage, and I need to talk to the staff at the

Durgapur Club. I want Harman Handa and Rakesh, or Ricki as he calls himself, together on the screen."

Inspector Banik replied, "My men are already working on it. But there is something wrong with the CCTV footage. The camera stopped working just a few minutes before Harman Handa entered the scene. It resumed working after a few hours. The barman, Sam, mentioned seeing a film producer, who might have asked Zinnia to meet him. We have the footage of the film producer. He was seen walking to the garden after Zinnia. And another curious thing is that Vivek Malakar has been missing since the night of the murder. He is a waiter at the club and is in love with the girl. According to Sam, Vivek was standing at the door of the garden to keep a watch on Zinnia as she went out with the filmmaker."

Detective Dipto Bhanu asked eagerly, "I want the footage of the film producer. Is he someone known popularly?"

Inspector Banik answered, "The film producer is Vanraj Joshi. He was known for B-grade Bollywood films, but now, he is the maker of two successful Netflix series. We are trying to locate him."

Detective Dipto Bhanu promised to help find the producer before ending the call.

Detective Dipto Bhanu looked more like an ordinary officegoer than a police detective when not in his uniform. He had a deep cut mark on his chin, the result of an injury caused while catching an offender. He was tall and fit. His well-maintained moustache suited his sharp features. He was in his early thirties and was already a well-recommended name as an honest and efficient police detective at the Lal Bazar Police Department, Kolkata. He missed nothing and was not much of a talker.

Detective Dipto Bhanu was in pursuit of a brilliant vehicle thief, Rakesh Gupta or Ricki. He had a network of men who worked as mechanics and drivers. Rakesh Gupta was very adept at changing his looks and identity. On several occasions, he had slipped away from being caught by inches. He was accused of stealing more than five thousand vehicles from different parts of the country.

Bhopal Police, Patna Police, Amritsar Police and Police of other states joined forces to find Rakesh Gupta and his close associate Jaipal Bajwa. The duo were like chameleons changing colours. Rakesh spoke several languages fluently and was known to act like a gentleman. They were successful as a team until they killed a well-respected and well-known professor in Bhopal in mid-December of the previous year. There was a witness to the killing. The much-loved professor was Faisal Ahmed, and he was a poet too. The witness to his killing was a local tradesman named Suraj Singh. He, too, was shot at by one of the duo. He was admitted to the hospital in a critical condition, and he gave his statement before his death. Later, he died in the hospital.

Suraj's statement was enough to identify the criminal Rakesh Gupta and his associate Jaipal Bajwa. They had three more close members in their team. Detective Dipto Bhanu was given the case as they had information about Rakesh being in Kolkata. He studied their method of stealing cars and vehicles. There seemed to be a systematic plan for each theft.

"What are you thinking, Sir?" Lakshman's thin voice broke Dipto Bhanu's reveries. Lakshman Kundu was Dipto Bhanu's assistant. He was a good listener and a big foodie.

"Lakshman, what would you have done now if you were Rakesh Gupta? I am trying to think like him. He is smart and keeps all information regarding the crimes he commits. So, by now, he must know that Professor Ahmed's murder witness, Suraj Singh, gave his statement before his death. And, accordingly, he must be planning to escape. Recently, he made a deal with the insurance agent Harman Handa. I know that Rakesh Gupta was stationed in Durgapur and is now in Kolkata. He can mingle with society without raising any suspicions. So, we need to keep vigilance on different clubs and garages." Dipto Bhanu walked to the evidence board and studied the vehicle theft map made from the shreds of evidence and reports from other state police.

"Sir, is Rakesh Gupta wealthy? After all, he has been stealing for many years now." Lakshman commented.

"He might be rich. He has a very expensive taste that we know. He goes to the Durgapur Club, founded by the wealthy local traders. He has a girl or more than one female associate. And he has pistols and guns, too. But he is well-spoken, can speak several languages flawlessly and seems like a well-read, cultured gentleman. He is in his mid-thirties or nearing forty, charming and sometimes irresistible to women. And lastly, he is like a magician with his looks. His associate, Jaipal Bajwa, is younger than him and looks handsome, too. The duo can open any locked car, truck, motorbike, and other vehicles. We have a definite description of Jaipal as he was some years ago, but Rakesh is a chameleon. He has been said to be tall, medium height, dark-skinned, fair, very handsome, bald, long-haired, thin, fat, big-nosed, nearly ugly and even lame..."

"Sir, he seems to be an impossible person. How can one person be all that? Finding him will be like finding a needle in a haystack. Maybe he is here in this building... how will we know him when we see him? Lakshman was more bewildered than ever.

The desk phone rang just then, and Dipto Bhanu picked it up at the first ring. He listened very carefully. The call was from one of his teammen. He had found Lawrence and Raghubir's hiding place.

Detective Dipto Bhanu put down the receiver and said, "Lakshman, get ready for a long night. We have found the den of Lawrence and Raghubir."

"Yes, Sir, pull the ears, and the head will follow automatically...," Answered Lakshman Kundu.

It was a hot, humid night when Detective Bhanu Chowdhury and his team positioned themselves in the area where the notorious criminals were hiding. The team kept vigil for over two hours, yet the criminals didn't return. Around midnight, Lawrence was seen coming with his motorcycle. He switched off the engine while still on the main road, walked stealthily into a pitch-dark alley, and parked his motorcycle in the shadows of a narrow passage between two tall buildings. Detective Chowdhury and his men were hiding near the alley. Lawrence opened a door almost hidden in a crevice and walked in the dark. He didn't look back in the dark alley, so he missed the inching and crouching dark figures approaching his door. Lawrence shut the door behind him but didn't lock it. There seemed to be the silence of a tomb, and suddenly, Detective Chowdhury and his team broke in with a shattering noise. The small room was shabby and smelt of stale food. A single yellow bulb illuminated the room, and they found Lawrence on the bed. He had just thrown himself down on the narrow bed when the police entered. Detective Chowdhury didn't give a moment to Lawrence to recover from the shock but almost pounced on him and put him in handcuffs.

Lawrence looked terrified and shaken. He was a reasonably decent-looking fellow and wore fashionable clothes. Lawrence looked to be in his late twenties. "Sir, there must be a mistake. I have done nothing. I don't work for any of the parties...," Lawrence pleaded.

"Where is your partner? When will he come here?" Asked Dipto Bhanu.

"I-I don't know, Sir. I have no idea what you are speaking about. Sir, I am just a mechanic and work very hard," Lawrence tried to plead with the Detective.

"No one will make any sound. I want the other one also. He is bound to return," Cautioned Dipto Bhanu.

Detective Dipto Bhanu's team left the room with the handcuffed Lawrence. They moved stealthily. Detective Chowdhury and Lakshman stayed in the dingy room and looked for his personal belongings. Dipto Bhanu found Lawrence's mobile phone in the crevice between the thin mattress and the wood of the bed's headboard. Two bank cards were on the small table, along with some cash.

Lawrence was led to the police van, and as he was being ushered, a man in a motorbike passed them. The biker wore a tight black outfit with a helmet covering his face. He passed by the police van and vanished into the nearest turn of the road. The police van with Lawrence proceeded towards the station by the same most immediate turn the biker had taken a few minutes before. The van had gone a few meters when the tires screeched, and the van careened. Somebody had thrown nails on the road, and the tires were punctured. They had to stop the vehicle and see the extent of the damage. Lawrence was inside the van with one constable. One of the other two members was busy arranging a change of vehicle, and the other got busy with the tyres.

Suddenly, a man in a black outfit with a face-covering helmet came out from a dark corner. He was riding his motorbike slowly. He came to the side of the police van and suddenly took out a revolver and shot at Lawrence. In a blink of an eye, he accomplished what he wanted. His aim was flawless and perfect. Larence was dead in a moment, and the biker sped past the police van. The whole thing happened within a matter of a few minutes. The constable sitting with Lawrence jumped down, but the biker was very swift, and before the team members could grasp the situation or take any action, the biker was gone. He was almost out of sight when the police team saw that Lawrence was shot. Lawrence was dying, and he tried to utter something. "Ric Ric Ri...," Lawrence died before finishing what he wanted to say.

Detective Dipto Bhanu came quickly, but the damage had been done. There was no life left in Lawrence. The other wanted criminal, Raghubir, didn't return to his den. Dipto Bhanu was angry because they had taken enough precautions to keep the operation secret, yet it seemed to have leaked.

"Who was the man with the motorcycle? How did he come to know about Lawrence's arrest? What did Lawrence try to tell? Was he trying to say that Rakesh was the motorbiker? How did he know that Rakesh would kill him? Will he kill Raghubir, too? Rakesh Gupta... Ricki... Raka..." Dipto Bhanu stood before his evidence board and thought about his next step.

"Sir, Raghubir has flown away, and we don't have any leads on Jaipal or Rakesh... What should we do now?" Lakshman came in with two cups of steaming tea and two jhalmuris. Dipto Bhanu looked at the clock and Lakshman. It was very late for jhalmuris, and he took the cup of tea while Lakshman smiled and munched the two jhalmuris happily.

In the early morning, in another small room, almost hidden behind a garage, a man was agitated and walked into the room like a caged lion. Ultimately, he came to a decision and dialled an unlisted number. He was the notorious criminal Jaipal Bajwa. He had light skin, brown hair, light brown piercing eyes and a beautiful smile. He was in his late twenties, about 5'8" tall and weighed about sixty-five kilograms. He looked robust but spoke in soft tones. He had an ugly cut mark on the left cheek, which seemed like a knife cut but could also be the result of some accident. He had a soft demeanour, and it was difficult to imagine him committing any crime or murder. He was the type that women found attractive and dependable. He was not a great talker and made friends rarely. But he had been in love with Zinnia, the bar dancer. They were planning to get married soon. He recalled Zinnia's last phone call and wondered if someone had eavesdropped their conversation. And he thought about Lawrence's murder a few hours earlier. He had gone to the dark alley and found the place swarming with police. He heard enough to understand the reason for the commotion. He came back to the safety of his hideout quickly. It had taken nearly an hour for him to analyse the situation, and he came to a decision. He called Rakesh.

"Lawrence is dead, and I did not kill him," Jaipal muttered as soon as Rakesh answered.

"Dead? Are you sure? Where is Raghu?"

"He is on the run; I haven't heard from him since the last few hours. His phone is switched off. But I shall get him, and he will sing me the truth." Hissed Jaipal.

"Did you get to see Zinnia before the police took away her body? I saw her dead body. It was not a pretty sight." Commented Rakesh.

"Ricki, where were you when Zinnia died?" asked Jaipal

"I was with Lawrence and Raghubir at the bar when Zinnia sang in the Hall. Then, I went to the card room and played a few rounds. Lawrence and Raghubir went to the bar for some time, and then suddenly, they rushed in with Zinnia's death news. They were looking awful and nervous." Rakesh answered calmly.

"I will find the murderer no matter what comes between," Growled Jaipal.

"You should know that Lawrence was sweet on Zinnia, but she was yours. Lawrence was becoming extremely jealous, unreliable, and problematic. Didn't Zinnia tell you about his lecherous attentions? But he was a coward, and cowards get killed. Other than Lawrence, Raghubir was also trying his best to impress Zinnia. Maybe they thought that your Zinnia was available for a price." Said the cold voice from the other end.

In another part of the city, the man switched off his mobile and took out the sim card. He broke the SIM and threw it away. He was Ricki to many people and Rakesh Nag to the general society. Rakesh Gupta for another set of people and had many other aliases. He stood in front of the mirror in his bedroom and smiled wickedly. He was wearing a charcoal grey blazer with dark trousers. He opened the blazer and looked at his image in the mirror. He was still wearing the body-hugging black suit inside the blazer. He took out the locally made pistol in the drawer of his dresser and started opening his suit.

"When did you come, Rik?" Asked a husky female voice from the crumpled luxurious bed.

"I didn't mean to wake you up, Layla... Mmm..." Rakesh kissed the woman passionately.

"What are we celebrating?" The woman cuddled him.

"Taken care of Lawrence and Raghubir. I also got rid of the number plate of the motorbike. I have given enough hints to Jaipal, and he should be going to Durgapur now. It's going to be sooner than expected." Rakesh whispered in Layla's ears.

"Then, you should call me by my new name." laughed Layla.

"H---- "the woman closed his mouth with hers before he could say her name. Their bodies became entangled with urgency.

The next evening, in another part of the city, Jaipal looked at the mirror and nodded in satisfaction. The mirror reflected the image of a woman with salt and pepper hair tied in a small bun at the nape. The woman wore glasses with a discoloured frame. Her blue salwar kurta was a bit dirty and loose fitting. Her skin looked unhealthy, and her lips were red with betel leaves. Jaipal looked like an ordinary female worker. He took out a burka and wore it over the salwar suit.

"Zinnia, I shall avenge your murder." Swore Jaipal under his breath. He took his belongings in a small bag and went out, locking the door.

Jaipal's hiding room was in the back of an oversized garage. A teenage boy was working on a bike when Jaipal went through the garage. The boy looked at Jaipal but didn't seem to recognise him in his disguise.

Jaipal went towards Howrah Railway Station in the darkness of the night.

CHAPTER XV

Spotlight on the Previous Year

18 May 2022

Jaipal Bajwa bought a second-class ticket and boarded the train from Howrah Junction. The train started at the right time, and Jaipal sat comfortably on one side seat. The opposite seat was still empty when the train pulled out of the station. Jaipal leaned back on the seat.

Two stations went by without interruptions, and then a young man came to sit opposite Jaipal. Jaipal watched closely at the young man sitting on the opposite seat through the heavy veil of the burka. The young man yawned and closed his eyes after a few moments. Jaipal loosened his muscles and sat comfortably. Soon, the ticket collector came, and Jaipal produced his fake ID. "Amina Khatoon... okay, here you are," the ticket checker returned the ID.

Jaipal relaxed with the train's rhythm and thought about that night when Zinnia wanted to go to the sea beach. The whole evening became vibrant in Jaipal's mind, and he could still hear the happy tunes when Zinnia entered the stage. The date was 17 May 2022.

The band was already playing a happy tune when she entered the stage. Immediately, the lights dimmed, and a spotlight fell on Zinnia. She looked provocative in her shimmering maroon dress. She crooned seductively, and everyone concentrated on her performance. Zinnia sang and moved amongst the guests. The spotlight followed her. She stopped at a table where Jaipal was sitting with a gorgeous couple. The gentleman had short hair like a soldier and dressed in a classy suit. He smiled at Zinnia and looked appreciatively at Jaipal. He was Rakesh Nag. The lady adorned a silk saree with coordinating jewellery and makeup. But something in her appearance made Zinnia notice her minutely. "Nirmala has been beaten, but she is hiding it well. Why did Rakesh beat her?

Interesting! Everyone has their firsts, and tonight, Nirmala had her first beatings. But why?" thought Zinnia while performing one of her regular sensual songs.

Twice, she noticed Jaipal looking at Nirmala with concern, and she felt pangs of jealousy. She recalled that Jaipal and Nirmala were often seen together. Rakesh didn't seem to mind. On the contrary, perversely, he seemed to enjoy seeing them together. "Are they in love?" thought Zinnia as she passed their table.

Jaipal had smiled inwardly because he knew what Zinnia was thinking. After her performance, she went inside for a short break, and Jaipal followed her stealthily. He wanted to surprise her. As Jaipal neared her tiny dressing room at the back of the Club, he saw Vivek Malakar standing in front of Zinnia's room. He was looking sad and dejected, like an unfortunate man.

Zinnia peeked out of her dressing room to look for Jaipal. Instead, she saw Vivek standing in the dimly lit corridor. Vivek had seen Zinnia before she could get inside. He had been waiting for her to open the door. Both of them didn't see Jaipal standing in the dimly lit corridor.

"Zinnia, please give me a chance. I promise to keep you happy, always. I love you and adore you. I will do everything to keep you on cloud nine. Zinnia – please..."

"Vivek, you are looking like a puppy begging for treats. I know that you love me, but I don't love you back. There is no future for us. Don't pest me with your love and puppy looks."

"Zinnia, I know that it is about money. I know I don't have the money to make you happy, but give me one chance, and I promise to show you my worth." Vivek was nearing tears.

Zinnia did not bother to answer him and went inside, shutting the door noisily. Her brows were knitted together, and she bit her lower lip thoughtfully. She did not notice Jaipal opening her dressing room door. He came inside and hid himself behind a row of shining clothes. Unaware of his presence, Zinnia looked at the mirror, reflecting her beautiful features. She had just crossed thirty but still looked like a twenty-plus-year-old. Her curly hair was adorned with red roses, and her sparkling dangling earrings and oval face looked perfect. She was blessed with healthy, dusky skin and an ideal figure. She said to her reflection, "Once, you thought of being an actress and singer in Bollywood films. But destiny has made you a singer in demand in many elite clubs. Now, you have accepted your status as the Club singer. And you've learnt to deal with obscene, lewd and drunkards. Now, you have Jaipal... Jaipal... Oh, I love you so much, Jaipal...But why do you torture me so much? Don't you love me? Not in the least..."

Zinnia drew out the gold bracelet she had bought for Jaipal and sighed. Then, she looked at herself in the mirror again and smiled confidently.

"Yes... Today is the day. I will not let anyone come between us." Vowed Zinnia as she closed the bracelet box. She had to leave for another performance. Jaipal remained in her tiny dressing room and smiled. He, too, loved her.

After her performance, Zinnia sat in the bar with Jaipal, Rakesh, and Nirmala. Zinnia was mainly talking while the other three sat quietly. Nirmala looked tensed and drank a lot of water. Rakesh smiled a lot and looked indifferent to Nirmala's tension. Jaipal was observing quietly. He heard everything and missed nothing. Zinnia was talking about a film by Vanraj Joshi. But no one shared her excitement about the filmmaker Vanraj Joshi. Nirmala looked scared and watched Rakesh furtively.

"This is the time of the year when I love to go to the sea beach. Let us plan something. Nirmala, are you in?" asked Zinnia.

"Hmm... seaside... no, no, I don't want to go anywhere..." Nirmala looked at Rakesh anxiously. She tried to hide her fear, but her eyes expressed everything clearly. Zinnia was interested.

Nirmala and Rakesh were an attractive couple who always maintained a friendly social appearance. Zinnia had never seen Nirmala to be frightened of Rakesh. She needed to know the details.

"I was thinking of a short trip to the sea beach, somewhere near, like Digha or Mandarmani. It would be fun for all of us together. what do you say?" Zinnia asked playfully.

"This is a great idea, Zinnia. Of course, we will join you both and will have fun together. This trip is on me. I will take care of everything. Jaipal, this girl is brilliant." Laughed Rakesh while Nirmala looked panic-stricken.

"Something is not right. I must find out everything about Nirmala. She is hiding something. Has Jaipal noticed her plight?" Zinnia's thoughts became busy concocting a plan.

She looked pointedly at Jaipal and was happy to see him watching Nirmala intently. "He has noticed, too."

The following day, the foursome were on their way to Mandarmani. It was a beautiful morning, and their car was speeding on a still-empty road. They started their journey well before the morning rush. Zinnia sat in the back seat with Jaipal. Nirmala was seated in the front seat and seemed unhappy still. "What is bothering her? Is she still scared?" thought Zinnia. She passed a message to Jaipal on WhatsApp. Jaipal looked at her in agreement.

"When will we reach Mandarmani?" asked Zinnia.

"In about one hour," Rakesh replied curtly.

"I need to go to the loo. Can we stop at the coming Dhaba?" Zinnia asked.

Some ten minutes later, they stopped at a Dhaba. Nirmala also went to the bathroom, and Zinnia had her chance to ask.

"Nirmala, you must tell me why you are so frightened of Rakesh. What have you done? Please don't pretend everything is okay because I know something has happened. Besides, you look like the picture of fear. Tell me about your problems. Maybe Jai can help," Zinnia coaxed her.

At first, Nirmala was too frightened to open her mouth, but Zinnia repeatedly persuaded her to speak up. Finally, Nirmala came to a decision. She agreed to speak.

"Wait, let me get you recorded. Then you can feel a lot safer." Zinnia started recording Nirmala's narration.

"I have finally joined the missing dots. Prakash Sur was also involved. Sajal Haldar was the man in question. He was killed. I do not know why or how, but I know that something terrible had happened that day. Both of them were in it together. Ricky, I mean Rakesh, knew them and cautioned me against him, but I was in love. Madly, truly, wholeheartedly in love with him. Then he came to me on a very wet monsoon night. He climbed up the rain pipe and came to me in secrecy. I was in love, and I gave myself. I was a fool and didn't obey my Baba or my grandfather. I became involved in the incident unknowingly and became his alibi. At the time, I had no idea about Sajal's death. Now, I cannot rewind the past and go to my Baba. I have to keep him safe. It had been raining very heavily that monsoon..." Nirmala stopped speaking as someone knocked urgently on the door. She looked terrified when Rakesh's deep voice floated through the thin door.

He was hurrying them. Immediately, Zinnia put her mobile in her bag and shouted to Rakesh to wait. He was standing in front of the door when Zinnia came out. She said teasingly, "Don't you know that it is bad manners to knock on the ladies' door? But I am jealous of you two love birds. You can't be separated even for this short while! Your lovely wife is in the toilet. She sounded like she was vomiting. Maybe she will take more time... have a little patience, Rakesh."

Rakesh glared at her and looked suspiciously. "What were you talking about?" He asked.

"Talking?! When did we talk? She went straight inside one of the coops and locked herself in. Why do you ask?" Zinnia sounded innocent and carefree.

After a few minutes, Nirmala came out looking disturbed. She said that her stomach was upset and she was sleepy. They resumed their journey to Mandarmani. Zinnia uploaded the video to the cloud storage while sitting in the back passenger seat. Jaipal was dozing by her side. Nirmala slept or pretended to sleep for the rest of the journey. Zinnia was perplexed at the narration. It was not at all clear. There were many names mentioned, and it seemed confusing. "Was she talking about this Rakesh or somebody else... she mentioned Ricki, but then who was the fellow with whom she had fallen in love?" Zinnia was frustrated at Nirmala's poor ability to narrate an incident.

"Will I get another chance to speak with Nirmala? I have to find out about Sajal Haldar's death. Maybe I should talk to Jai. Will he be interested in knowing about Nirmala's secret? I think that she was talking about two different people. This video could be our security. When did it happen? Where are the other men she mentioned? Who is Ricky or Rakesh? Ugh! Nirmala is such a lousy storyteller..." Zinnia's train of thought was broken as Rakesh chirped that they had reached Mandarmani.

They had stopped in front of a lavish-looking resort. It was almost on the sea beach. They went in together. Nirmala looked uneasy and glanced at the security cameras in the reception area. Zinnia noticed that Rakesh didn't bother taking off his cap or sunshades. Rakesh had already reserved two deluxe rooms overlooking the sea. Zinnia and Jaipal readily went to their room while Nirmala hesitated. Zinnia saw Rakesh's face and trembled to think of herself in Nirmala's shoes. Nirmala followed her husband to their room like a goat going to the sacrificial altar.

Zinnia found their room to be large and airy. The bed was large and inviting, and Zinnia popped on it as soon as the bellboy left them. She and Jaipal were alone in their bedroom.

"Jai, I will give you a map of a big treasure. The treasure may give you power over Rakesh. But we both have to be super careful about it." Zinnia said in a low tone.

"The treasure is something that Nirmala told you. Correct?" Jaipal said with a poker face.

"You guessed?!"

Jaipal nodded in agreement. He had effectively surmised the situation.

Zinnia told him everything that Nirmala told her and showed him the video. Jaipal watched the video several times and was impressed with Zinnia's detection. He said, "I think the Nirmala is talking about another fellow. I know that this Rakesh is using an alias. It is not his real name. Is Nirmala her real name, or is she also using an alias? I will find out about Rakesh and Nirmala. Finding out about her past will be easier as she keeps relations with her grandmother."

Zinnia and Jaipal planned to go to the grandmother to get Nirmala's details.

"Enough of plans... I've been waiting for this..." Zinnia kissed Jaipal sensuously.

Her dream came true when he professed his love for her, and they made love.

After an hour, they stepped out and walked to the sea. Rakesh and Nirmala did not come out. Zinnia asked a waiter about them, but he had not seen them. Zinnia and Jaipal bathed in the sea. The beach was empty, and on their way back to the resort, they met a preoccupied Rakesh on their way back to the room. He walked away absentmindedly towards the dining room. Nirmala was nowhere in sight.

Zinnia and Jaipal came to the dining hall after changing into fresh clothes for lunch and saw Rakesh. He was waiting for them. "Where is Nirmala?" asked Zinnia. "She is sleeping. She does not want to have lunch because of her stomach problem," Rakesh replied seriously. He became good-humoured by the time the food arrived. He told funny incidents and discussed exciting concepts. Zinnia wondered at his friendliness. She thought, "If I hadn't known him, then I would have been charmed at his knowledge of things. He is surely a good entertainer. He knows how to play with words and emotions. I wonder, where is Nirmala?"

Rakesh was keenly watching Zinnia, who acted normal. She laughed and appreciated at all the correct places appropriately.

After lunch, Rakesh took a jug of lime water he had ordered for Nirmala. He said, "We had a fight, and now she is not feeling good. I feel bad that we are in such a lovely place, and she cannot even walk by the sea."

"Something is not right. I am afraid for Nirmala. Shouldn't we intervene?" Zinnia sounded worried when they were alone in their room.

"I know she is in danger, but she has been handling him since she married him. I have known them for the last five years. She is used to his ways. She will be alright." Jaipal tried to dissuade her worries.

They remained in their room the whole afternoon and made love. Zinnia was happy that Jaipal had confessed his love for her. In the evening, they went out together and walked along the shore. They behaved like teenagers in love. It was pretty dark when they returned from their walk, but Rakesh or Nirmala was nowhere to be seen. Dinner was a quiet and cosy affair. They dined alone without Rakesh or Nirmala joining them.

After dinner, they sat cosily in a loving embrace on their big balcony and watched the sea. It was a beautiful, starry night. One big spotlight was roving, casting a massive disc of light. The light moved in circular movements. Zinnia was humming something romantic, and suddenly, Jaipal sat up straight, disturbing her.

"What?" Zinnia asked worriedly.

"I think I saw someone move in the darkness. The person was dragging something heavy," Whispered Jaipal. He had become very alert instinctively.

Zinnia tried to follow his direction but could see nothing.

That night, they were making love again when they a commotion, and they came out of their room to find the chaos. Rakesh looked like a person hit by lightning. He was sitting alone in the lounge. The manager was consoling him.

"What happened, Rakesh?" Jaipal was immediately by his side.

"Its... Nirmala. She went for a swim and drowned. We cannot find her." Rakesh spoke through his tears.

"She went for a swim! But she was suffering from a bad stomach... were you with her?" Zinnia Asked.

"No, I was not with her, and that is why I feel so responsible for this accident. Why did she go for a swim at night? What will I tell our daughter?" Rakesh sounded depressed.

Jaipal looked sternly at Zinnia. The stare was enough to caution her into silence.

"She drowned very conveniently at the perfect time. But I will find the truth, Mr. Rakesh Nag," Zinnia promised to herself.

CHAPTER XVI

Tezz the Car Rental Company

7 March 2023

Detective Dipto Bhanu Chowdhury was scrutinising Lawrence's murder details. He was angry as the motorbike, and the biker seemed to have vanished. Both could be traced to Tiljala by the street cameras, where the biker was seen to go in an alley but hadn't come out of the alley. Dipto Bhanu concentrated on the map of the Tiljala area.

"This is interesting!" Exclaimed Dipto Bhanu.

Lakshman was also looking at the map but needed help understanding what interested the detective.

"Tezz... the garage cum car rental can be reached from all the three entrances. This company's name comes up on many occasions. Lawrence and Raghubir worked at the car rental, and now this biker goes missing near it. What happened to the follow-up on Tezz, the car rental company? Did you visit them?" Dipto Bhanu mused.

"No... I mean, I was meaning to, then this..." Lakshman stammered excuses.

"We must pay them a visit on our way to Durgapur now. I have to see the archived video footage of the club. I am sure that Rakesh, Lawrence, Jaipal, Raghubir and Harman Handa were regular customers at the Club. We have to ask the staff at the club for evidence. People often see important things but don't realise they have seen something important. I will surely find some links between Tezz and the Club in Durgapur. Is Raghubir hiding or silenced like Lawrence? Jaipal has also gone underground... Zinnia's phone is missing, too... Harman Handa was last seen in Durgapur. Is he still there? Where is Rakesh now?" Mused Dipto Bhanu.

"Sir, the post-mortem report has come for Lawrence. He was killed with a locally made bullet," an office orderly came in with the report.

"Rakesh seems to be dealing with locally made firearms. We must tap all the regular informers for details on recently made firearms dealings. There were no firearms at Lawrence or Raghubir's den. I think that the motorbiker is none other than Rakesh. He was cooking something with Harman Handa but without Jaipal, Raghubir or Lawrence. If he was the biker, he must have used the garage to change his mode of transport." Commented Dipto Bhanu.

Lakshman asked, "This Rakesh fellow is slippery like a fish and changes appearances like a chameleon. Sir, how would we recognise him if we met him? There is no information on any Rakesh Nag or Rakesh Gupta. What if he uses other aliases?"

"We will see the archived video footage of the Club and get details of each guest. Something will definitely come out," Dipto Bhanu answered thoughtfully.

The car rental company called Tezz has been on the police radar for a while. The company was new, but its name appeared on several car theft reports. Some of their drivers had been charged in cases of accidents. Their cases were still pending at the court. Dipto Bhanu suspected Rakesh and his associates to be connected with the car rental company. Dipto Bhanu and Lakshman started on their way to the garage called Tezz. They were in plain clothes. They reached the premises of Tezz and found the place empty. It was thirty minutes past ten in the morning, and the open place seemed unusual. Lakshman looked into the garage area and found no driver or mechanic working or even lazing around.

Dipto Bhanu walked into the so-called office of the car rental. The office consisted of a dingy, dirty room. There was no one in the office. He checked the little table drawers and some other billing books on the desk. He took photos of some of the bills. Lakshman had joined him by this time.

"I did not see anyone, sir. Should I go again and see if I can find anyone?" Asked Lakshman.

Dipto Bhanu nodded in agreement, and Lakshman went out pretending to be a customer while Dipto Bhanu remained in the office half-hidden behind the door.

"Hey, is there anyone? Hey, you, where is the office manager? I want to rent a big car – like an eight seater for two days," Lakshman could be heard from afar.

Dipto Bhanu understood that the person with whom Lakshman was speaking must be a little away from him. Dipto Bhanu couldn't catch the answer. He continued his search of the office and took many photographs of the things lying on the table. He finished his search in the office before joining the scene.

A man in a sleeveless t-shirt was lying beneath a car. His face and a little portion of his chest were exposed as he had put his head out to talk to Lakshman. He was working on the car and had grease marks all over his face and exposed skin. His short, spiky hair had streaks of yellow and brown. It was challenging to guess his looks, age or height. He didn't get up from the floor but looked at Dipto with interest as he came to stand beside Lakshman.

"Who is in charge of this car rental? Where are all the drivers and the cars?" Asked Dipto Bhanu.

"I- I am S-S-Subho... I am the m-mech-anic, sir. You can tell me what you want. Our owner is Nirmala Devi, and she is not here. There are only two *perment* drivers; they are also out with customers," said the man from his position on the floor. Dipto Bhanu noticed the mispronounced word permanent and his name with emphasis on the s, which sounded like a hiss. Subho's voice was shrilly and nasal.

Dipto Bhanu took Nirmala Devi's number and asked, "Where is Raghubir?"

"R-Raghu ... I know R-Ramcharan... he is one of the d-drivers. But no, R-Raghubir." Subho replied while resuming his work with the wrench.

"And Jaipal... you should know him. He works here as a mechanic." Said Dipto Bhanu.

"J-Jai-ram ji ki... but no J-Jaipal. I, S-Subho, work here. Sir, s-someone gave you the w-wrong information." Replied Subho, the mechanic.

"I would like to see all the motorbikes on the property," said Dipto Bhanu.

"Motorbikes... over there, you will find six bikes that came yesterday. One was in an accident, sir."

Dipto Bhanu checked all the bikes and took their details. There was no trace of the last night's motorbike.

"How long have you been working here?" Asked Dipto Bhanu.

"About five years, sir."

"Where were you last night?"

"Last night...I was here, sir. Sometimes, I stay here at night and sleep in the office.

Dipto Bhanu took his address details and phone number. Lakshman poked at the other three standing cars for a few minutes. They watched Subho working for some time before leaving.

On the way to Durgapur, Dipto Bhanu called several times at the number given for Nirmala Devi. Still, it was switched off. He forwarded the number and address he had seen at Tezz to his office for verification. He had seen nothing to incriminate Rakesh with any of the crimes at the office.

Lakshman was sitting beside the driver and turned back to ask for a stop for a tea break and noticed Dipto Bhanu looking stern and a little disturbed. Something bothered him.

"Sir, what is bothering you?" Lakshman couldn't help but ask.

"Sssubho... he is too theatrical. Who is he?" Dipto Bhanu almost whispered the last words.

"Sir, shall I send his details to the office for checking?" Asked Lakshman.

Dipto Bhanu gave him a look of hopelessness.

"Already sent... sorry, sir." Said Lakshman in a low tone.

The police jeep sped away from the heart of Kolkata towards Durgapur.

CHAPTER XVII

Patravali's Letter

8 March 2023, Kolkata

Mayurakshi Bose spent the whole journey thinking about Patravali. She was perplexed at the development. She often asked herself why Patravali chose to elope when she could have stayed there or even sold her property and started life elsewhere.

Bidyut had tried to cement the misunderstanding and said, "Mou, your ego is hurt, and so you are trying to find problems. I bet that Patravali has fallen in love with the handsome Professor. And she didn't want to stay back in Simlipur to avoid being the talk of the town. After all, people do talk and spread rumours and tarnish reputations. I do not blame Patravali for choosing life; you should also give her time. She will definitely tell you all about it. She must have her reasons to be secretive. Besides, you were not taking calls for a few days."

Mayurakshi had no choice but to wait until she got to Simlipur to hear about the whole episode first-hand from a more reliable source than Indu Raha. She refrained from calling her other acquaintances in Simlipur to find out the situation.

The journey from Copenhagen to Kolkata included several flights with long waits in the transit. Mayurakshi started her trip on the morning of 7 March and reached Kolkata the next day. Mayurakshi and her husband owned a fair-sized flat in a multi-storied building in Kolkata. As she entered the gate of the housing society where her flat was located, she felt a little unhappy at the prospect of entering a lonely flat. She pictured the dust protection draped furniture and the empty pantry.

Mayurakshi dragged her luggage and walked inside the apartment building. The security person, Bablu, who worked as a receptionist and security at the entrance lobby, came forward and helped her carry the luggage to the lift.

After the initial greetings, Bablu handed her a big, thick, padded envelope and informed her that while she had been away, he had received the envelope on her behalf.

Mayurakshi thanked him and saw the sender's name. It was from Patravali. They had been writing letters for the last fifteen years, but this was the first time Patravali had sent a letter in a padded envelope, which seemed very light in contents. Mayurakshi was curious and a little apprehensive about its contents. Mayurakshi opened the envelope as soon as she was alone in her flat.

To her surprise, there was a photograph of a girl along with the letter. The coloured photograph was 8x6 inches. Mayurakshi recognised the girl. She was Jhimli at the age of fifteen. On the back of the picture, Patravali had written Jhimli's name, date of birth, and the year it was taken. That was eighteen years ago when Patravali was a newly married wife. Mayurakshi calculated Jhimli's present age to be thirty-three.

It was about fifteen years since anyone had seen Jhimli. Nobody knew the whereabouts of Jhimli and her husband. In the photograph, Jhimli resembled her mother a little. But she had the same beautiful eyes. "How does she look now? Did she contact Patravali? Does Jhimli know that her father is no more? Mayurakshi had many more questions forming in her mind.

Mayurakshi opened Patravali's letter. It was written in Patravali's neat handwriting on thick, personalised letterhead. Mayurakshi read the letter twice to understand the meaning hidden between the lines.

The letter read accordingly:

25 February 2023

Senjuti, Simlipur.

Dear Mou,

It has been long since I wrote anything to you. A lot has been happening here at Senjuti, my home, which is infested with dangerous pests of the kind not in the insect category. To me, home means security + privacy + a place where I can be myself without judgment. Yet, I feel like I am being watched constantly in my home. Their piercing, vigilant eyes are on me, but they hide behind friendly, smiling faces when I turn back. Somebody is going through my papers and diaries. In my own home, I am moving and writing furtively. I am keeping my private papers and journals hidden under lock and key. When I am in the company of friends and acquaintances, I feel their eyes judging me, measuring my every move.

Why do they bother about my personal life? I am not responsible for what others feel. I don't control anyone's actions. My heart still beats at Timir's name. I am not ready to move on yet. Their menacing whispers ruin my peace.

I do not know whom to trust anymore. Inside and outside, I am surrounded by people with friendly masks. I have to cross-check certain information given to me by Mrs Sneha Mitra. I want you to help me to do some detective work. I have kept a record of all my findings and suspicions.

Our dear Doctor Dutta is much better now and is back in Simlipur. Sometimes, I feel like confiding in him, but then the dear doctor needs peace, not anxiety, after his stroke.

You wrote several ghost and supernatural stories, and they were pretty convincing. So, do you believe in ghosts? Can the past become real? I don't know what to make out of Rimjhim's ghost. In the past eighteen years I have never seen her famous ghost yet now, every night, at late hours, she walks in the garden when I am alone working in the study.

I love Senjuti and will never allow it to go into the wrong hands. I am not technology-savvy like them and cannot compete with their evil mechanics. But I am gathering clues to make a whole picture. I believe in my old-fashioned, straightforward ways to protect all I love.

My journals are essential documents. They can be vital in case something needs to be investigated. I cannot lose them. Neither can I risk them falling into the wrong hands. I have kept them safe.

I like working at my Lilliputian Lily Ponds. I have created a heaven, and I am proud of my creations. I know you will love it when we have tea at the Gazebo again. Do you remember those lovely evenings of reading poetry and music? It is important to me that you never forget those beautiful evenings spent at the Rose Arbour and Gazebo. The Lilliputian Lily Garden is vital to my writing and keeping my documents safe.

*The positive thing is that my **boat** is ready to set sail.*

How is Gitisha? She promised to visit during the Christmas break. And how is Bidyut da? Convey my love and regards to him.

With much love and warm regards.

Yours ever loving

Patravali

The letter was perplexing and seemed to be written in an anxious mind. It was obvious that Patravali felt threatened afraid, and thought she was secretly under observation.

Patravali had never written anything so mysterious, and Mayurakshi felt that Patravali had meant the letter to be used as a witness. But witness to what or which event that was not clear to Mayurakshi. The letter was full of hints. Mayurakshi read the letter twice and reasoned, "Patravali has not eloped. Maybe she is hiding somewhere to feel safe until the trouble clears. The letter is dated 25th February, and she confirms her devotion to Timir Babu. There is no mention of any new love interest. She talks about doing some detective work for her. She tells about hiding her documents. She mentions Rimjhim's ghost. She sent me a photograph of Jhimli. And yet she elopes just three days after writing such a mysterious letter! I do not think she has eloped but is hiding for safety."

Mayurakshi called Patravali on her mobile. The phone was switched off. It was only thirty minutes past seven in the evening. She knew that Patravali did not sleep before eleven.

Mayurakshi called her husband and told him about the letter. He could only say the same things that Mayurakshi herself was thinking. She emailed a photocopy of the letter to her husband as he asked.

Mayurakshi was dead tired after the long journey, but she felt restless and thought about her next step. This was the first time that everything was becoming like a riddle. She ordered food and searched social media for Sneha Mitra. There were several Sneha

Mitras in Kolkata. It wasn't evident to pinpoint the same Sneha Mitra whom Patravali referred to.

Mayurakshi's dinner arrived, and while eating, she booked a train ticket to Simlipur the next day. The biriyani from her favourite restaurant made her sleepier. She called it a day and promised to resume her comprehension and unravelling of the letter in the morning.

CHAPTER XVIII

The Dark Labyrinth of Lies

9 March 2023

Jaipal Bajwa was strolling on the streets near the bazaar in Durgapur. He has been in Durgapur for the last two days. The roads were not yet busy, but the greengrocers and other daily market was ready for customers. It was only six in the morning. Jaipal came to a chicken shop and asked for Chotu. The man overseeing the shop looked closely at Jaipal, still dressed as Aminah Khatoon.

"I do not know any Chotu...," said the chicken shop in charge.

"Tell him that his maasi has come from Kolkata. He will know." Jaipal said in a low female-like voice.

The man looked at Jaipal's strong-looking hands and said, "Ali Chacha's shop, next to the rice shop... he knows."

Jaipal went to Ali Chacha's shop, which happened to be a barbershop. Jaipal found a customer perched on a wooden plank supported by several bricks. He had foam all over his beard, and another man was preparing to shave him. Jaipal surmised the second man to be Ali Chacha and asked him about Chotu. Ali Chacha didn't reply in words but pointed the razor at the customer.

Jaipal understood that the customer was the same Chotu he wanted to meet.

"I have come from Kolkata... in search of Vivek Malakar. I was told that you might help me." Jaipal said in the same female-like voice.

Chotu did not open his eyes for once but remained quiet. He was still perched on the wooden plank. Jaipal waited for Ali Chacha to shave him, which he did slowly. Jaipal surveyed Chotu. He was a tiny man, rather skinny and dark. Jaipal had been working in the dark alleys of Durgapur for the last two years but had never met Chotu before. In Jaipal's profession, everyone knew the opponents and the co-workers. Chotu was a local goon, and he worked for the local politicians. He was also a police informer when it suited him.

"You said Kolkata... Maasi? Who gave you my name?" Chotu asked and scrutinised Jaipal.

"Let's say someone whom you know well and whom I searched out told me you can help me," Jaipal said softly.

"Why do you want to know about Vivek Malakar?" Chotu asked curiously.

"I am looking for a murderer. He killed Zinnia. Do you know about her?" Jaipal asked earnestly.

"Vivek Malakar did not kill her. He is afraid. Look elsewhere for her killer." Chotu said dismissively.

"But Vivek might know something about the killer. Give me his whereabouts." Asked Jaipal.

"If you came here in your clothes, I might have thought about it. Now leave. You may come to Raju's tea stall in the evening. But don't wear the same clothes." Chotu replied and walked away. Jaipal was going after him, but Ali Chacha stopped him and said, "Chotu hates men wearing bangles. He will help you when you ask for his help as a man."

Jaipal took his advice and went in search of food.

That afternoon, Jaipal went to the Club dressed as a typical gardener. He waited for Sam, the bartender in the vicinity of the Club. He did not have to wait long as Sam came in just after three. Jaipal halted him before he entered the Club. They talked for some time, and Jaipal learned about the filmmaker Vanraj Joshi. The police were also looking for the filmmaker.

Jaipal knew that the police would never find any connection between the murderer and the well-known filmmaker. He was certain that Rakesh had orchestrated the murder as he must have come to know of their plan and their possession of the fatal video. Jaipal was frustrated and thought, "Zinnia, why did you play with fire? Why did you not wait for me before confronting Rakesh? Why did you go out to meet someone whom you never met before? Zinnia... why did you forget our pact and get killed...Zinnia..."

As Jaipal thought about the whole thing, he remembered they had kept the video in the cloud storage. He took out his phone and opened the video with their common password. Jaipal copied it on a memory stick. He wanted to ensure the police would get it if something happened to him. He had thought of several places to hide, but Zinnia's dressing room seemed the best place to hide the memory stick. He was sure that police would tooth-comb it soon. He made a simple plan to visit the Club incognito.

That evening, he went to the Club dressed as a housekeeping staff member and entered the narrow back corridor leading to Zinnia's tiny dressing room.

"Hey, what are you doing here?" a sweet female voice called Jaipal as he was trying the doorknob of Zinnia's room.

He turned and faced a woman dressed in a glittering sari. She was voluptuous and dusky. She asked again, "What are you doing here?"

"Cleaning." Jaipal's monosyllable did not dissuade her interest. And she said interestedly, "You do not look like a cleaner... I am Preeti, the new dancer. I was recruited after the death of the former dancer, Zinnia. Did you know Zinnia?"

Jaipal hated this conversation and denied knowing anything about Zinnia. Preeti seemed unaffected by his ignorance and told him how the other girl was murdered. She was describing how she got the job as a dancer when a serviceman came to fetch her. Preeti left as soon as he came onto the scene. The serviceman looked very young and inexperienced, and Jaipal had not seen him before. Jaipal resumed his work and was able to open the room. He went inside and let his tears flow freely as he saw Zinnia's things on the tiny table and her clothes. He spent some time touching and smelling her things. He took out the memory stick and tried various places to hide it. There were only two solid pieces of furniture besides the two plastic chairs. He had to hide it in a place that would not be too obvious or complicated.

After some time, Jaipal left the room and saw Detective Dipto Bhanu and his assistant walking into the corridor. Jaipal did not wait any longer but started walking away. "Hey, you, we would like to talk to you. What do you do here?" Asked the assistant. Just then, another waiter came in with some keys and opened a door. The assistant turned to his boss momentarily, forgetting the oldish-looking cleaner. Jaipal took the opportunity and walked out of the Club.

In the evening, Jaipal walked into Raju's tea stall, a small brick room with red tiles for the roof. He asked for tea and waited to talk privately to Raju, the proprietor. He was a heavily built man in his early sixties. He paid no attention to anyone in particular. He just worked like an automated machine, maintaining rhythm. There were few people in the little shop, and they looked like regular officegoers. Jaipal was sitting on the outside bench, and he came inside. He sat near the table where Raju had his cooking arrangements. Jaipal said to Raju when no one was paying attention, "I have come from Kolkata. Chotu said he might have something for me."

Raju looked straight at Jaipal for a fraction of a second before turning his head away in the back direction. Jaipal followed his gesture and saw a closed door behind the small cooking area. He stood up to go inside, and Raju nodded his approval.

At the Durgapur Police Station, Dipto Bhanu and Lakshman were reviewing the statements taken at the Club when Dipto commented, "I think we left one person. Who was he? Where did he go? I remember seeing him in the corridor when that serviceman opened the door of the musicians' room. I thought you were talking to him. Then he went out."

"You mean that oldish-looking man? I thought he would be amongst the others." Lakshman commented.

"But he was not... how did I forget him? Who was that man?" Dipto Bhanu checked the list of employees' names and the list of interviewed staff. He did not find anybody missing in either of the lists. Dipto Bhanu was annoyed at the miss. He considered all the possibilities.

In another section of the town, Jaipal knocked on the closed door, opened by someone standing behind it. Jaipal entered the dimly lit room. Chotu sat on a comfortable chair, and two other men played cards. Jaipal scanned the room briefly and said, "I am looking for the murderer who killed my Zinnia. Vivek might know something because he liked Zinnia."

Chotu replied leisurely, "You are Jaipal Bajwa, wanted by the police of more than four states. You came here without any disguise. Are you reckless and stupid or intelligent and daring?"

Jaipal seemed to consider the question. He replied after a few seconds of contemplation, "It is important that I know who killed my girl."

Chotu said smilingly, "I help lovers, and so I will tell you to look for the murderer in the film business."

Jaipal replied, "I propose to Vivek to film his opinion and tell elaborately all that he knew and saw that night. He doesn't have to meet me personally but can give me a copy of his statement film."

Chotu considered Jaipal's idea and agreed. They were discussing the venue and medium of transferring the video of Vivek's statement when suddenly, there was an urgent knocking on the door. Chotu looked at Jaipal and pointed to the back door. Jaipal did not waste another minute and ran through the back door into the darkness of the night.

One of the card players strolled to the door slowly and opened it to find constable Chandan Das standing outside. He often acted as the liaison between Chotu and the police. He was rewarded handsomely for leaking news of police activity.

"Is someone hiding here? He was dressed as an oldish-looking man in little dirty clothes," Asked Constable Chandan Das.

"Already left. Why? What's he done?" Asked Chotu.

"He is Jaipal Bajwa, and we are looking for him. Detective Dipto Bhanu from Kolkata will visit you shortly with our Inspector Banik. Today, he went to the Club when the detective interviewed the staff. The Detective from Kolkata had seen him. Now, our Inspector Banik will bring the Detective to you for questioning." Constable

Chandan Das elaborated.

The next hour went by swiftly as Dipto Bhanu and Inspector Banik collected news of the fleeing Jaipal, who had not gotten the opportunity to change his disguise. He was trying to hide himself at a known garage where they did business often. Unseen by him, a man in dark clothes followed him on the way.

Jaipal became aware of a moving shadow when he took a turn in the dark alley leading to the garage. He started running. He suddenly turned, hid behind a wall, and took out his knife. While waiting for the man in dark clothes, he heard a police whistle near the alley. Jaipal didn't wait any longer and ran to the wall at the end. He jumped the wall in the other direction without much difficulty and ran.

The man in dark clothes also chased him. But the chase was very short-lived as two things happened simultaneously. The man in dark clothes fired two shots at Jaipal, and at the same time, the police fired, too. Jaipal fell on the rough stone-strewn side of the railway tracks and saw the other man limping away before he lost consciousness.

Jaipal closed his eyes with the satisfaction that the other man had also been hurt.

CHAPTER XIX

The Train Journey

9 March 2023 at 11:30 p.m.
Howrah Junction

Mayurakshi reached Howrah Station thirty minutes before time for departure. Many trains were going to Simlipur, and Mayurakshi found this train's time comfortable. She was feeling fresh after the long sleep and rest. She was a little absent-minded as she thought about Patravali and her mysterious letter.

It was fifteen minutes past eleven at night, yet people jostled, pushed, and became overactive at the sight of the approaching train. Families were shouting at each other; porters ran with multiple pieces of luggage balancing on their heads and each arm. It was chaotic as a typical scene in a busy railway station like Howrah Junction. Mayurakshi waited on the side and let go first, the most eager ones to get on the train. She finally embarked on her designated compartment when others had already settled in. She found her seat and settled down when a woman came in with a suitcase. Mayurakshi's berth was on the lower level, and the woman took the lower berth opposite hers. They were the only passengers in their compartment, consisting of four berths. Mayurakshi sat in one of the window seats, and the other woman sat opposite her. She was wearing a cheap-looking nylon sari with a mismatched blouse. The woman had tied her hair in a tight bun in a non-fashionable, simple manner, although her hair looked treated at the salon. The cheap glass bangles on her hands made a tinkling sound. She seemed to be in her late twenties. Mayurakshi scrutinised the woman sitting opposite to her out of habit of a writer. She had fair hands with mehndi and long, manicured nails and wore expensive shoes. The woman was good-looking, but somehow, she had managed to look very common. Mayurakshi briefly thought that something was not right, but as her mind returned to Patravali's letter, she didn't pay much attention.

The train pulled out of the station at thirty minutes past eleven. Many of the other passengers in the adjacent compartments had switched off the bright fluorescent lights and drew the curtains dividing the compartments. The woman sitting opposite Mayurakshi asked to switch off their lights, too. In a moment, their cubicle became semi-lit with a faint blue night lamp. The woman unrolled the blanket and pulled the curtain that enclosed their compartment in privacy. Mayurakshi likes reading while travelling by train and seldom sleeps on a moving train. She took out her notebook and sat comfortably with her legs covered by the blanket. She had turned on the reading lamp. The whole compartment went into sleeping mode within ten minutes of leaving Howrah. Mayurakshi wrote in her notebook the description of her fellow female passenger. Mayurakshi was puzzled by the woman's sophisticated manner and conflicting attire. Mayurakshi was intrigued by the woman.

Mayurakshi wondered when the ticket collector would come as the station of Shrirampur left. As she was thinking, the ticket collector came. He looked like a friendly fellow and exclaimed when he saw Mayurakshi's ticket, "Surely, you are not the writer, Mayurakshi Bose! I have seen your photo on one of the book covers. My wife and daughter are your fans."

Mayurakshi smiled and thanked him. The following five minutes were spent talking about her best-known books and taking pictures with her. The ticket checker, Mr Sayantan Mukherjee, sat beside Mayurakshi and checked the other woman's ticket. Mayurakshi saw the woman's name when Mr Sayantan Mukherjee was ticking it on his list. The writer in Mayurakshi wondered, "Bina Naskar! Well, she doesn't look like a Bengali woman. Is she trying to portray a different persona?" Mayurakshi asked Mr Sayantan Mukherjee, "Who are in the upper berths in our compartment?" He answered, "Mr Madhav Kothari will board the train at Barddhaman Junction. He has the upper berth. And Abhilash Kundu will board at Durgapur, and he has the upper berth opposite you.

Mayurakshi tried to resume reading, but her mind was astray with many conflicting thoughts. The rest of the passengers had returned to sleeping mode, and the compartments were drenched in a low bluish light. Mayurakshi switched off the reading lamp and lay down on her berth. She woke up suddenly as she heard many sounds. The train had stopped moving and was standing at a station. Mayurakshi checked her watch. It was forty-five minutes past two in the morning. The station was Durgapur. Mayurakshi turned towards the opposite berth. Bina Naskar was still sleeping, covered in her blanket. Their compartment was still curtained, and a man in the upper berth was also sleeping. His heavy snoring could be heard in the quietness. "Why are we stopping for so long," thought Mayurakshi as the train did not start moving even after ten minutes.

Then she saw the police officers searching everywhere. One of the men entered their compartment and asked to switch on the bright fluorescent light. Mayurakshi was a large man sleeping on the upper berth. Mayurakshi remembered being told that a passenger named Madhav Kothari would board at Barddhaman. The Policeman looked at the sleeping man and turned to the opposite berth. The woman was sleeping on her berth. The Policeman went to the next curtained compartment. Mayurakshi's curiosity was piqued, and she followed him and asked, "What has happened? Are we under some threat?"

"We are looking for a man. You can go back to sleep." Answered the policeman rather importantly.

"How does he look? Is he dangerous? It would be helpful if I knew the details." Mayurakshi offered to help.

"He is tallish, has a ponytail, very rough-looking fellow... he might be hurt in his leg. He is alone and may need medical assistance. If you see him, then tell the ticket checker or the security guard in the compartment." The Policeman was almost done checking the other compartments.

Mayurakshi nodded and returned to her berth. The woman named Bina Naskar was not in her berth. The train started moving again after twenty minutes. Mayurakshi was wide awake, lying on her berth, thinking about the whole experience. The train's low light and rhythmic movement made her drowsy, and she closed her eyes. Suddenly, she sensed a movement in the compartment and looked furtively at the woman named Bina Naskar returning to her seat. In the dim light, Mayurakshi noticed that she had a large canvas bag in her hand, which she shoved under her berth. "Did she have the bag when we started the journey?" Mayurakshi wondered. Mayurakshi sensed being watched and kept her eyes closed, pretending to be asleep.

After about half an hour, Mayurakshi noticed a man entering their curtained compartment. He limped a little, alerting Mayurakshi, but then she remembered being told about a passenger boarding at Durgapur. Bina Naskar gave him her berth and went up to the upper berth. The newcomer laid down on the berth and turned towards Mayurakshi. She closed her eyes and pretended to sleep. She looked furtively at the man, but he seemed harmless as he went to sleep immediately after lying down. The rhythmic movement of the train, combined with the sound, made Mayurakshi sleepy, and she dozed off.

"Mrs Bose... Madam Mayurakshi, your station... Madam...," someone was calling her name. Mayurakshi opened her heavy eyes and saw Mr Sayantan Mukherjee standing near her.

"What..." Mayurakshi was surprised to see the light. It was ten minutes past seven in the morning.

"Simlipur is coming in fifteen minutes. The next station is your stop, Mrs Bose. I remembered your station, wanted to see you off, and found you sleeping," said Mr Mukherjee.

"What happened to the fugitive? Did they catch him?" Asked Mayurakshi.

"No, I think he did not board the train. The police made a mistake. Nobody was unaccounted for." Answered Mr Mukherjee.

"That is a relief. And thank you, Mr Mukherjee, for waking me up." Said Mayurakshi. She organised her things swiftly and became ready to get off at Simlipur. The large man in the upper berth was still sleeping. Bina Naskar and the newcomer, Abhilash Kundu, were also up. Bina Naskar was getting ready to get off, and the man sat as if he had nothing to organise. Mayurakshi noticed that Bina Naskar looked a little pale and alert. Abhilash Kundu was a man in his early forties. He looked tired, but his eyes looked sharp and keen. He had bouncy shoulder-length hair and a healthy moustache. He wore an ordinary cotton shirt and trousers with sneakers. He seemed like an insurance agent. He was reading a newspaper. Mayurakshi looked outside. The scenery had changed from lush green fields to semi-dry land strewn with black and grey boulders. The sky was clear and blue, with white clouds floating lazily. The flame trees and simul trees were laden with bright flame-coloured flowers. Mayurakhsi thought about her home in Simlipur and felt happy. She loved being at Suprabhat.

The train was running a little late, and they reached Simlipur at twenty minutes past seven. It was a beautiful sight, and Mayurakshi felt happy to come to Simlipur again. Mr Sayantan Mukherjee came as the train stopped. Bina Naskar was the first to get off the train. Mayurakshi noticed an ugly cut mark on Abhilash Kundu's right hand near his thumb. She wondered briefly, "Insurance agent with a knife cut mark on his hand! There must be a story related to the ugly scar." Mayurakshi noticed him limping badly. He managed to get down on the platform with a bit of difficulty.

Getting off the train became a memorable affair for Mayurakshi. Mr Sayantan Mukherjee had arranged for a porter and another railway personnel to meet her at the station. As they talked sociably, Mayurakshi noticed Bina Naskar walking ahead with her suitcase and bag. Abhilash Kundu walked slowly, limping as he walked. They seemed to be going separately. Mayurakshi saw Abhilash Kundu carrying the same canvas bag that Bina Naskar was shoving under the berth at night.

"I wonder why did she shove his bag under the berth. Does she know him? But, they seem like strangers...," Mayurakshi's thought was interrupted as a well-known voice greeted her happily. He was Umanath Ji, the priest of the old Kali Temple near Mayurakshi's house, Suprabhat. He was also returning home, and they went off together towards the exit.

CHAPTER XX

The Favourite Window

10 March 2023

On the way to Suprabhat, Umanath Ji was telling her about his visit to his daughter. Mayurakshi could not concentrate on what Umanath Ji was saying. Her mind was excited with many questions regarding her co-passengers, Bina Naskar and Abhilash Kundu.

"...it was Amavasya, the new moon night, and I was late... Patravali..." Umanath Ji was talking about a puja on a certain night.

"What did you say, Umanath Ji?" Mayurakshi caught Patravali's name being mentioned, and she became interested.

"I was telling you about the night Patravali went away with the Professor. There was a late-night Kali Puja for Amavasya Tithi. The date was the 28th of February; I was returning home very late, probably around midnight, when I saw a car coming out of Senjuti. I stopped under the big tree so as not to be in the way; as you know, the path is narrow at the bend. I saw the professor sitting in the driver's seat and a lady sitting in the passenger's seat beside the driver. I thought that she looked familiar, but then I did not give it much thought. Indu and Savita visited the temple two days later and told me about Patravali's elopement. I recalled seeing the professor with the lady. She had been wearing the same coloured sari that Patravali had worn to the party. But somehow, I was not convinced. There was something different...I still do not know if she was Patravali or someone else. I had seen Patravali before she went to the party, as she had stopped at the temple on her way. She told me you would be coming, and she would go with you to Kolkata," Narrated Umanath Ji.

"So, you are not sure if the woman was Patravali... Would you know her if you saw her again? Asked Mayurakshi concernedly.

"Dear Mayurakshi, my eyesight is not what it used to be... I cannot be sure... I think that Patravali would not do anything rash like running away... but then you can never tell. Life is full of surprises. At my age, I am not surprised easily. Indu and Savita were so very sure. I heard that Indu had talked to Professor Ahmed, and he had confirmed their relationship. Patravali had come to offer puja and asked me about Timir's old friends a few weeks before her elopement. We had a long chat." Umanath Ji said.

"If you recall anything more, promise to tell me about it first. I think something is wrong with this elopement business," commented Mayurakshi.

"You should be very careful because if something is wrong, you should involve the police. Writing thrillers and being a part of something mysterious are different," Umanath Ji sounded concerned. He had known Mayurakshi since she was a kid. Mayurakshi promised to be careful.

The taxi entered Mayurakshi's favourite lane. She called it an avenue of flowers. From February to April, Simlipur dresses like a bride, adorned in red, flame-coloured flowers on trees with a blue veil of clear sky. People come to Simlipur for tranquillity, solitude, peace and the taste of the old-world charm seldom found elsewhere. Gradually, Mayurakshi felt at peace by the time the taxi came to a halt in front of Umanath Ji's house. He made her promise again to be careful before going inside. Mayurakshi went to her house, Suprabhat, inherited from her grandparents.

Time stood still at Suprabhat. It looked the same. Mayurakshi had spent much time at Suprabhat when she was growing up. She had spent her pregnancy period at Suprabhat and after her daughter Gitisha was born. That was nineteen years ago.

Mayurakshi sighed gratefully as she reached the outer gates of Suprabhat. The much-loved iron grill gate was flung open in welcome. It was her haven far from the madding crowd where, many years ago, she had discovered her writing skill.

Nimmo was standing on the front porch when her taxi stopped at the gate. She was smiling in a matronly welcoming smile, making Mayurakshi feel at home. Nimmo and her husband Gangadhar have looked after the Suprabhat for over thirty years. They lived in a small cottage in the garden, as is the custom of most of the old properties in Simlipur. The old houses have servants' quarters built on the premises of their properties. Nimmo was in her late fifties and was still very active and strong. She did all the housework; when the family was visiting, she also cooked for them. Gangadhar worked as a gardener and a handyman. He was in his mid-sixties and in great shape. He was a very reserved man with only a few friends. He came forward smilingly and took Mayurakshi's luggage to her room.

Suprabhat was a fair-sized family house. The living room, dining room, kitchen, bathroom, laundry room and guest room were on the ground floor. The first floor consisted of four bedrooms and bathrooms. One of the four bedrooms was smaller and was Mayurakshi's favourite. Whenever she was visiting alone, she stayed in the small bedroom with a big window opening to the back garden. Senjuti was on the other side of Suprabhat, sharing a part of their back garden fence, and could be accessed through a small back door. The study window of Senjuti was visible from the window of the small room at The Suprabhat, and it was the only window in The Suprabhat from which a part of Senjuti was visible.

Mayurakshi entered the small bedroom and saw that Nimmo had cared for it. The bookcase by the table, the comfortable sofa in the corner, the writing table in front of the window and her favourite red chair were kept in tip-top shape. Here, she had written her first book and sat at her desk. She could become anyone, do anything, have adventures, and live any life she wanted.

"It is good of you to come here at home, Mou. Your mother had called several times. Call her once you get settled. And I am making your favourite dish of *posto and macher jhol*. But would you like to have breakfast now?" Nimmo asked in her loving motherly way.

"Oh, Nimmo, you spoil me so dearly. I spoke to Mother last night. And I will have coffee, but before anything, I need some information from you." Mayurakshi declared.

"Doctor Dutta had also called. He wants to talk to you, too. Shall I inform him about your arrival?" Nimmo asked, ignoring the information part.

"I will call him as soon I finish talking to you. Tell me what you know about Patravali. Umanath Ji saw Professor Ahmed in a car. A lady was sitting beside him in the passenger's seat. She was wearing the same sari that Patravali had worn to the party. They seemed to be leaving Senjuti. The date was February 28th. But he is not certain if she was Patravali." Mayurakshi commented.

Nimmo looked puzzled and said, "Dhaniram visited us on the morning of the First of March. He was perhaps excited or a little intoxicated and full of self-importance. He was repeating something about Patravali leaving in her car with Professor Ahmed. He said the professor was seen putting something heavy in the back seat of Patravali's car. He told about the lady accompanying him wearing the same sari... but just then, Ganga practically showed him the way out as he dislikes gossiping. I wanted to hear more but could not ask Dhaniram about the night. Bindi has also not been here since the 27th. Ayah is hopeless as a reliable source of current news as she becomes obsessed with the past. Later, everyone started discussing the news of her going away with the professor. But I believe Patravali Chatterjee is a strong woman and will never run away like a teenager." Nimmo spoke her mind.

Mayurakshi admired Nimmo's ability to speak her mind without any frills. She had become like a family member.

Mayurakshi asked, "Is Indu still spreading rumours about Patravali?"

"Now, there is no need to spread rumours any more as Indu Raha, Savita, Mrs Sinha, and a few others took responsibility for spreading the news like wildfire. They do not have any other way to get entertained and feed on gossip. The gossip mongers," Nimmo was angry at Mrs. Raha, and now she couldn't hide her feelings.

"Nimmo, tell me everything from the beginning, how the two met, what happened afterwards, and everything related to Patravali. I had talked to her about a month ago, but then she did not mention the new love. Her letter was waiting for me when I landed home in Kolkata. Her letter is dated 25th February, and there is no mention of Dr Ahmed. Her letter is mysterious and disturbing. She has mentioned secret vigilance, someone going through her documents, Rimjhim's ghost, me playing detective and something about Lily Pond. There was an old photograph of Jhimli with the letter. After reading her letter, I think she is in trouble, yet everyone believes she has escaped with a new love." Mayurakshi was perplexed.

Nimmo retorted, "I know why Ayah and Dhaniram are acting strange. Dhaniram is drinking a lot more now. Bindi went away to see her son on the 26th or the 27th of February and still has not returned. It seems Dhaniram has more money to spend on gambling now. How could he forget what Mr and Mrs Chatterjee did for him."

Mayurakshi remembered the gazebo at Senjuti, designed and named by Patravali as The Rose Arbour. She thought about the beautiful evenings spent at The Rose Arbour. Mayurakshi had an idea suddenly, and she took out Patravali's letter. She had mentioned creative reading sessions at the Rose Arbour.

Mayurakshi asked, "Nimmo, did Patravali make any recent changes in her garden? I mean, like a pond or something... with water... you know, landscaping with water and plants..."

Nimmo thought momentarily and replied, "I am not sure about water or pond, but often I have seen her working in the garden. Recently, she was creating pottery or something with cement. She is a creative person and keeps on doing something."

Mayurakshi said reflectively, "Why did she send me the photograph of Jhimli? Who was keeping a watch over her every move? Why did she feel threatened? I am sure that Patravali has gone away willingly somewhere. Maybe she is hiding. I hope that Professor Ahmed is not a bad person. Yet... Should I go to the police and lodge a missing person report?"

Nimmo said in her matronly fashion, "Mou, better discuss the issue with our Doctor Dutta over a cup of tea. I am sure that he is at the door at present..." Nimmo went hurriedly to answer the door. Mayurakshi had not heard the faint ringing of the bell. She, too, went downstairs to meet the doctor.

Mayurakshi came into the living room when the Doctor was entering. They greeted each other happily. Doctor Dilip Dutta was in his early sixties. He was a widower. His son, Sumit, lived in Mumbai, while his daughter, Ranjana, resided in Canada. He had a head full of silky white hair and sported a beard matching his hair. He would have made a nice Santa but was a little thinner. Timir Chatterjee and Doctor Dutta had been friends since their school days.

"Mou, I am so happy that you have come. How is Bidyut and Gitisha? Is she coming during the Christmas break?" Asked Doctor Dutta.

"They both are doing fine. Bidyut is very busy with a new project. He has a new PhD student. Gitisha is enjoying her first year at college. When did you return from Sumit's?"

Doctor Dutta and Mayurakshi exchanged more news about their families, and Nimmo brought them breakfast and coffee. After the initial friendly chat, Doctor Dutta became quiet.

He said, "Something is bothering me very much. I attended Indu Raha's anniversary party and met Patravali. She said to me something very curious. Was she drunk? But, I have never seen her drunk and as far as I can remember, she never drank too much. Patravali's own words were, *'I have read about Queen Nefertiti. Doctor, please remember that I read about the most beautiful Egyptian Queen Nefertiti. It is most important for you to remember and tell Mayurakshi that I have read about Queen Nefertiti.'* She told me this puzzling thing, and the next day, I heard she had eloped with the Professor. Was she trying to give me some hints? I am perplexed and do not know what to make of the whole episode. I kept repeating that Patravali had found love and friendship again, which was good for her. After all, she is only forty and has many lonely years ahead, but my other mind is unrest with concerns for her."

Mayurakshi took several minutes to digest the party episode and said thoughtfully, "Do you think I should lodge a missing person report with the police? Patravali wrote me a letter, which deepens the mystery. I hope that she is not in danger."

She showed the letter to Doctor Dutta, and he, too, became concerned about Patravali's safety.

Doctor Dutta read the letter with utmost concentration but could not reach any conclusion about reporting it to the police. Mayurakshi thought of waiting one more day before going to the police. She decided to visit Senjuti the next morning and talk to Ayah and Dhaniram. Besides, she needed to see the Rose Arbour and the gazebo to identify the changes made since her last visit.

That night, when Nimmo put a coverlet on the bed, Mayurakshi remembered something, and she asked, "Nimmo, have you seen Jhimli in recent years?"

"Jhimli! No, I remember her as she was when she visited Senjuti for the last time. Patravali had just been married, and Jhimli had just come from her boarding school. She was about fifteen then. She must be... thirty-three or four now."

"Do you remember her friends or teachers? How was she as a girl?"

"She went away to the boarding school when she was still a small girl. I remember her looking a lot like her mother. She must be a beautiful woman now. She might have kept in touch with Ayah, as Ayah was like a mother to her. Mou, take my advice and go to sleep. It is already eleven, and you have had many journeys since starting from Copenhagen. Tomorrow is another day, and you can start with a fresh mind." Nimmo said in a severe tone before leaving.

Mayurakshi thanked Nimmo lovingly and promised to retire soon. But she couldn't sleep and made tea for herself.

Mayurakshi sipped her tea, sitting on her favourite chair facing the big window. She was in deep thought and glanced at Senjuti casually. The portion of the garden that could be seen from her window looked deserted, and Mayurakshi felt very sad. Two study windows at Senjuti could be seen from Mayurakshi's window, and both windows were tightly shut. Mayurakshi took out her journal and noted everything happening since she boarded the train at Howrah, Kolkata.

In the quiet night, her mind became alert and focused as she progressed with her writing. It was nearly two in the morning when she looked outside. It was a very dark night with dark clouds threatening to rain. The tall trees looked like giants, and the rustling of the leaves created mysterious whispers. Somewhere, a night bird's sharp whistle pierced the night's stillness. Mayurakshi looked at the darkened study windows of Senjuti and felt a shiver of apprehension run through her. Suddenly, she saw a flicker of light moving in the study of Senjuti. Instantly, Mayurakshi became alert and concentrated on the moving light. The windows were still closed, and thick curtains were drawn closely. Yet through one of the gaps, she could discern the restless light. Mayurakshi switched off her desk light and sat in the darkness, vigil on the moving light.

"Is that Patravali?! Or someone else is looking for something?" Mused Mayurakshi. She sat there for another half hour, and suddenly, the moving light vanished. It was almost three in the morning. And Mayurakshi couldn't resist calling Patravali.

Patravali's phone remained switched off.

CHAPTER XXI

Visiting Senjuti

11 March 2023, 4:45 Hours.

Mayurakshi had spent most of the night tossing in her bed and fell asleep only in the wee hours when the pitter-patter of rain created serene music. She woke with a start as the sudden gust of wind toppled a small vase kept on her desk. She squinted her eyes and saw the phone. It was 4:15 in the morning. As her eyes adjusted to the room, everything came rushing to her. "Who was there in her study when Patravali was still absent?"

She got out of bed and considered going out in the darkness. After a brief war of conflicting thoughts regarding the pros and cons of visiting Senjuti in the dark, she decided to call.

Mayurakshi dressed in a jogger's suit and put on the raincoat before locking the door behind her. Nimmo had all the necessary keys and could enter in her comfort. Mayurakshi walked towards the back of her garden from where she could access Senjuti. It had been raining, and now only a light drizzle made the wind heavy. The ground was soggy, and the narrow, muddy path made it difficult for Mayurakshi to walk fast. She walked as fast as she could on the slippery path and reached the small service gate, which was never locked. As she entered the premises of Senjuti, she felt strange sneaking into her friend's property. In the past, she had crossed the distance without having second thoughts, but now her sixth sense was heightened, and she pulled the raincoat tightly around her. Slowly, Mayurakshi reached near the house, which seemed deserted and empty. No one was around, and she inched close to the study windows. The windows were tightly shut, and the blinds were drawn, but Mayurakshi tried to peep in through the little gaps in the blinds. Inside, it xxas dark and slowly, her eyes adjusted to the darkness. Gradually, she could see the things in the study. Patravali's favourite Murano glass blue lamp was on the table, and many things were strewn on the floor and elsewhere. It was a chaos. "What happened here?!" thought Mayurakshi. Somebody must have searched the room for something. But where was Patravali? Who was in the room? Are the staff involved?"

Suddenly, a sound somewhere within the house broke into her reveries. Somebody had shut a door, which made the sound in the stillness of the morning. Mayurakshi hid herself, as best as she could, against the wall. A window was opened somewhere upstairs, and within a few minutes, it was shut again. Then, all became quiet once more. Mayurakshi waited for further developments, but nothing stirred again.

Slowly, Mayurakshi walked towards the Rose Arbour. It was the space in the garden designed and created by Patravali and her late husband, Timir. A spacious platform with sitting arrangements was at the top of the Rose Arbour. It was the Gazebo. They regularly spent time at the Arbour and the Gazebo, reading together or listening to music. On many occasions, Patravali had referred to the Rose Arbour and the Gazebo as her secret garden and oasis. They gave musical and poetic parties at the Gazebo. Nimmo had said that in the last few months, Patravali spent many hours working on the landscape at the Arbour. Mayurakshi thought of the letter, referring to the reading sessions and music-filled evenings. "Did she hide something there?"

"Mou didi..."

Suddenly, a thin, shrill voice called Mayurakshi from the mist of the rain. She could barely see a ghostly, frail-looking figure approaching her. Mayurakshi stopped in her tracks.

It was Ayah. She was in her mid-seventies and looked frail with her thin and bony structure, yet she was still very active. She could walk quite fast, and within a few minutes, she came close to Mayurakshi.

"How nice to see you! But your friend, Patravali Bahuji, has gone away with her new lover. She is not here." Said Ayah, baring her tobacco-stained big teeth.

"Ayah! You startled me." Said Mayurakshi.

Ayah continued in the same conversational manner, "Bahuji fell in love with the excellent Professor. It's good for her. She had no children, and the master was also dead. She found love again. And money, too. Good for her. She is fortunate with money... The professor is also loaded and can keep her warm in bed."

Ayah laughed maliciously. Looking at Ayah made Mayurakshi understand Nimmo's meaning of 'acting strange'. She looked like a witch with her head full of grey hair and a thin, frail frame. Mayurakshi regained her composure, then asked, "Did you see her going away with the Professor? Did she tell you that she was going away with him?"

Ayah said indifferently, "I saw them together on many other occasions, and Dhaniram saw them leaving together in her car. She had dressed in a pale pink silk sari for the party and wore gold jewellery. And she went away wearing the same sari. Her new love, the Professor, had phoned Dhaniram to tell him about their happiness. I knew she was in love again. It is time that everyone knew about her lustful nature. She sniffed money again with the excellent professor..."

Mayurakshi looked hard at the strange woman and wondered at her maliciousness. Ayah relished speaking ill of Patravali. Her whole frail frame shook with an unpleasant pleasure. Mayurakshi thought, "She was not so spiteful when I last saw her. She seemed to be boasting. Is she hiding something? Or is she working for someone?"

Ayah spoke in her shrill voice, "You look very thoughtful. Mou Didi, no need to think so hard. Your friend is not a child; neither is she poor anymore. She posed as the devoted, unselfish, all-loving wife. But she was dying for an adventure. And her husband left all his money to her. Think of my poor darling Jhimli. Oh! How she was deprived. Rimjhim Madam will rest in peace now. She came to avenge her daughter's deprivation of the property. And now, Jhimli will surely take over what is truly hers. I am sure that everything will be okay now..."

Mayurakshi was surprised to hear Jhimli's name and asked, "Why do you think Jhimli is deprived? What do you know about Rimjhim's ghost? Jhimli went away and did not look back at her father for even once. Jhimli did not want to keep any relationship with her father. Why are you blaming Patravali for what Jhimli did?"

Ayah became angry and blurted out in hatred, "This house belongs to Jhimli. Your friend could not be a mother to Jhimli. And that's why she couldn't bear children of her own. The barren woman. The unfaithful woman. The adventuress. The gold digger. She was a nobody before our master married her out of pity. Now that the master is dead, she plays love games with the nice professor. He also has money. And he is good-looking, younger than our master. Your friend is nothing but a whore."

Mayurakshi was stunned to see the frail woman shake with hatred, her eyes darkened with venom, and her mouth twisted with malice. Ayah's perception of Patravali was warped and contemptuous.

Mayurakshi wanted to flee from the venom-spitting woman and started walking towards the Rose Arbour.

"Why are you going away? You should know the truth. My Jhimli will come back home at last. She is the rightful owner, not your friend..." Ayah's shrill could be heard from miles away.

Mayurakshi did not stop walking, and Ayah stood watching her walk away towards the Rose Arbour. The rain had stopped falling, and the first ray of dawn appeared through broken clouds.

The arbour was laden with red, white, pink, orange, and yellow roses. The zig-zag path leading to the Gazebo at the top was paved with flat granite slabs. Mayurakshi stood at the entrance to the Arbour and looked towards the gazebo. Big concrete tubs full of water lilies were placed artistically in ascending order near the gazebo. The colourful ixora plants in full bloom bordered the paved winding path. Patravali's creativity was evident in the arrangement of the little decorations and the waterlilies placed at different heights.

Mayurakshi felt a lump of sadness as she remembered all the beautiful occasions spent with Patravali in this picturesque garden. Suddenly, someone called her from behind. Mayurakshi turned to see Dhaniram standing behind her. He asked, "When did you come, Mou Didi?" His speech was slightly slurred. He looked a little drunk, unkempt and tired. Dhaniram was the gardener and did odd jobs of fixing and mending things. He looked older than his sixty-five.

"You saw Patravali sitting in the passenger's seat beside the driver's. Professor Ahmed was driving? What else do you remember, Dhaniram?" Mayurakshi scrutinised him and asked.

Mayurakshi's question seemed to stir some memories in Dhaniram. He said confusingly, "I saw her sitting in the passenger's seat when she left with the Professor. It was raining... raining... she waved at me... the night of the party... she and the professor...he put a big, heavy bag in the ...back seat... she waved at me..."

"Have you seen Rimjhim's ghost recently?" Mayurakshi asked him.

"R-Rim-jhim- Madam! No – no..." Dhaniram looked frightened.

"What was Patravali wearing when you saw her getting in the car?"

Dhaniram stared strangely at Mayurakshi but didn't answer. He was still frightened and confused.

"Please, may I know who you are?" A nasal-tone male voice asked suddenly from her behind.

Mayurakshi and Dhaniram turned to see a man in jeans and a t-shirt standing behind them. He wore rimless spectacles and had a short crew cut. He looked fit like an athlete, and his clothes enhanced his looks and physique. He looked to be in his mid-thirties. He could have been good-looking save for his high teeth. His hands were jammed inside the pockets of his jeans.

Mayurakshi introduced herself. The newcomer exclaimed cheerfully, "You are the writer, Mayurakshi Bose! I am so happy to have you as my neighbour. Am I correct in surmising that we are neighbours?"

Mayurakshi looked puzzled, and he apologised for not introducing himself. He said smilingly, "I am Sanjay Lahiri, and I have bought this property. I would have invited you for coffee and breakfast, but my wife is still up. But you must promise to visit us someday soon."

Mayurakshi had missed something and asked confusedly, "Do you mean that you have bought Senjuti? Did my friend make the deal, or did her lawyer act on her behalf?"

Mr Sanjay Lahiri looked puzzled and asked interestedly, "Why do you ask? Is there any dispute regarding this property? I was looking for a quiet property with large grounds and open spaces. Mrs Chatterjee was looking for a customer with ready money, and we made a deal that suited both parties. Of course, our lawyers did everything needful."

Mayurakshi nodded and said, "My friend is missing, and it is doubtful that she sold out her beloved Senjuti."

Mr Lahiri's reaction was confusing as he laughed heartily and said, "Lawyers are wonderful creatures, Mrs. Bose. They can make a person change their mind with various arguments and deals. Mrs Chatterjee changed her mind since she spoke to you last, and then the lawyers did everything, and this magnificent property is ours. Mrs Chatterjee is happy with the ready cash, and we look forward to a peaceful life. Mrs. Bose, tell me, are the neighbours nosey here?"

Suddenly, Mayurakshi felt herself wrapped in an antagonistic atmosphere. Mr Sanjay Lahiri spoke with a ready smile, but his eyes remained cold. He was standing with his legs a little apart in a rigid stance. He did not seem friendly anymore. Ayah had withdrawn and couldn't be seen anywhere around. Dhaniram also had departed from the scene. In the vast garden, she was alone with a stranger who was probably not speaking the truth. Mayurakshi shivered slightly in apprehension.

"Why do you seem a little afraid? After all, we are neighbours now. We believe in love thy neighbour. Don't forget the tea, dear lady," Laughed Mr Sanjay Lahiri in a nasal tone.

Mayurakshi smiled warmly and bid goodbye to Mr Lahiri. Walking towards the main gate, she looked back at the arbour where they had been standing. Mr Lahiri was still standing with his legs a little apart. He waved his hand in farewell without a smile. Mayurakshi turned back and increased her pace.

CHAPTER XXII

Whiff of a Trail

11 March 2023

Simlipur, 7:00 Hours

Mayurakshi returned home in an agitated state. She was thinking about the absurdness of the situation. Here, she was concerned for the safety of her friend Patravali because of the handwritten letter she wrote regarding her property. Yet, a new owner claimed that he had legally acquired the property. Mayurakshi debated with her inner self, "Would Patravali willingly sell the property on such short notice? Was she compelled to sell or forced to sell by threats? Is she safe now? Did she go with the professor voluntarily? Was the elopement part of the game to secure the property? Is Jhimli responsible in some manner? Why did Patravali send Jhimli's old photograph? Ayah mentioned Rimjhim's ghost would rest in peace now. What did she mean by Jhimli coming to...

"Good morning, Mou! You are up so early... where did you go? I saw you walking back home. Did you go to the temple?" Nimmo smiled pleasantly as she came in with a flask of tea.

Mayurakshi told Nimmo about her experience. Nimmo also became puzzled and asked, "Could Ashok Trivedi be involved in all these?"

"Ashok Trivedi, the lawyer? Why would he be involved? Does he do business with realtors?"

Nimmo nodded in agreement and said, "Maybe he is in touch with Jhimli... you know, once he was very close to her mother. Besides, he has been working for a lot of builders lately. He does all the buying and selling of properties, etc. He had kept connections with Jhimli's grandmother. Doctor Dutta has his number."

"I will call him and see what he knows. I hope he is up; it is only fifteen minutes past seven in the morning..." Mayurakshi messaged Doctor Dutta for the lawyer's number. Within minutes,

Doctor Dutta sent her the lawyer's number, and she called him.

The phone rang several times before Mr. Ashok Trivedi answered. Mayurakshi had known him for many years and was also an acquaintance of the family.

Mayurakshi was about to abort the call when Mr Ashok Trivedi answered in a low tone, "Hello."

After initial greetings, Mayurakshi did not beat around the bush and immediately asked about the sale of Senjuti. He did not answer at once and Mayurakshi could hear the shuffling of papers in the background. His heavy breathing could be heard.

"You are saying that Senjuti is sold. Patravali did not mention to me about selling the property, and I did not initiate any negotiation." Mr. Ashok Trivedi sounded worried when he answered at last.

"Did you make any will for Patravali recently? Or are you working for Jhimli?"

"My dear Mayurakshi, surely you are not asking me to divulge personal legal matters! That would be unethical of me."

Mayurakshi was more confused at Ashok Trivedi's answer. She called the Doctor and told him about her experiences since morning. He became utterly silent, and Mayurakshi thought that the phone was disconnected.

"Hello... Doctor Dutta..."

"I can hear you, but words fail me. There is more than meets the eye. I want to meet you and ..." Doctor Dutta trailed off in a thoughtful silence.

"I think we should lodge a missing person report to the police," Mayurakshi said firmly.

Doctor Dutta said, "One of my patients knows the Sub-inspector in charge of Simlipur police station. He can introduce us... so that he will know that we are serious people..."

Mayurakshi was puzzled and asked, "Why must we be introduced? Law is equal for all citizens."

Doctor Dutta answered frustratingly, "Yes, everyone is equal before the law. It applies when the person in charge is reasonable and honest. In our case, we need an introduction."

They agreed to go to the local police station after the introduction and breakfast.

Durgapur, 9:30 Hours

At the Police station, there was a meeting in progress. Inspector Ramprasad Banik, detective Dipto Bhanu and Lakshman were seated around a table. Detective Dipto Bhanu looked at the spread-out map in anger. "I know in my blood that the other man was Rakesh. He tried to silence Jaipal. Why did they fall out? Money or girl? Did he take one of the trains standing at the station in Durgapur? And how did he escape without leaving a trail? I must be missing some important factor in the scene... first Zinnia was killed. Next, Jaipal was targeted. Why did they fall apart? If we could know their recent deals, it would be easier to track down Rakesh. I have to confirm the identity of that oldish-looking man at the Club. What was he doing near the back rooms? Was he Rakesh or Jaipal? Was he taking out something important or leaving a trail behind?"

"Chotu will help us... once the MLA gives him the green signal. The waiter, Vivek, is also in hiding. Does he know the killer?" Inspector Banik said.

"I surely hit the second man near the station. He fled away with a wound. He has got a bullet wound! He cannot escape far. The more I think about the whole thing, the more I become certain that he was Rakesh, trying to kill Jaipal before we caught him. Lakshman, call at the hospital to find out about Jaipal's condition. And I will call the MLA to speed up the process. We cannot sit here waiting for some development to happen." Dipto Bhanu declared and proceeded to make his call.

Dipto Bhanu connected with the MLA and asked for permission to interrogate Chotu. He spoke briefly and answered many queries. At the end of the conversation, Dipto Bhanu looked triumphant and declared happily, "We can bring in Chotu for a friendly chat. He seems to be a useful fellow, and the MLA would not like him scathed. I gave him my word of honour to be gentle with Chotu."

Lakshman was still speaking to the nurse at the hospital, and he wrote down something before hanging up the phone. He gestured at Dipto Bhanu and showed him the slip of paper on which he had taken notes.

Constable Chandan Das was dispatched to fetch in Chotu. While waiting for Chotu, Lakshman told them, "Early in the morning, Jaipal regained consciousness briefly. He tried to say something. She could only understand two names. One is 'club', and the other is 'Zinnia'."

"It is not surprising or new information. Jaipal and the girl were lovers. And the girl was murdered in the club premises." Inspector Banik commented.

"I wonder... we have to pay another visit to the club. Visit Zinnia's room in particular," Observed Dipto Bhanu.

By ten o'clock in the morning, Chotu was sitting opposite Dipto Bhanu. Chotu gave his statement eagerly on his own. He said, "Jaipal came to me asking about Vivek Malakar because he thought he might know about the murder and the murderer. Jaipal was confident that the filmmaker who wanted to meet Zinnia was someone whom Vivek knew well. He was dressed as the filmmaker but was not the famed filmmaker himself."

"Where is Vivek Malakar now? And where is Jaipal?" Asked Inspector Banik.

"Jaipal came to me, and then you went after him... I can only tell you about Vivek. I told him to flee, and he did that. I did not take the responsibility of hiding Vivek. He couldn't afford to pay me anything and would not work for me, so I had no interest in taking responsibility for his safety." Chotu said.

"So, Vivek told you that he was in danger. Did he tell the reason why he was in danger?" Dipto Bhanu asked.

"Vivek had seen the filmmaker from close. He had seen her talking to him, and then they had left his range of vision. Vivek was the first person to see Zinnia's dead body, and he fled in terror." Chotu replied readily.

"What did Jaipal tell you?"

"Jaipal wanted to avenge his girl's murder."

Dipto Bhanu repeated the same questions several times, but the answers remained the same. He let Chotu go and became very pensive after he had left. He opened the video of the club and sat watching it. Lakshman knew Dipto Bhanu too well and took the opportunity to go for a bit of munching. They had already eaten a hearty breakfast with an omelette and toast, but Lakshman loved eating sweets and always waited for short breaks to satisfy his cravings. Lakshman returned an hour later to find Dipto Bhanu looking pleased.

"Vivek Malakar saw more than a dead body that night. He must have heard something about Harman Handa and Rakesh too. Here, Vivek is seen moving between the tables when the band is playing... and after this... there is no more video for the rest of the night." Dipto Bhanu pointed to the video footage of the club. Inspector Ramprasad Banik had made a note of the time and date. He looked through his notes about the staff at Durgapur Club. He found the desired information and said with conviction, "We have to find Vivek. He is from a village near Kalipahari, and we should find him there. I will dispatch someone now."

Simlipur, 11:00 Hours

Back in Simlipur, Mayurakshi and Doctor Dutta went to the police station. The sub-inspector in charge of the thana was Bishnu Jana. He was not in a good mood when Doctor Dutta and Mayurakshi entered his station.

He was beating a man with a ruler, and his constable stood watching him.

"...where did you hide... Ahh... tell... what colour..." The commotion could not be avoided. Mayurakshi tried to think of something else to be able to ignore the situation. But the beatings and the Sub-Inspector's bombastic questioning methods were too loud to ignore. It was evident that the unfortunate man had taken somebody's goat.

Mayurakshi instantly disliked the Sub-Inspector, but she knew to control her speech. Doctor Dutta hesitated momentarily and then went near sub-inspector Jana and said humbly, "I am Doctor Dilip Dutta…"

They were offered chairs and asked to wait. Mayurakshi sat looking angry and disturbed, but Doctor Dutta gestured for her to calm down.

The sub-inspector came to his seat about fifteen minutes later, looking strangely satisfied. He indicated the direction of the beating and said significantly, "These people speak only after a good beating. Doctor, you do not need an introduction. You might not remember me, but you had treated my son last year. Well, what can I do for you?"

Doctor Dutta introduced Mayurakshi and said they wanted to complain about a missing person. Sub-inspector Jana became interested, and Doctor Dutta told him about Patravali's letter, disappearance and the sale of her property.

"I think she might be having a wonderful time with the Professor. She is hiding, you know, the social impact of a woman like her having a relationship with a person like the Professor can be overwhelming in a small town like Simlipur. It would be best if you waited before lodging a report. Maybe she wrote the letter for fun. And she sold her property to start a new life elsewhere," Sub-Inspector Jana said.

Mayurakshi asked, "She did not write the letter for fun. Is it not proof enough that she felt threatened in her own house? How can you be sure she was not forced to sell her property? She might be living in danger, after all."

Sub-Inspector Jana laughed sarcastically, "Mrs Bose, I am surprised at you! You are a writer, too, of psychological thrillers. Yet you find it difficult to see through your friend's plan to deceive you all. She is afraid of societal pressure and is in hiding. She was trying to create a picture of being victimised. I think she is a great manipulator."

"You will not look into it? Can you suggest in writing that we wait for some more time before lodging any report about Patravali Chatterjee? She was last seen on the night of 28 February, and today is 11 March. All these days, no one has spoken to or seen her." Mayurakshi sounded cool, but Doctor Dutta, who knew her too well, sensed her anger.

Sub-Inspector Jana fumbled for papers and said uncertainly, "I-I was just suggesting. If you think writing a missing person's report will bring back your friend, you are wrong, Mrs Bose. It will be difficult to find them since they are deliberately hiding."

Sub-Inspector Jana gave them the complaint lodge book and left the thana on the pretext of other appointments.

CHAPTER XXIII

Lump and Else Together

11 March 2023, Simlipur at 13:30 hours

Mayurakshi walked into the Club with Doctor Dutta. They felt emotionally exhausted. Their experience at the Police Station was not good. They decided to have lunch at the club and discuss their next move.

Some of the many new faces and families were the guests of existing Club Members. The cafeteria was brimming with people. Doctor Dutta and Mayurakshi were standing at the junction of the cafeteria and on the way to the restaurant when suddenly, a stout, broad-shouldered man jostled inside the cafeteria, pushing Mayurakshi on his way. She almost lost her balance.

"Sorry, Madam." The stout man said with a grin and grabbed Mayurakshi's elbow to support her from falling. He looked at her with piercing small eyes placed closely in his swelled face. He held on to Mayurakshi's hand even after she had regained her balance. His chubby fingers grasped her hand in a painful grip.

Mayurakshi furrowed her brows and pulled away from the offending person. He leered at her, baring a missing tooth. Mayurakshi noticed that he was well dressed and exuded a strong perfume. The short man bounced through the tables with the agility of a lizard and went to sit in a corner.

"Mrs Bose, Doctor Dutta, how are you?" asked a pleasant voice behind her.

Mayurakshi turned to see Mr Phagun Das, the manager of the Club, standing behind them. Mayurakshi smiled and exchanged pleasantries.

"We have a new chef from Kolkata. It would be best if you tried some of his special dishes. People are happy with his culinary expertise." Mr Das said happily.

"Thank you for the information. It is good to see our old Club thriving. There are so many new members. It is good for business." Smiled Mayurakshi.

"Some are new members, but most of the visitors are guests of old members." Mr Das looked at the corner of the room while speaking, and he nodded at someone in recognition. Mayurakshi followed his direction and saw the stout man with whom she had collided a few minutes earlier. Mr Das took their leave and waded to the corner table where the burly man was sitting.

"Come, let us sit in the restaurant. I do not think there would be so many people there," said Doctor Dutta.

But Mayurakshi lingered momentarily and noticed as Mr Das settled in the chair opposite the stout man. After a moment, they became absorbed in a deep conversation. As Mayurakshi was leaving the cafeteria, Ramanuj, the old waiter, came into the cafeteria with an empty tray and gave a pleasant salute.

"How are you, Madam? It is wonderful to see you again," said Ramanuj, baring his tobacco-stained teeth.

Mayurakshi smiled appreciatively, "It is nice to see an old face. There are so many new members I do not know, like the person in that corner with whom Mr Das is talking."

"Oh, that is Mr Harman Handa. He is a prominent businessman. Now he is a member of the Club. Mr Das introduced him here." Ramanuj informed after glancing at the designated table.

"Was Professor Ahmed a regular visitor in the club?" Asked Mou.

"Professor Ahmed? Yes, he came to the club regularly... but I don't remember seeing him in the last two weeks. He was also introduced by our new Manager, Mr Das." Ramanuj looked a little nervous as he spoke.

At that moment, a customer waved at Ramanuj, and he excused himself and went towards the customer.

Mou looked at them for a few seconds, then proceeded to the restaurant. They ordered food suggested by the waiter. When the waiter left them, Doctor Dutta spoke, "Do you think Mr Jana might be correct? Like, societal pressure..."

Mayurakshi looked troubled and said thoughtfully, "Why do you ask, Doctor Dutta? Are you having second thoughts? What Mr Jana suggested could have been true if the concerned person was not Patravali. She is not the scheming type. I trust her and can feel that something is wrong. I am worried, Doctor. Why do you think she wrote me such a mysterious letter? What about Rimjhim's ghost? Why did Ayah mention Jhimli? Patravali also sent me the photograph of Jhimli... I will take out my diary, and let's list things happening since that night."

She took out her pen and little notes diary and wrote,

1. "1. Patravali is having an affair – confirmed and specified by Indu Raha and other ladies.
2. Patravali writes a letter and does not mention the affair or the man – why?
3. She is in fear of being stalked – why? By Whom?
4. Ayah is spitting venom against Patravali – why?
5. Umanath Ji saw a lady with Professor Ahmed – but he is unsure about her identity – why?
6. Why did Professor Ahmed tell Dhaniram and Indu about their being together? Why did not Patravali call me and tell me the same?
7. Who is Sanjay Lahiri? How did he buy Senjuti? When did the sale happen?
8. Why did Patravali write me such a letter if she was willing to sell her property?
9. Where did she hide her documents? Could Rose Arbour be the hiding place?
10. Who gains most if something happens to Patravali? Can Jhimli sell the property without involving Patravali?
11. Who started the rumours of Patravali and Professor's love affair?
12. And lastly, who is Bina Naskar? Why did she shove Abhilash Kundu's bag under the berth? How are they related? What happened to Abhilash Kundu?

I need answers to these questions. Then only my mind will rest. Do you have any questions to add to the list, Doctor?"

Doctor Dutta read the list and added, "13. What did she mean by '*I have read about Queen Nefertiti? Doctor, please remember that I read about the most beautiful Egyptian Queen Nefertiti. It is most important for you to remember and tell Mayurakshi I have read about Queen Nefertiti.*'?

14. Why did she ask me if I remembered any of Timir's and Jhimli's friends?"

"What? When did she ask you about Timir Babu's and Jhimli's friends?" Mayurakshi was excited.

"Sometime in January, after my heart attack, she visited me and, on occasion, had asked me casually about their friends. I had completely forgotten about it until you made this list." Doctor Dutta said thoughtfully.

As the duo waited for their food, a familiar figure approached them. He was Mr Ashok Trivedi, the lawyer. He came to their table and sat down. He was in his mid-fifties and had bags under his eyes. His tallish frame looked lean save for the protruding belly. He looked curiously at the notes diary, which Mayurakshi had closed as soon as he came onto them. He looked at Mayurakshi and asked, "What did you mean by Senjuti being sold to someone? Mr Raha did not employ me to make the deal."

Mayurakshi did not show her surprise, but she was intrigued by the information. She thought, "So, Indu Raha had a motive. She wanted Senjuti and tried her best by spreading the rumours of Patravali's love affair. She thought Patravali would feel uncomfortable enough to sell her property to Indu. But that's absurd..."

"What are you thinking, Mayurakshi?" Asked Ashok Trivedi.

"Why does Indu need another property? She has her beautiful abode and the hotel. Has she bought anything after Patravali refused to sell her Senjuti?" Mayurakshi asked.

"They will open another resort soon. I have a few offers... let's see what clicks. Patravali Chatterjee refused to sell Senjuti to the

Rahas, but why did she sell it to someone unknown? I find this very interesting." Mr Ashok Trivedi said with a curious look.

"Ashok, do you know where Professor Ahmed stayed while he was in our town?" Asked Doctor Dutta.

"Professor Ahmed? Well, Mrs Rosie Alvarez would be able to answer you better. Sometimes, I help her with the leases. She keeps tenants and has a wonderful house." Replied Ashok Trivedi.

They were sitting in a pensive silence when the food arrived. Mr Ashok Trivedi said, "My client should have been here, but since he is not, I guess I have to order something to eat..."

"You can join us, and we can order for more..." Doctor Dutta said pleasantly.

"When did you last see Jhimli?" Mayurakshi asked Ashok Trivedi.

The suddenness of the question made him almost choke on his food. He drank water and waited to get back his breath. Then managed to ask, "Jhimli? Why do you ask about her?"

"If something happens to Patravali, then Jhimli would benefit most. I am just considering her as a suspect. She might be involved in Patravali's disappearance and also in the selling of the property."

Mr Ashok Trivedi looked astonished. He could not reply at first. Slowly, he understood the accusation and said in a panicky voice, "Mayurakshi, I am a well-wisher, and I want the best for them. All of them. Jhimli has not been able to live here because Patravali was here. But Jhimli would not be involved in all these; if she were involved, she would live here. Right? Besides, she is the rightful heir to the property after Patravali. I know Jhimli. She has money and is too proud to be involved in Patravali's affair."

"Ashok, you are a true promoter of Jhimli's interests. But when she eloped at nineteen, she forgot her family. Never in these fifteen years did she contact her father. I know how Timir grieved for her, and he tried to contact her many times." Doctor Dutta said rather rudely.

Ashok Trivedi answered coolly, "Dilip, you are defending your friend, but people change. Especially when they become lonely and with lots of money at their disposal. I saw Patravali and the Professor together on several occasions. The professor and Patravali being so lovey-dovey at Indu's anniversary party..."

Doctor Dutta replied hotly, "Remember, I was there too. She looked uncomfortable, more than happy. Everyone congratulated her and pushed her onto the Professor. I didn't find them lovey-dovey... Ashok, you are showing your dislike for Patravali in an unprofessional, ungentlemanly manner."

It was evident that the doctor was angry at the lawyer and was trying to get a grip on his emotions when suddenly he became very still. His eyes were fixed on the camera near the ceiling of the restaurant. He had a look of trance for a brief moment. Mayurakshi had noticed the look and saw the camera. They both became silent and thoughtful. Ashok Trivedi had finished eating and left early before the bill came.

Mayurakshi said as soon as the lawyer left, "I think we should check the video footage of that day. Was there any private photographer at the party?"

Doctor Dutta nodded in agreement and said, "She had gone somewhere for some time during the party. I remember the professor asking some of the guests about her whereabouts. Then she came to me and said the puzzling thing about Queen Nefertiti... we can check the Club CCTV archive and Indu's photographer's video."

They finished lunch and went to the surveillance room adjoining the maintenance room to look for Raghupati. He was the security guard in charge and was also responsible for the maintenance of the surveillance cameras at the club. The Club manager, Mr Das, was nowhere to be seen. It was a small room stuffed with a few cartons. There were about ten monitors mounted on one wall. Mayurakshi looked at the screens and watched for a few seconds. The café, restaurant, swimming pools, lawn tennis courts, and everything else could be seen. Raghupati watched a football game on a small TV on his messy desk. His back was turned towards the entrance. He turned to get his cigarette packet and was startled to see

Mayurakshi and Doctor Dutta standing.

"Ma-May I k-now- wha-t..." Raghupati stammered tensely.

Before he could finish his questions, Mayurakshi cut him short and said sweetly, "I am a writer, and I am looking for inspiration. I thought you might help me with stories that you see here." She indicated the monitors.

Raghupati answered apologetically, "Mr Das has given strict instructions that no one should come here without his permission."

"Must he know that we are here? Something secret and rewarding can be arranged between us." Mayurakshi kept a folded five hundred rupee note on the table beside him.

"Madam, our Das sir is very strict. I might even lose my job if he knows I am part of this..." Raghupati's eyes glittered as he eyed the note on the table.

Mayurakshi slipped one more two hundred rupee note and waited for the results.

Raghupati looked at Mayurakshi and pocketed the notes silently. He turned to the monitors and the controls. "What do you want to see, Madam?"

"The evening of the 28th February. Mr and Mrs Raha were celebrating their marriage anniversary. We want to see the footage of the party hall, garden, pool, and the first floor." Mou became business-like.

"Saturday, 28th February?!" Raghupati looked pale and almost trembled.

"Why, any problem?" Mayurakshi asked.

"The- The – c-ame-ras were no – not working... o – o - out of order... Das sir knows." Raghupati was very nervous.

"Since when?" Mayurakshi sounded angry.

"I – I – don't know. Das Sir knows." Raghupati looked cornered.

"Okay, let us check. You can keep an eye out for Mr Das. We will be quick." Mayurakshi started clicking at the footage.

"25 February, 26... 27... 3 March...Hmm... So, 28th February is missing. Who else has access to these videos?" Mayurakshi asked in a professional tone.

"Only Das sir and the man who comes for maintenance every month. I have not done anything. I only sit here and keep an eye on when the children are swimming." Pleaded Raghupati.

"Yes, Mr Das also has the keys to this room... and... there is no camera here... but you have a camera at the parking lot. Check the footage of 28th February at the parking lot." Mayurakshi was business-like.

Raghupati checked all the footage and found no video from the 28th of February to the 2nd of March.

"We have to depend on Indu's photographer solely... are you brave enough for an encounter with Indu?" Mayurakshi asked Doctor Dutta when they came out of the building.

"You are better with words, Mou. Besides, we must look for Rosie Alvarez... maybe she can help us with the Professor's abode." Doctor Dutta said sweetly.

"You better go home and take a break, doctor Dutta. I will invite Indu for a cup of tea and play the part of a listener, and words will flow out of her mouth incessantly... we can go to Rosie Alvarez's house tomorrow." Mayurakshi agreed and went home to Suprabhat.

CHAPTER XXIV

Witness

11 March 2023, 17:30 Hours

Mayurakshi returned home from the club with plans for the evening. She phoned Indu and said sweetly, "I was hoping to have tea together with you, Indu. Will you come to Suprabhat...please."

"When did you come? How did I miss your arrival? I feel slightly under the weather but would be delighted to have tea with you. I cannot miss this opportunity. You must come to my house and we can chat... what will you have? Chicken pakora? Jalebi? Chaat? Samosa? Pa..."

"Indu, please do not become the menu. We can have tea and chat about our differences. See you in the evening." Mayurakshi cut short the word faucet which Indu cannot control.

"She can show me the album, and the video. Maybe she will give me all the other information... In the meantime... Google the professor." Mayurakshi said to herself and searched for Professor Ahmed.

She found the news regarding The Professor within a few minutes of her search. The news was brief and had appeared in a local Hindi newspaper of Bhopal. The news read as follows:

18 December 2022, Bhopal

A shocking tale of twin murders and vehicle robbery

Professor Faisal Ahmed of Bhopal University was found dead near a wilderness area between Ralamandal Wildlife Sanctuary and Bhopal. According to the Police, the university Professor was visiting the Sanctuary when another vehicle approached him for help. There were two men in the other car, and they were stranded on the road. The Professor stopped to help them and one of the men shot him. The Professor fell, and simultaneously, another vehicle approached the scene. The newcomer was Suraj Singh, a local businessman. He had seen the whole thing happen: two men and the murder. On his arrival, the robbers sped away from the scene, and he called the police. But when police arrived, they found Suraj Singh wounded and the professor dead. Both of their vehicles were also stolen. Suraj Singh passed away in the hospital two days later from the fatal bullet wounds. Professor Faisal Ahmed was a well-known poet who taught Hindi literature at the university. His two sons and his wife survive him. The parents and wife survive Suraj Singh.

Police sources say that the ill-famed vehicle robbers Rakesh and Jaipal are suspected of the crime. According to the police, Rakesh and Jaipal are adept at disguises and speak several languages.

Mayurakshi sent the link to Doctor Dutta and called him. He answered on the first ring, "Hello, Mou."

"I have sent you a link. Please read now. It is about Professor Faisal Ahmed. The news says that he had been killed on the 18th of December last year, near Bhopal." Mayurakshi almost shouted the news.

The Doctor took time to digest the news, and Mayurakshi gave him time to read and understand the situation.

Now, she knew for sure that Patravali was in danger. Her heart sank as she realised it had been eleven days since she was last seen. "Is she alive? Who was behind the fake Professor Ahmed's smile? Why did Patravali send me the photograph of Jhimli? Who is Mrs Sneha Mitra? Why did the phoney Professor choose Patravali, of all people? I must find out about these vehicle robbers, Rakesh and Jaipal."

She Googled Rakesh and Jaipal but found almost nothing on them, except for a few vehicle thefts. They were good at their job of stealing, and the police of several states wanted them.

Mayurakshi thought for some time about all her connections who might help her find more details about Rakesh and Jaipal. She was sure that Patravali's disappearance had a connection to the vehicle robbers.

As she thought about her connections, she realised she had not returned her husband's call, but it was almost time for the tea at Indu's place. "Will call you later at night," she messaged Bidyut and left Suprabhat.

The path that led to Indu's house was lined with big trees casting huge shadows. Mayurakshi strolled, looking at the well-remembered trees home to many birds. She rang the bell at Indu's house dot at thirty minutes past five. The live-in maid opened the door and led Mayurakshi to Indu, who was sitting on a recliner with a hot pad placed on her knees.

Indu was excited to see Mayurakshi and gave numerous instructions to the maid. Mayurakshi settled in one of the brightly coloured sofas and looked around the big room. There were too many objects with contrasting colours. It felt a little chaotic.

After passing the initial excitement and exchanging pleasantries, Mayurakshi said, "Senjuti has a new owner. Mr Sanjay Lahiri and his wife are already living there."

Indu looked shocked. And for once, Indu had nothing to say. There could not have been more impact if Mayurakshi had dropped a bomb.

"...and she did not want to sell her property to me! I thought she was sentimental about it; after all, it was her home, but... how could she sell it to some stranger? Mou, now I am furious. And I thought I was doing her a favour by bringing them together... I thought... oh my God! Now, I understand why she ran away... she wanted more money... but she has so..." Indu would have continued lamenting, but Mayurakshi interfered and said firmly, "The man who claimed to be Professor Faisal Ahmed was a fraud. The real Professor Faisal Ahmed was shot on the 18th of December. He was killed and his vehicle stolen."

The news was too much for Indu Raha, and she almost jumped out of the recliner. Mayurakshi showed her the news that she read before coming. "I need to see your party photographs and the event video footage. I have to know about the man behind the disguise of the Professor. And you can help by remembering small incidents that didn't fit Patravali."

An hour later, Mayurakshi had seen all the photographs. She needed to see the raw video footage of the day and said so. It was arranged that Gajanan Dubey, who had done the video, would provide the raw footage.

Indu had recovered enough to be her chatty self again. She remembered a lot of incidents that didn't help further the case. Indu was saying something about a picnic arranged by her hotel staff when Mayurakshi recalled the name, Rosie Alvarez.

"Indu, do you know Mrs Rosie Alvarez? She rents out flats and rooms."

Indu took her phone, scrolled through the names, and handed it to Mayurakshi. "That's her number. Rosie Alvarez. Sometimes, I refer her name to students and single employees with transferable jobs who want something cheaper and for longer periods. She has a nice brick house and lives with her granddaughter. She is a nice old lady."

Mayurakshi telephoned Mrs Rosie Alvarez. She answered after the first ring. They talked briefly. As the call ended, Mayurakshi told Indu, "He stayed at her place. He had rented a flat and paid in advance. Mrs Rosie Alvarez had secretly seen a lady visiting him several times in the week. She doesn't know the timing of the lady visitor coming and going. He left on the 28th of February at night. She has Xerox copies of his ID. I will inform the sub-inspector about the living arrangement of the imposter. Let's hope he will be able to find him and the lady. Who could she be?"

"No, I am as spellbound as you are. I am confused. I have no idea about the lady. The real professor was dead by the time this fake Ahmed came here. Then how did he manage to look the same as the real person? It is just like the movies. The actors put on makeup, and the sound engineer works on the voice, resulting in a different person. Mou, do you think the fake Ahmed did the same thing?"

"I think he did not look like Professor Ahmed as he was unknown here. I am more concerned about this lady... everything is fitting into their scheme. They were working together..." Mayurakshi mused.

Mayurakshi was ready to leave when Gajanan Dubey came in with the raw video footage of the party. She took the video home.

Mayurakshi went to her room and opened the pen drive given by Gajanan. The party came alive on her computer screen. The Rahas had made lavish arrangements for the party. There were fresh flowers, a centre stage, food, beverages and beautiful lighting. She stared at the monitor while glimpses of guests moved on, people eating and talking in small groups, children floating in and out of the frame. Suddenly, the camera swivelled to the entrance, and Patravali was seen standing at the gate for a second, then she moved into the hall. She waved at someone, not in the camera and started walking towards that person. She looked lovely in a pale pink silk saree and gold pendant with matching danglers. Indu Raha came forward, blocking that unseen person and laughed happily as Patravali gave her a wrapped box and flowers. Indu said something to Patravali, which was inaudible. Patravali's face clouded while Indu laughed teasingly. Then Mr Raha came forward and said something to the duo. Mayurakshi's eyes filled with tears as Patravali smiled and posed with the host and hostess. In the footage, she could be seen blending in with other guests. There was nothing suspicious about the guests or her movements. Mayurakshi watched closely and froze the frame when the imposter, Professor Ahmed, came into the scene. He looked impeccable in a classic charcoal grey suit. His shoulder-length curly hair framed his handsome face. He sported a well-groomed moustache and French beard. The expensive-looking retro horn-rimmed glasses suited his wheatish complexion. There was a touch of grey near his temple. He had full cheeks, which did not mar his good looks. He was in great shape and looked to be in his late forties. He was tall, and Patravali's petite form looked pretty beside him. He moved slowly among the guests but always seemed to be in the same frame as Patravali. Mayurakshi watched the video fascinatedly and thought that the man posing as the professor looked too perfect, like an actor fitting in a role. The imposter Professor seemed attentive to Patravali; twice, he was seen handing her drinks and snacks. Patravali looked overwhelmed and a little ill at ease at the intentness of his open devotion. Mayurakshi observed the ladies' delight at the Professor's obsession with Patravali. Doctor Dutta was seen sitting in a corner. He waved a hand to someone in greeting or recognition while talking to a couple. Once, Ashok Trivedi was also seen talking to Patravali.

There were many guests at the party, and the footage was extended.

Then Patravali and Professor Ahmed were seen with a group of ladies and gentlemen. They seemed to be entertained and happy about something. The Professor was gloating like a teenager. Then there was the singer singing a Bollywood romantic song. The hall lights were dimmed, and couples were dancing.

Mayurakshi noticed Patravali walking unobtrusively out of the hall through the side door. Mayurakshi replayed the part and confirmed that Patravali had stepped out of the entrance at quarter to nine. Mayurakshi watched the imposter Professor missing in all frames at the same time. The Professor's departure was not recorded. Patravali was seen again in the video at twenty-five minutes past nine. At that time, the imposter professor was already present in the frame. She played the video several times and noted the professor leaving the hall at thirty-five minutes past eight and returning before Patravali.

"Patravali had walked out, and so had the imposter... he was gone for about the same time. Where did he go? He left the hall by the side door... that could lead to the garden and the first floor... did he know that she was also out? The side door can lead to the garden or the first floor through the corridor... did she go to the first floor? Perhaps to evade the intentness of attention, Patravali had gone to the first floor... library?! She was gone for about forty minutes, enough to see something... or hide something..." Mayurakshi mused.

Mayurakshi was excited at the thought and continued watching the video footage. Patravali was seen talking to Doctor Dutta when some women approached them along with the imposter Professor. Patravali seemed excited and a little frightened.

"'*I have read about Queen Nefertiti. Doctor, please remember that I read about the most beautiful Egyptian Queen Nefertiti. It is most important for you to remember and tell Mayurakshi that I have read about Queen Nefertiti.*' Mayurakshi remembered the words that Patravali had told Doctor Dutta.

"Did she mean that she had seen something in the library? Or was she referring to a book about the Queen?" Mayurakshi thought of the options that Patravali might have meant. Doctor Dutta had said that Patravali insisted vehemently about the Queen Nefertiti. Mayurakshi decided to visit the Club library and Mrs Rosie Alvarez the following morning.

It was almost ten, and Nimmo came into her room looking stern. Mayurakshi knew the look and said sweetly before Nimmo could utter, "I know I am late for dinner... please Nimmo..." Mayurakshi put on her slippers and followed Nimmo to the dining room.

"Did you call your mother or your husband? Mou, it would be best if you gave them also some attention. Your mother called me, and on your behalf, as an excuse, I had to tell a bunch of stories to the dear lady. And Bidyut said he wants to speak to you before you sleep."

"I love you, Nimmo. You've always helped..." Mayurakshi couldn't finish because the bell started ringing continuously.

"Who is this Maharaja? It is almost thirty minutes past..." Nimmo's grumble trailed off as she went to answer the door.

There was a little commotion, and nothing could be heard distinctly. Nimmo sounded angry, and a deep voice was saying something in a slurred speech.

Mayurakshi had finished her meal and went to the door to see the cause of the tumult. To her surprise, Dhaniram was arguing with Nimmo, who stood like a warrior at the door. He seemed a little drunk, but he insisted on talking to Mayurakshi.

"Dhaniram, you may come in if you have anything to tell me," Mayurakshi said.

Dhaniram, the gardener, looked unkempt and walked a little unsteadily, yet he seemed insolent, which irritated Mou.

"The other day when you visited her favourite arbour, I was surprised and couldn't answer your questions. Later, I realised I had seen our Bahuji sitting in her car with the Professor. It was very late at night, the party night... that same night, they went away. He was carrying a large sack-like backpack. He put it in the back seat. She was wearing s-something p-ink or purple... sari. It started to rain, and I called them... she waved at me. I saw her look... a little different, I mean... too white... perhaps the night or the rain... too glowing... " Dhaniram seemed to pull himself together as he answered.

"Dhaniram, can you tell why Ayah is spreading words of hatred for Patravali? As far as I know, she always treated you with care and sympathy. She always paid you handsomely. And she got you treated for your drinking problems... the list of her goodness as an employer is long, yet suddenly, Ayah is spreading hatred. Why?" Mayurakshi sounded angry.

"Ayah Di wants justice for Jhimli... Jhimli, like her own daughter,... her child. She had brought her up as a daughter. Jhimli has told her that she will come to Senjuti to live. Bahuji did not allow Jhimli to come... to Senjuti to live. Now Jhimli can come. She talks to Ayah Di. She is pretty like her mother," Dhaniram said in slurred speech.

"When did Jhimli speak to Ayah? Did she speak to you also? And why are you lying about Patravali? What do you mean by 'too glowing'?"

"That- I don't know the details. I cannot remember... no I did not talk to Jhimli... Bahuji is now gone with the professor... he called me to tell me about their happiness. She is good, but she is young. Our Master is no more, and she is still young and beautiful. Jhimli... will come... she will stay. She is pretty like her mother," Dhaniram suddenly stopped and looked confused.

"Do you know anything about Rimjhim's ghost, Dhaniram?" Mayurakshi's question acted like acid on Dhaniram. He shook a little and looked frightened.

Dhaniram mumbled something unintelligently under his breath. He excused himself and wanted to go.

"Who was keeping vigilance over Patravali? Were you and Bindi involved, too? Why did Bindi go away before Patravali went missing? The police will make you say everything you know," Mayurakshi muttered angrily.

Dhaniram was decidedly very frightened, and he fled.

That night, Mayurakshi could hardly sleep as she thought about all the probabilities of what might have happened to Patravali. She was also excited because, in the morning, she would find the mystery of Queen Nefertiti.

It was very late, and everything else seemed to be sleeping. The crickets made a humming background, adding to the night's mystery.

Mayurakshi pondered over her notes and looked distractedly at the window. There was a slight drizzle, and the trees murmured in the windy night. The trees looked like giants with shivering hair. She looked on abstractedly. Suddenly, she sensed a movement near Senjuti's study window. Mayurakshi looked with attention in the darkness. A light was put on in the study of Senjuti. The windows were closed, and curtains were drawn, but a thin light line could be seen through a gap. Then she saw a shadow move from the nearing bush. Quickly, Mayurakshi switched off her table lamp and stood in the dark while observing the black shadow move furtively. The shadow seemed unsure of itself and walked unsteadily.

It was challenging to decide with certainty if it was a man or a woman. The human figure was crouching near the study window. She took out her field glasses and looked closely at the stealthy figure. Suddenly, the light in the study of Senjuti was extinguished, and the shrouded person slowly walked unsteadily away. Nothing could be seen anymore. She wondered with excitement if the person she had just seen was the same one Patravali had noticed in her garden and thought to be the ghost of Rimjhim. But then Patravali had mentioned a red dress, and she had seen only a shadowy figure draped in a dark shawl.

She could not sleep; tumultuous thoughts kept her vertical on her chair. She had a premonition of evil, and the shadowy figure lurking in the garden made her very uneasy. It was half past two in the morning and was still drizzling, making the night gloomy. The chorus of the crickets and the monotonous sound of the dripping water falling on the tin roof of the outhouse at regular intervals created a soothing lullaby. Mayurakshi closed her eyes, "Nefertiti... Dhaniram... Lahiri... Rimjhim's ghost is walking... the dead professor..."

Suddenly, she was walking down a semi-dark corridor; she knew the place well. It was Patravali's house, and she was walking down the middle corridor that connected all the rooms on the ground floor. She was all alone, walking stealthily to the study. The empty room was dimly illuminated, with the light cascading softly from the Murano glass table lamp. The desk was neatly arranged with Patravali's journals and books and a vase of bougainvillaea. Mayurakshi smiled at the neatness and the artistic arrangement of Patravali's things. She said laughingly, "I will always envy your ability to keep things in perfect order and harmony. Somehow, my desk always looks like a storm hit it." Mayurakshi's smile died on her lips as she looked at a clump of cold and wet soil on the table. She looked on in terror, and suddenly, the light dimmed, and with a short, sharp, penetrating sound, the Murano glass table lamp broke, scattering tiny blue fragments of glass everywhere. A dark shadowy figure approached her and held a muddy hand towards her. Mayurakshi shouted in horror.

She woke up with a start. She had fallen asleep on her comfortable recliner. Her body felt wet with sweat. One of the windows had opened, and a fine mist of rain was coming through it, creating a cold and damp atmosphere. Her heart sank with apprehension as she remembered her dream.

CHAPTER XXV

The Withered Rose

12 March 2023

It was a beautiful morning without any trace of rain of the preceding night. The weather was just perfect for a picnic. Five young friends were preparing to spend the day at the famous lake near Simlipur. They were staying at the Blue Peaks Hotel, which the Rahas owned. Kalipada Das was an expert driver and cook. He was in charge of the picnic parties arranged by the hotel. Kalipada checked all his supplies for cooking and started the journey.

The lake was the most favoured picnic spot for visitors. Giant boulders were scattered around the lake, home to many wild geese and cranes. Many tourists visited Simlipur from February to April. The five youngsters were university students, and they were excited about the journey.

The drive to the picnic spot was very scenic and pleasant. The thin dirt road crawled through clumps of trees and scattered boulders. Several ponds and many expanses of green fields lay between the hotel and the picnic spot. It was only half past seven, and people were busy working in the fields while their animals grazed in the unploughed wilderness. The five youngsters were happy and played music on their car stereo while their car jumped and shuddered on the uneven dirt road and moved at a leisurely pace.

As their car moved along the dirt road through a stretch of wilderness, they saw a small group of kids shouting in terror. They were looking at something on the ground in a horrified fascination. There was a mongrel dog with them, and it was digging madly in the ground at the place of their interest.

"Hey, let's stop and see. Maybe they have found something interesting." Cried Asim, he was one of the young men.

"They are local kids, and maybe their idea of having fun is to look at some buried nuisance." Remarked Firoz philosophically.

"What if it turns out that the buried nuisance is a treasure map leading to a fortune? Let's join in." Laughed Asim. He was a reckless and adventurous type.

"It might be a dead body. We should at least enquire to see if they need help." Suggested the horror-loving young man named Supriyo.

"Hey, not a dead body! You seem to enjoy only the grotesque. But I do agree to investigate. Maybe we will have an experience of some kind." Assented Anuj.

"I think it is serious business. We should stay out of it. We are here for a holiday, and let's not get involved in local nuisance." Observed Pranjal. He was the serious one amongst them and always thought about everything with a practical perspective. His friends teased him and sometimes called him "Chacha, " meaning uncle.

"Chacha is afraid... Chacha, don't worry, you can stay out of this adventure." Teased Asim.

The others laughed at the comment and ordered Kalipada to stop the car. The driver, Kalipada Das, was a local man who was also curious about the commotion. And he stopped the car. The four young men hurried to the spot, and the 'Chacha' of the group lagged reluctantly. Although Kalipada Das had second thoughts for a moment, he joined the five young men.

Six of the adults progressed towards the kids. They smelt a stench as soon as they came near the spot. Then they saw the horrible thing protruding from a little hole where the dog had dug some dirt away. The ground was soft and wet.

"Oh my god!"

"It's a foot! A human foot!"

"A lady's foot!"

"Yes, I can see the nail polish."

"I cautioned not to jump into this mess. Now, this horrid dead body will lead to a police investigation. We all will be implied. And we have to forget our holiday. We were here to have some quality time amidst nature..."

"Shut up, Chacha!"

"Move away! Do not touch anything. We have to call the police."

There was chaos as the young men shouted with the kids. Kalipada was also disturbed at the sight of the human foot. But he kept his head and phoned the hotel's owner and the police. He had the sense to shoo everyone away from the body.

Within an hour, the area was swarming with police and local people. The young men went back to the hotel when the police arrived. The news spread like wildfire. The crime scene was about twelve kilometres away from Simlipur, and many workers went to work in Simlipur from the area of the crime.

Sub-Inspector Bishnu Jana took charge of the scene as the area was in his jurisdiction. He arranged for the forensic team. "Sir, is this the same woman that writer and Doctor Dutta referred to?" Asked Constable Shyamlal. Sub-Inspector Jana considered the possibility.

"Let us wait for the forensic team to help us dig out the corpse first. We can call them for identification afterwards," said Bishnu Jana.

In another part of Simlipur, Mayurakshi woke up with an ill omen. She dressed quickly and phoned Mrs Rosie Alvarez, who answered at the first ring. Mayurakshi came straight to the point and declared, "I would like to visit you today to discuss the professor and the lady. Do you still have their details?"

"I have the Xerox copy of the professor's driver's license, but the lady came here secretly, so I don't have anything related to her. I saw him so little during his stay, and he was so quiet that I mostly forgot his existence."

"But, you saw the lady with him... can you describe her?" Mayurakshi asked eagerly.

"Why are you so much interested? I should know what I am getting into before I tell you about any of my past or present tenants."

Mayurakshi told her about Patravali's disappearance and the Professor's role in the affair. Mrs Alvarez became alert and readily agreed to help her. She said, "The lady lived here like she did not exist. But I have eyes on the back of my head. And my ears are quite good. You come here, my dear, and I shall tell you all I know about the couple."

Mayurakshi ended the call and took out the notes diary. She started preparing an evidence board.

Around ten, Nimmo came in with tea and breakfast. She set the tray on her bed and sat on a chair.

"Nimmo... please go now... I am working..."

"Okay, I will leave you, but where is your phone? Your mother has been calling again. She is very excited about meeting someone."

Mayurakshi sighed in defeat and called her mother. She picked up at the first ring and said happily, "Mou, I am so happy... I have met my school friend, Sushmita, after almost twenty years. She is now my neighbour in Kalimpong. And she is a big fan of your books." Mayurakshi's mother chatted about her school friend Sushmita and her family. "...Sushmita's younger son is a police detective at Lal Bazar Police Department..."

"Ma, tell me about her son..." Mayurakshi interrupted her mother as soon as she heard the word detective. She had been thinking about her connections in the police, and here was an opportunity.

Mayurakshi was still talking to her mother when another call came in. She would have ignored it, but the call was ongoing.

Mayurakshi ended her mother's call and answered the incoming call.

"A dead body is found! A woman's body! Clad in a salwar suit. Our driver Kalipada Das found it. And the stench... Oh! I think that the poor thing must have been dead for some time." Busted in Indu and would have continued her train of speech, but Mou cut her short.

"Where was this body found? Whose body? Did anyone identify her?" Mou was pressing her nails in her palm as she spoke.

"She seems to have been a lady. Kalipada said that she had nail polish on her toes. I will find out the details. And the guests who were going to the picnic were shocked. Poor things. They are a bunch of university students on a break..." Indu would have continued, but just then, Nimmo came in looking agitated and pale. Mayurakshi asked her what had happened. "Come... Police..." Nimmo ran downstairs again, and Mayurakshi followed her.

Constable Shyamlal was waiting for her, and he said without any preamble, "You and the Doctor have to come with me for identification of a woman's dead body. She has been found this morning. The Doctor is coming here to pick you up."

Just then, Doctor Dutta came in his car, and they went to the crime scene.

"I hope to be proven wrong." Commented Doctor Dutta unconvincingly. The veteran doctor looked ill at ease, and she was clenching and unclenching her palms. The journey to the crime scene seemed too long.

As they neared the place of crime, they saw a small team of police working on the dead body, and some ordinary people flocked to see the proceedings. Mayurakshi and Doctor Dutta were ushered to the shallow grave. The body lay exposed on the ground. There was an awful stench, and the body looked bloated. It had a blue-greenish hue. It was a woman's body clad in a salwar suit. Mayurakshi could barely look at the toes with maroon nail polish. She closed her eyes and, in her heart, knew that she would see Patravali lying on the ground.

Doctor Dutta muttered something in a hoarse voice.

"What did you say, Doctor Dutta?" Asked Inspector Jana. The Doctor repeated hoarsely, "She is Mrs Patravali Chatterjee."

At last, Mayurakshi was able to look at the dead body of her beloved friend. Seeing the gentle, charming, and gracious Patravali lying in the dirt with a blue-swelled face was shocking. It was not a pretty sight, and she wished to forget this distorted, ugly face of Patravali. She had been shot in the chest. The blood had dried, leaving a hole in the chest. There were bushes and a few tall trees around the grave, making the place grimmer and more shadowy.

"Yes-s she is... was our friend, Mrs. Patravali Chatterjee..." Mayurakshi uttered painfully as she hurried to a nearby tree to throw up.

Mayurakshi was angry, outraged, frustrated, and in pain. She had known that Patravali would never leave her beloved Senjuti willingly. And if she loved someone, she had the integrity to stand by her love and not run away like a teenager. But the neighbours and friends believed what they wanted. They did not care for Patravali's disappearance and would have continued to believe in her elopement. The children had found the grave accidentally. It was coincidental that the guests were travelling by that road at the same time.

"What a devilish plot! First, there were rumours of a false love affair between Patravali and the imposter Professor Ahmed, and then there was the news of her elopement, confirmed by the imposter. Who gained from this intricate falsehood? Was Jhimli responsible in any way for all these? Where is Jhimli now? Who is her husband? Would Jhimli inherit everything as next of kin? Are Ayah and Dhaniram part of the game? Did Patravali write a new will? Who was dressing up as the ghost of Rimjhim? Is Jhimli involved ..."

"Mayurakshi... Mou..." The gentle touch at her elbow made her return from her reveries with a start. "Oh, Doctor Dutta... Patravali..." She could not hold herself together anymore and started sobbing like a little girl. Her tears rolled down her cheeks unchecked. Doctor Dutta sadly nodded his head. His old frame suddenly looked older than ever.

It took some minutes before Mayurakshi had her emotions under control. She looked at the forensic people working at the grave and said, "If she hadn't written me that letter, then I would also have believed in the nonsense of her elopement... Someone brilliant has been orchestrating the whole affair. All these elaborate fabricated stories have been circulated very systematically. I want them punished... Patravali, I promise to avenge your horrible murder."

CHAPTER XXVI

Bring to Light

12 March 2023

The forensic team worked at the crime scene while Patravali's dead body lay in the muddy grave where she was found. Sub-Inspector Jana was discussing the details with the police doctor. Mayurakshi and Doctor Dutta also joined them to listen.

The police doctor said, "I think that she died about two weeks ago. The death occurred due to the bullet wound. The bullet is still inside the body. After performing the autopsy, I can confirm the date and time."

After the body was dispatched for post-mortem Mayurakshi and Doctor Dutta went to the police station with the sub-inspector. After settling down, he asked Mayurakshi, "Where were you about two weeks early?"

Mayurakshi replied calmly, "In Copenhagen."

"And you?" Sub-inspector Jana indicated to the Doctor.

"How did you know that she might be in danger?" Sub-inspector Jana's sarcastic attitude had returned with full force.

Mayurakshi could not control her temper and without any diplomatic method said, "Yesterday, we told you everything in detail yet you did not pay attention. We told you about the letter, the Professor, the new owner of her property ... yet you are accusing us? Are you shielding anyone? What about the house staff who worked for Mrs Patravali Chatterjee?"

Sub-inspector Jana was aback at the retaliation but he composed himself. He pretended to look into some files and drank water.

Doctor Dutta tried to calm Mayurakshi and advised her to be more diplomatic with the sub-inspector.

After what seemed like a lifetime to Mayurakshi, Sub-Inspector Jana asked, "Who saw her for the last time on the night of the party? I want all the information regarding the party. Who were the guests, who left early and who was with your friend… everything."

Mayurakshi was glad that, ultimately, the Sub-Sub-Inspector was ready to listen.

"I was at the party and saw her leave around nine forty-five. I can't recall if anyone left immediately after her. She was alone when she left and was a little agitated at the time." Doctor Dutta sounded sure of himself.

"I think Dhaniram, the gardener at Senjuti, saw her last on the night of the party. Umanath Ji of the old Kali Temple had also seen someone like her the same night." Supplied Mayurakshi.

"Senjuti? Dhaniram? Umanath Ji? How do you know all this? Are you sure Dhaniram was the last to see her alive that day? You said you were in Copenhagen, but you know all the details. Interesting!" Sub-Inspector Jana looked at Mayurakshi curiously.

"Senjuti is the name of Mrs. Patravali Chatterjee's property. Dhaniram is the gardener at Senjuti. I went to Senjuti and talked briefly with Dhaniram yesterday morning before I came to the police station to lodge the missing person report. He was pretty sure that he had seen Patravali on that Saturday night. He was drunk on the night of the party but remembered seeing Patravali in a pink saree leaving with Professor Faisal Ahmed. Ayah had been working at Senjuti for a long time. She knows many things that would help to find the murderer. And now, Senjuti has a new owner, Mr Sanjay Lahiri." Mayurakshi said patiently as if she were talking to a half-wit person.

"Wow! Madam, you have done your homework well. Why are you so much interested in other people's lives? You said you were a writer, so get busy with your writing… and let us do our job." Sub-Inspector Jana said sarcastically.

"I would gladly finish my writing if you were involved in finding the culprit. By the way, you would be interested to know that Professor Faisal Ahmed died; I mean, he was murdered near a place in Bhopal. He was killed in mid-December last year. And here in February, he was trying to romance my friend, Patravali Chatterjee… the same one who was found dead." Mayurakshi spoke angrily.

"How do you know so much, Miss Marple? I would like to know about your friend's lifestyle and attitude towards men. Where is the professor now?" Sub-Inspector Jana took out a short notebook and wrote several names.

Mayurakshi was becoming frustrated at the laid-back attitude of the sub-inspector, and she opened the news of the death of Professor Faisal Ahmed on her mobile and passed it to the sub-inspector.

"Read... and you will know what I said is true."

Suddenly, the attitude of sub-inspector Jana changed as he finished reading the article. He looked worried and took out notices sent to all police stations nationally. He also made calls to several other police stations.

"Yes, the news is not fake. Professor Faisal Ahmed and Suraj Singh were killed on 18 December 2022. The police of many states want the possible killers, Rakesh and Jaipal. They are vehicle robbers and have stolen thousands of vehicles in the past seven years." Sub-Inspector Jana was agitated, and Mayurakshi instinctively knew this was his first big case.

"I need all the information that you have collected so far. Mrs Bose, I want you and the Doctor to join us. Please share your thoughts and any advice that you think necessary." Sub-Inspector Jana's attitude appeased Mayurakshi.

"We have photographs and video footage of the fabricated Professor Ahmed. Dhaniram and Ayah are still at Senjuti and know more about the incident. The new owner, Sanjay Lahiri, might reveal something important if his documents are checked. I am sure that you are going to bring them in for interrogation. And the imposter Ahmed had rented a flat at Mrs Rosie Alvarez's house," Mayurakshi said to Sub-Inspector Jana, who listened carefully. He wrote everything in his little notebook and asked, "Doctor Dutta, how well did you know Patravali Chatterjee?"

"I have known Timir Chatterjee since we were in school. We went to the same class, the same school. He was my closest friend, and I was among the few invitees when he married Patravali. They made a nice couple. She was very artistic and a good person. She was completely devoted to Timir. Then suddenly, Timir died of a heart attack. Patravali became depressed and completely shut off her social life. That was in May last year. Now, Patravali was beginning to live again. And ..." Doctor Dutta had his eyes closed. He did not attempt to wipe the tears rolling down his cheeks.

"When did she meet Professor Ahmed?" Sub-Inspector Jana waited for a few seconds before asking.

"I had a mild stroke in the last week of December and went to live with my son in Mumbai to restore my health. I returned in mid-February. I had not seen or heard any rumours until the last week of February. One day in the last week of February, I went to her house, Senjuti, but she was not home. Bindi, the housemaid, told me that Patravali was busy with an event related to some school. That same day, Indu Raha visited me to invite me to her party. She told me about the affair. I did not know what to believe. Then, on the 28th night, I met Patravali and the professor at the party. She didn't seem like having an affair with anybody. Rather, she seemed embarrassed by that person's public display of devotion." Doctor Dutta recalled slowly.

Sub-inspector Jana looked puzzled. Mayurakshi elaborated, "The Professor was trying to impress others about her having a relationship with him. He was trying to show that she was romantically involved with him. In a way, he was successful because most of the party's guests practically congratulated Patravali."

"Publicly trying to impress others about their relationship?" Sub-Inspector Jana sat straight in his chair. He was the picture of attention.

"Mr Jana, I know my friend. She is... was a straightforward person. She would not run away like a schoolgirl if she had fallen in love. I didn't believe it when I heard that Patravali was having an affair with Professor Ahmed. But then, it is not a crime to be a widow and fall in love. My ego was hurt that she didn't confide in me. When I returned from Copenhagen a week ago, I found a handwritten letter awaiting me. She wrote it. The letter was disturbing and initiated my queries." Mayurakshi said after a few minutes.

"You must give the letter to me for evidence." Sub-Inspector Jana said.

"You can have a copy. I am sending it to your phone." Mayurakshi forwarded the letter to the Sub-Inspector's phone.

"This copy will do for now, but I want to see it in the original later." Sub-Inspector Jana said while looking at the letter on his phone.

"If you have any questions, you know where to find us. Now, with your permission, we would like to go home." Doctor Dutta sounded very tired.

Both were silent and immersed in their worlds on their way home. Mayurakshi felt a void that could not be filled. She was trying to remember the last time she had spoken to Patravali. It seemed like a lifetime away. There were no goodbyes between the friends, and Mayurakshi realised for the first time that she would never see Patravali again.

"Life is so unpredictable. Yet we take everything, every day, everyone, for granted. Why didn't I call her in the last month? Why didn't she call me either? I saw her missed call and thought of calling later..." Suddenly, Mayurakshi sobbed like a little girl.

Doctor Dutta stopped the car and sat in silence. It was almost four in the evening, and everything around them looked fresh and beautiful. Red simul-flowering trees and flame trees shaded the avenue. Mayurakshi sobered gradually, and Doctor Dutta started the car.

"We had planned to spend Holi together at her Rose Arbour..." In mid-sentence, Mayurakshi became quiet. She opened her little notes diary, read something, and looked on absentmindedly. The Doctor knew that look and did not disturb her.

"I think that I have got it. She said that I should remember that she read about the Queen. She was referring to my first book. We have to go to the Club." Mayurakshi was motivated.

"You want us to go the Club, now?" Doctor Dutta sounded confused.

"Yes, now, before anyone else gets the wind of the idea."

Doctor Dutta stopped the car and looked at Mayurakshi with admiration. He was also motivated.

"What makes you so certain about the book?" Asked Doctor Dutta.

"My first book was titled, 'The Effigy of Nefertiti'... and Patravali wanted you to remember the beautiful, courageous queen, Nefertiti...So... 2 + 2..." Mayurakshi nodded her head in contemplation.

"Yes, I see the logic. Let's go." Doctor Dutta started the engine.

"Did you take your medicines? It would be best if you didn't become sick," Mayurakshi reminded him.

"I am fit now, Mou. Besides, I am quite responsible. And we need to eat also." Smiled Doctor Dutta.

They reached the Club. No one was around the lift, and silently, they headed towards the library. The library on the first floor was deserted. A mild humming was coming from the billiards room on the other end of the first floor, which Mayurakshi and Doctor Dutta avoided cautiously.

The well-stocked library was empty, and they proceeded towards the Bengali books section.

They searched the racks, but the book was missing. Mayurakshi's face clouded as she thought someone had been more innovative and quicker than them. Did anybody else hear her say about the Queen?"

Doctor Dutta nodded, negating the thought. Mayurakshi thought for some time, and suddenly, she walked into the history section.

Doctor Dutta was rechecking the Bengali books when Mayurakshi returned with the book. She looked excited and said smilingly, "Patravali did a fine job. She hid this amongst the other historical books. Now let us find out what she wanted us to find."

Mayurakshi flipped the pages carefully. On the dedication page, she found a short poem written in Patravali's neat handwriting dated Saturday, 28th February. The poem was dedicated to Mayurakshi.

"Doctor, I have found it." Mayurakshi almost whispered with excitement. She showed the note that was dedicated to Mayurakshi in Patravali's handwriting.

The note read like this:

"Dear Mayurakshi,

Red Roses- White Roses

leading to the nymph,

sitting with her feet,

dipped in the spring,

Look at my dreams;

Deep in water

with petals pink

and leaves green.

Yours ever-loving Patravali."

"Do you have any idea what she was referring to?" Asked the doctor after reading the note several times.

"I think I can guess a little, but I need to confirm something first," Mayurakshi bent down and stealthily put the book inside her bag.

Doctor Dutta looked enquiringly at her. "For safety purposes," Mayurakshi whispered and pointed to the camera installed in a corner.

They came out of the library and started walking towards the lift. "I need a plan to sneak into Senjuti. I have to search the Rose Arbour and the Gazebo." Mayurakshi confided her thoughts to the Doctor.

"And how are you going to do that? Don't forget that now Senjuti has a new owner." Reminded Doctor Dutta.

"I do not know if this new owner, Mr Lahiri, is also a part of the scheme... What if Jhimli is involved with Mr Lahiri... or..." Mayurakshi's thoughts trailed off.

Mayurakshi wanted to go home and invited Doctor Dutta for an early supper. They had not eaten since breakfast and were hungry.

They remained silent and thoughtful on the way to Mayurakshi's home, Suprabhat. As the Doctor stopped his car in front of the house, Nimmo opened the door. Mr Ashok Trivedi also came out and stood beside Nimmo. He looked pale and distressed. He came forward to meet them.

"It is so sudden and unfortunate... I cannot envisage the horror of finding our dear Patravali in such a horrible state." Mr Ashok Trivedi said in gloomy tones.

"Please, Mr Trivedi, I would be grateful for not talking about the morning. It was most unpleasant, and now we are exhausted." Mayurakshi did not mince matters.

"Doctor Dutta, will you stay or ..." Mr Trivedi did not finish his question because Nimmo almost pounced and said, "Our Doctor needs food and rest. Let them take a breath... please. I think they would be in better shape after they eat proper food."

Mr Ashok Trivedi took the broad hint and excused himself. He promised to visit again.

"Nimmo, call Dhaniram and tell him to come here right now," Mayurakshi said as soon as the lawyer had left.

They waited for Dhaniram while having coffee.

Mayurakshi told the Doctor about Mrs Rosie Alvarez. They decided to meet her the next day.

CHAPTER XXVII

Needle in a Haystack

12 March 2023

Detective Dipto Bhanu Chowdhury had remained quiet and thoughtful for a long time. Jaipal was still unconscious and would probably remain so for a long time. He had tried to say something about Zinnia, which bothered the Detective. He decided to test his theory.

"Where are we going, sir?" Asked Lakshman as Dipto Bhanu started the car.

"Lakshman, we need to visit Zinnia's room at the Club. I am sure that the oldish-looking man went there for some hidden evidence. Maybe he wanted to retrieve something important. Or he might have hidden something..."

"And, he was not found also!" Observed Lakshman.

Zinnia's tiny dressing room was locked, and the Club manager opened it with his key for Detective Dipto Bhanu and his associate. There were two plastic chairs, one small dressing table with several drawers and makeup neatly stacked, one open wardrobe with a few flashy clothes still hanging with matching pairs of shoes and one framed poster of Lata Mangeshkar. Dipto Bhanu checked everything in detail and sat on a plastic chair in front of the mirror. He seemed puzzled.

"Sir, I think that the man was a cleaner. Jaipal did not come here. He wouldn't have dared to come while you still interrogated the staff." Lakshman said confidently.

"...he dared... but why... Zinnia...dressing table...," Dipto Bhanu looked into the mirror and suddenly became very still. Lakshman smiled satisfactorily because that look indicated success.

Dipto Bhanu moved the dressing table away from the wall and started feeling under the wood. "I don't think that he had time to take this apart. He would rather..." Dipto Bhanu talked to himself while he checked the dressing table thoroughly. After a few minutes, he took out a small Pen drive hidden behind one of the drawers.

"He is intelligent and smart. He wanted this to be found, but not quickly. Now, let us see what he hid with so much care." Dipto Bhanu smiled with satisfaction.

The Detective was given a laptop, and he opened the Pen drive. There was only one video file named Nirmala.

Dipto Bhanu clicked open the file, and a beautiful woman appeared on the computer screen. She looked frightened. Dipto Bhanu paused the frame and looked closely. There were faint bluish bruise marks near her eyes and on her cheeks, which had been attempted to hide. He played the video and heard her say:

"I have finally joined the missing dots. Prakash Sur was also involved. Sajal Haldar was the man in question. He was killed. I do not know why or how, but I know that something terrible had happened that day. Both of them were in it together. Ricky knew them and cautioned me against him, but I was in love. Madly, truly, wholeheartedly in love with him. Then he came to me on a very wet monsoon night. He climbed up the rain pipe and came to me in secrecy. I was in love, and I gave myself. I was a fool and didn't obey my Baba. I became involved in the incident unknowingly and became his alibi. At the time, I had no idea about Sajal's death. Now, I cannot rewind the past and go to my Baba. I have to keep him safe. It had been raining very heavily, that monsoon..." Suddenly, urgent knockings were heard in the film, and the woman stopped speaking. She looked panicked. She joined her palms together in prayer. Another female voice, close to the microphone, said, "shit." And the video ended.

Dipto Bhanu was surprised. Many questions came rushing to his mind. "Lakshman, we have to go to the police station. Call our archive department and ask for the details of the murder case of Sajal Haldar. In the meantime, I will find out about this lady. She must be Nirmala. Nirmala... Nirmala...Nirmala Devi is the proprietor of Tezz. Is Nirmala of the video the same Nirmala Devi, the proprietor?"

They returned to the Durgapur police station, and Dipto became busy with computers and phones. In the evening, Dipto Bhanu had a list of names and dates. He had found out the latest news related to Prakash Sur. Lakshman was waiting for news from the archive department.

"Sir, in the video, she mentioned Ricki and Rakesh. Is he the same Ricki or Rakesh we are looking for?" Lakshman asked.

Dipto Bhanu did not answer him because he was puzzled by the statement. She seemed to be referring to two separate persons...

In the evening, Inspector Banik came in looking excited. He blurted out, "A fraud posing as Professor Faisal Ahmed was romancing a widow in Simlipur. Her dead body was found this morning. The real person, Professor Faisal Ahmed, was killed near Bhopal by Rakesh and Jaipal on 18 December 2022."

Dipto Bhanu also became excited at the news and said, "Yes, I know about the case because that was the only murder that Rakesh and Jaipal did not finish properly, and the witness had given his statement before he succumbed to his injuries. Suraj Singh was the witness who was shot but did not die on the spot. The Professor died before the police reached them. I must go to Simlipur and look into the matter. Inspector Banik, please let me know when Vivek is found."

Simlipur, 13 March, 1:30 Hours

Mayurakshi was tossing in her bed but could not sleep. She could see Patravali's bloated body lying in the ditch. She did not speak to her husband, Bidyut when he had called earlier in the evening. She did not shed any more tears, but her mind was revolting. Dhaniram had not come, and his phone was also switched off. "Did Mr Jana arrest Dhaniram and Ayah? Did he call Mr Sanjay Lahiri for questioning? Is there any guard posted at Senjuti? Patravali's murder was definitely premeditated. Where is Jhimli now? Was she dressed as the ghost of Rimjhim? Ayah knows the ghost, very likely Jhimli dressed up ... Patravali has given me all the clues in her letter and note, and I must read them correctly to understand the clues..."

She took out the library book and re-read the short note.

"Dear Mayurakshi,
Red Roses- White Roses
leading to the nymph,
sitting with her feet,
dipped in the spring,
Look at my dreams;
Deep in water
with petals pink
and leaves green.
Yours ever-loving Patravali."

"Red roses must be the Rose Arbour. Is the 'nymph' a statue? The statue is dipping her feet in the spring. But where is the spring? Is it near the Lilliputian Lily Garden that she mentioned in her letter? I need to visit the garden without interruptions. Is now a good time to visit? But first, I must have a definite plan. What if I am caught stealing into somebody's private property... how did he buy it in the first place...No, I need to concentrate..."

Mayurakshi took out the letter and reread it. This time, she started making notes while reading it.

The letter read accordingly:

25 February 2023

Senjuti, Simlipur.

Dear Mou,

It has been long since I wrote anything to you. A lot has been happening here at Senjuti, my home, which is infested with dangerous pests of the kind not in the insect category. To me, home means security + privacy + a place where I can be myself without judgment. Yet, I feel like I am being watched constantly in my home. Their piercing, vigilant eyes are on me, but they hide behind friendly, smiling faces when I turn back. Somebody is going through my papers and diaries. In my own home, I am moving and writing furtively. I am keeping my private papers and journals hidden under lock and key. When I am in the company of friends and acquaintances, I feel their eyes judging me, measuring my every move.

Why do they bother about my personal life? I am not responsible for what others feel. I don't control anyone's actions. My heart still beats at Timir's name. I am not ready to move on yet. Their menacing whispers ruin my peace.

I do not know whom to trust anymore. Inside and outside, I am surrounded by people with friendly masks. I have to cross-check certain information given to me by Mrs Sneha Mitra. I want you to help me to do some detective work. I have kept a record of all my findings and suspicions.

Our dear Doctor Dutta is much better now and is back in Simlipur. Sometimes, I feel like confiding in him, but then the dear doctor needs peace, not anxiety, after his stroke.

You wrote several ghost and supernatural stories, and they were pretty convincing. So, do you believe in ghosts? Can the past become real? I don't know what to make out of Rimjhim's ghost. In the past eighteen years I have never seen her famous ghost yet now, every night, at late hours, she walks in the garden when I am alone working in my study.

I love Senjuti and will never allow it to go into the wrong hands. I am not technology-savvy like them and cannot compete with their evil mechanics. But I am gathering clues to make a whole picture. I believe in my old-fashioned, straightforward ways to protect all I love.

My journals are essential documents. They can be vital in case something needs to be investigated. I cannot lose them. Neither can I risk them falling into the wrong hands. I have kept them safe.

I like working at my Lilliputian Lily Ponds. I have created a heaven, and I am proud of my creations. I know you will love it when we have tea at the Gazebo again. Do you remember those lovely evenings of reading poetry and music? It is important to me that you never forget those beautiful evenings spent at the Rose Arbour and Gazebo. The Lilliputian Lily Garden is vital to my writing and keeping my documents safe.

*The positive thing is that my **boat** is ready to set sail.*

How is Gitisha? She promised to visit during the Christmas break. And how is Bidyut da? Convey my love and regards to him.

With much love and warm regards.

Yours ever loving

Patravali

Mayurakshi reread the last part of the letter many times and came to a decision. She was looking unmindfully through the study window at Senjuti when she saw a small light, which seemed to get brighter. In a moment, she became alert. "Is that Mr Lahiri? Or is she Mrs Lahiri? Or are they together? What are they doing in the study in the dark hour at half past one?" Mayurakshi took out her binoculars and watched fascinatedly. The flickering light in the study extinguished about half an hour later. "Were they burning something? What? Did they find some important papers that might prove the crime and point to the criminal? I have to hurry before they wipe out everything important pertinent to Patravali's murder. There is no tomorrow for me, and I must act tonight."

She wrote a few lines on her writing pad addressed to Nimmo in case something went wrong and kept it on the dining table. She took some plastic packets as she thought Patravali had hidden some documents inside one of the tubs. In her mind, she thanked her husband for being an excellent critic of her written fiction, which made her more careful about details. She dressed in a black sports tracksuit with a hoodie and running shoes. Again, she felt grateful to her perfectionist husband for pushing her to do exercises to keep fit. She knew that today, she would need all her fitness to do what she would do.

Mayurakshi had to cross the expanse of her back garden and the expanse of Senjuti to reach the Rose Arbour. Both properties shared the boundaries of their back gardens. The night was pleasant, with a full moon shining in its full glory. Senjuti's rear garden was also as shady as her Suprabhat's. The cluster of big trees towered over the thin trail leading to the back gate with their dense foliage. Walking through the dark trail was an ordeal that was not used regularly. Generally, Mayurakshi was afraid of snakes, lizards, and all creeping insects, but tonight, she found the strength to ignore her fear. She knew her adventure might prove dangerous if she was found out.

Mayurakshi reached the back garden of Senjuti. It was completely dark as the orchard at Senjuti created the darkest shadows, making Mayurakshi apprehensive to go forward. She stood briefly and watched around her to ensure her loneliness. The house could not be seen from the orchard. Mayurakshi had to reach the Rose Arbour from its behind roundabout through the vegetable garden to avoid the house and the servants' quarters.

Mayurakshi started running, her senses heightened with excitement and fear. The house came into view. It looked dark and deserted. "Are they sleeping now? Or preparing to go somewhere?" Mayurakshi thought to herself. The servants' quarters were also draped in darkness. She reached the Rose Arbour, but it was at least two stories high with boulders and sharp-edged stones jutting out at the behind part. She couldn't climb the stony wall. Mayurakshi walked to the other side, away from the house, and came to the front of the Rose Arbour. "*Red roses, White roses...* I think she meant the entrance of the Rose Arbour". Just then, the dark cloud floated away, revealing the shining silver full moon again, flooding the stone steps of the Rose Arbour with the silver glow of the moon. "*leading to the nymph ...*" I have to find a statue of the nymph..." Mayurakshi started climbing the steps adorned by little tubs of blooming lilies on each side. Mayurakshi saw a big tub with a solar-powered fountain, making a gurgling sound like a brook. To her delight, she saw a statue of a nymph sitting with its feet in the water. There were little lilies in bloom around the nymph's feet. The sculpture was about four feet tall. "Brilliant, Patravali! Your thoughts are crystal clear to me."

Mayurakshi plunged her hand into the cold water and touched the nymph's feet. Something hard was protruding under the tiny feet of the nymph. She felt the thing with her fingers. It seemed like a small packet. Excited at the finding, she started sticking it out with her nails. A few minutes later, she pocketed a tiny plastic packet.

"Now, to find the other things," thought Mayurakshi. Mayurakshi's mind was working overtime as she started climbing the broad steps leading to the top of the Gazebo. "I hope to find another lily pool in the sitting area...".

The Gazebo looked different from her memory. There were new flowering plants and a big cement tub with water lilies. But there was no boat in the tub. She was puzzled and tried to remember the last part of the letter. The tub was about five feet in diameter. "Did she hide her documents here? But I have to get inside the tub to look for it... She wouldn't get inside to put something because someone might have seen her... if I had to hide something here..." Mayurakshi put her hands in the water and started feeling near the edges.

As her hand explored underwater, she felt a hard box-like thing. It was placed beneath some ornamental stones. The corners of the rectangular box could be felt protruding from the bed of stones. It was kept on a platform of flat rocks. Mayurakshi had to use her strength to pull out the little heavy box. It was wrapped in plastic and weighed nearly five kilograms. Mayurakshi put the box in another plastic packet before putting it inside her backpack. She cautiously looked at the house and the servants' quarters before walking down the steps.

Suddenly, she stopped in her tracks and heard the mechanical sound of a car. Mayurakshi took out her binoculars and looked. She couldn't see any car. The sound had also stopped. She zoomed in on the house, but there was no light. She was about to continue her walk, still puzzled about the mechanical sound of a car, when she saw the tail lights of a receding car. She looked at her watch. It was nearly four in the morning.

Mayurakshi resumed her slow walk. The rest of the return journey was uneventful. She stepped inside the safety of Suprabhat long before dawn.

CHAPTER XXVIII

Skeletons in the Cupboard

13 March 2023

Simlipur Police Station, 5:00 Hours

Dipto Bhanu and Lakshman reached the police station when the sky was beginning to light. The police station looked deserted as Constable Shyamlal slept and Mr Jana had left the station at night. Dipto Bhanu and Lakshman had to wake Shyamlal and call Mr Jana to the station. Sub-inspector Jana came in looking tired and sleepy. He was cursing the detective inwardly but tried to answer calmly the questions related to the murder of Patravali Chatterjee. Dipto Bhanu made notes about the incidents and lists of people involved.

"Mr Jana, did you interrogate Dhaniram and Ayah and any other staff of Patravali Chatterjee? I suppose the household is still functioning? Is anyone keeping guard at the property?"

Sub-inspector Jana looked ill at ease. He was used to a more laid-back work schedule. He was in his mid-fifties and enjoyed his freedom. Simultala was a peaceful town; most cases were of petty thefts of goats or cycles. Patravali Chatterjee's case was the first case in his career where he had to take initiative and do a lot of hard work. And he did poorly.

"We will start as early as possible before they are prepared. Let us pay a visit to Patravali Chatterjee's house now. Sanjay Lahiri and his wife bought the property, but how did they buy it? Have you checked their papers? I want to get started as early as possible." Dipto Bhanu said while checking his arms. Mr Jana had to accompany the detective when he left for Senjuti, while Lakshman stayed back at the station to get refreshed.

Their police car stopped inside the premises of Senjuti in front of the house. The household was not yet up. Dipto Bhanu walked around the house and then went to the servants' quarters, which looked deserted, too. He knocked on Dhaniram's and Ayah's cottage doors but received no response. "Mr Jana, you stand on guard here at the front; I am going to check the cottages from the back," Dipto instructed the Sub-Inspector and went to the back.

Dhaniram's cottage was closed and locked from the back. Ayah's cottage's kitchen door was ajar. Dipto Bhanu entered the small cottage using the half-opened door. The small kitchen was empty, and Dipto Bhanu proceeded to the adjacent single room. The bedroom cum living room was empty, too, and he was about to leave when he saw her. The frail, thin body of Ayah was lying down on the floor, half hidden by the bed. She seemed to have rolled over in her sleep. Quickly, he knelt beside her and felt her pulse. It was beating faintly. Her thin, claw-like hands were icy cold, and she did not respond to the callings. The next few minutes went in, arranging for the ambulance and searching the other cottage. Dipto Bhanu took photographs of Ayah's room. Soon, the ambulance came, and Ayah was transferred to the hospital. Dipto Bhanu sent all the remaining food, drinking water and garbage to the forensic department. Surprisingly, no one from the house came to investigate the commotion of the ambulance and the police jeep.

Dipto Bhanu and Sub-Inspector Jana went to the house and knocked. They knocked several times before Mr Sanjay Lahiri opened the door. He wore comfortable pyjamas and a T-shirt. He looked sleepy and confused as he ushered them inside after being introduced. The entrance to the house was spacious and tastefully decorated, which opened into a large hall. The furniture and the décor looked elegant and beautiful. "Mr Jana, you may sit with Mr Lahiri while I satisfy myself..." Dipto Bhanu said casually. The Sub-Inspector flopped down gratefully on one of the comfortable sofas.

Sanjay Lahiri stood confusedly to one side while Dipto Bhanu satisfied himself by looking around. Everything was neatly arranged. Dipto Bhanu went to all the rooms on the ground floor. The rooms were in excellent condition and decorated tastefully. Sanjay Lahiri stood quietly. He had no questions but seemed alert.

"I would like to see your documents. And the sale deed," said Dipto Bhanu.

"Certainly, Detective," answered Sanjay Lahiri.

"What happened to your leg? When did it happen?" Dipto Bhanu asked him when he started walking towards the door.

"I had a little accident with a motorbike just a few days ago. My wife also was injured. She is better now, and I am still recuperating," Sanjay Lahiri said nonchalantly.

"Where is Mrs Lahiri? Please, tell her to come here. May I see your wound?"

Sanjay Lahiri seemed to hesitate momentarily, but he showed his wound. It was bandaged.

"How did you cut your hand? Was it stitched?"

"This happened when I worked in the mines. That was long ago." Answered Mr Lahiri.

"What do you do now for a living?"

"I am a builder and in the construction business." Sanjay Lahiri answered smoothly.

"Where is Dhaniram, the gardener?" asked Dipto Bhanu, apparently satisfied with his answers.

"That man is a nuisance, officer. He drinks all through the day and night. He must be sleeping somewhere, intoxicated. I don't know how Mrs Chatterjee tolerated him," Sanjay Lahiri answered readily.

"What does Ayah do for you?"

"Ayah, that old woman is completely off her mind. She is a crazy woman but is quite old and probably has nowhere to go. We are uncertain about her. We cannot just throw her out, yet we do not know what work she can do..." Sanjay Lahiri replied hesitatingly.

Mr Jana was about to say something about Ayah's plight, but a stern look of caution from Dipto Bhanu stopped him.

"You cannot leave Simlipur without informing us. A team of forensics will be here shortly for inspection. Mrs Chatterjee might have been killed here after all," declared Dipto Bhanu. Sanjay Lahiri seemed puzzled and unhappy at the prospect.

About fifteen minutes later, Mrs Lahiri came downstairs in her sleeping attire. She looked a little tense.

Suprabhat, 8:00 a.m.

A different scene was unfolding at Mayurakshi's house, Suprabhat. Doctor Dilip Dutta had arrived, and he was sitting with Mayurakshi. Both were thinking hard. Mayurakshi's laptop was kept open beside a small steel safe. They had seen a video and were contemplating their next move. Mayurakshi had found a sim containing a video in the small packet taped to the nymph statue's feet. The footage showed three persons talking in a hushed tone. The sound and picture quality were not good. It was evident that Patravali's hand had shaken when she was filming the secret meeting. Mayurakshi recognised Harman Handa in the film and thought the second person to be Mr Das, the club manager with Harman Handa. But she couldn't recognise the third man, who had his back to the phone camera. Doctor Dutta and Mayurakshi decided to hand the SIM to the police for investigation.

The plastic-wrapped box that Mayurakshi had found hidden among rocks had turned out to be an electronic-code-locked steel safe. They needed the PIN to open it. Mayurakshi wanted to open the safe, while the Doctor wanted to consult some experts.

They were discussing their disagreements.

"I think we should consult the specialists to open the safe. It is an electronic-code-locked safe, and it will be challenging to open if we make mistakes more than thrice." Doctor Dutta expressed his concern.

"I am sure Patravali has left the pin in her letter to open the safe. Let's read this together and see if we can find any combinations. She provided the safe and the SIM's whereabouts, and I am sure she also mentioned the pin," Mayurakshi replied and reread the letter.

Doctor Dutta looked sceptical, and Mayurakshi continued reading.

Mayurakshi kept the letter aside after reading it several times. She looked disturbed and took out her notes diary. She read it and said," I have a list of questions... maybe you can add more.

1. Rimjhim's ghost haunted Patravali. Was Jhimli playing the ghost? I think that might be Jhimli.
2. Professor Faisal Ahmed was murdered. Was Jhimli's husband playing the Professor's role? Yes, most probably.
3. Harman Handa, Shyamlal Das, and the third man are planning something. Was Patravali murdered because she heard their plan, which means that her murder was not premeditated? *No, her murder was planned because someone was trying to frighten her and was keeping watch over her.*
4. Where is Dhaniram now? Whom did he see that night? That person could not have been Patravali, as she was seen wearing the party sari.
5. Did Dhaniram hear any pistol shot that night? Or was the sound drowned by thunder? Did anyone hear the bullet sound?
6. Who gave money to Dhaniram? Why?
7. Why is Ayah angry with Patravali? Does she know anything about the ghost?
8. Who are the Lahiris? How did they buy the property when Patravali was dead? Did Jhimli pose as Patravali and sell the property to the present owners? *Possible. The second possibility is that the wife is Jhimli, and the husband is Jhimli's husband, posing as Mr. and Mrs. Lahiri.*
9. Where is Jhimli now? Did Patravali know about her?
10. Who is Mrs Sneha Mitra? What did she mean by detective work?
11. Who is Hemangini Lahiri? Why did she push the canvas bag under her berth? Who was the other man?
12. Patravali must have written the code for the safe in the letter. But which is the code?"

Doctor Dutta was satisfied with Mayurakshi's list and said so. They again broached the subject of opening the safe. After a few more disagreements, they decided to try decoding the lock.

"Let us try to make a code with the date… so 25-2-2023 will be seven digits… 2522023…," Mayurakshi wrote the number in her small diary and tried to open the safe with it. But it didn't work.

"See, the word HOME is mentioned more than once. Perhaps she used the alphabet in place of numbers. Some letters can be written in the digital format like we used to write names in the calculator," The Doctor suggested.

They tried to write the word HOME in digital formats, like 4 = h, 0 = O, 3 = M, and 3 = E, which made 4033. They tried to open the safe with the number 4033 but could not.

Mayurakshi closed her eyes and saw images of Patravali writing at her desk while a shadowy figure peeped in from the study's doorway. A shapely woman walking in the garden at dark hours. Someone draping a dark shawl is looking at Patravali's papers. There was noise of glass door breaking... No, I must get a grip on myself.

"We are reading it wrong. I am sure Patravali had written a simple code. She mentioned not being technology savvy and doing things in more straightforward ways... so we must think differently," Said Mayurakshi and started reading the letter loudly once again. Suddenly, she stopped reading and looked surprised, as if she had seen a ghost. Doctor Dutta watched her quizzically.

"I think I have found the code to the safe," Mou told Doctor Dutta.

"This will be the third try," Doctor Dutta cautioned.

"I found the manual on the internet, and it says that we have three more chances before it would lock," said Mayurakshi while writing numbers for each alphabet. She showed the result to Doctor Dutta.

"A = 1, B = 2, C = 3, D = 4, E = 5, F = 6, like this, we can count till 26 because there are 26 alphabets ... See, this is a number substitution cypher and we can read the word HOME in numbers. The numbers for HOME are H=8, O=15, M=13, E=5, which is 815135. Let's try." Mou started to punch the number 815135.

But the safe didn't open. There was no clicking sound; an 'error' appeared in the small space above the punching numbers.

"No, no... I think the word is not home but boat. She has underlined the word boat. Now, let's try BOAT. B = 2, O = 15, A =

1, T = 20, making the numbers 215120." Mou started punching the new numbers.

To their joy and surprise, it worked. The safe opened with a clicking sound. The little steel safe was full of documents, journals, bank passbooks, a copy of a will, one key for the bank locker with written instructions, Patravali's passport and a lawyer's card. Mayurakshi found an envelope addressed to her.

She opened it with shaking hands and read:

25 February 2023

Senjuti

Dear Mou,

If you are reading this, then I have been proven correct. I am feeling threatened, yet I do not have any concrete proof to go to the police. But now I know for sure that the shocking news had killed Timir. Months later, after his death, I started looking into the details of that fatal night. He had received a call from Jhimli's grandmother, Narmada Sengupta, moments before his heart attack, and he died that very night. However, he had uttered something like 'Nir, Nirma or Nar', I was not sure what he had tried to say.

I went to Kolkata to meet Jhimli's grandmother. Her house was locked up, and she was not there. I could not return without any message or news from the lady, so I went to her neighbour, Mrs Sneha Mitra, who told me many things about Jhimli and her grandmother. Jhimli has a daughter, aged thirteen, at a boarding school in Kurseong, Darjeeling. I do not know her details yet. I do not know the whereabouts of Jhimli or her grandmother either. However, I have a few leads, which I hope to explore with you when you visit Kolkata.

I filmed Rimjhim's ghost walking in the garden. You will find the film among these documents. I have my suspicions about the ghost. I think she achieved the ghostly float with the help of a hoverboard because she always stayed on the short paved path that led to the flame trees. It would be easy to walk on a hoverboard on that paved path. I can only guess her identity. I am confident that Ayah knows about this ghostly lady. And I am sure she is helping her hide her identity because she is very dear to her. She raised her like her own daughter. Every morning, Ayah eagerly waits to hear about my nightly frightful experience. I caught her looking through my things, and she stares strangely at me as if waiting for something to happen. Sometimes, I feel like sending her away, but then she is an old person... nowhere to go... like me.

Mou, I am trying to finish what I have started, but in case I fail... I can only depend on you.

I have made a new will, and all the paperwork is done and ready in case you need it. I have made you the executor of my will. Sorry, I did not have time to ask your permission. You can approach my lawyer, Ms Angana Deb.

I remain in debt to you forever for your kindness and friendship.

With love and best regards

Yours

Pats.

Mayurakshi's voice broke as she finished reading. Doctor Dutta also sat in silence. Nimmo had come in with coffee and heard the last part of the letter, and she, too, was tearful.

After a while, Mayurakshi recovered enough to look into the contents of the steel safe. She made a list of the things that Patravali had kept so carefully.

"You have to hand over these to the police. They would want it for evidence," said Doctor Dutta.

"I would, but first, I need to read everything. Do you think we should depend on Mr Jana, the sub-inspector?"

The Doctor looked unhappy about leaving Patravali's things with the sub-inspector.

"I think I will contact the Police, Detective Dipto Bhanu, the son of my mother's old friend. I am yet to find his details... Doctor, you go through one of the journals while I look for the video first," Mayurakshi said and handed one of the journals to the Doctor.

The Doctor looked quizzically at her regarding the Police Detective, and she narrated to him about her mother's phone call and her finding a school friend after many years.

Mayurakshi scanned the things in the safe and found a memory stick that fit a video camera in one of the sealed envelopes.

"I would need a card reader to open this," she said, pointing to the little SanDisk.

After a while, the duo sat glued to the computer screen as they saw Rimjhim's ghost walking in the garden at night. She had a deathly sheen and seemed to be floating. The ghostly figure was zoomed in, and Mayurakshi marvelled at the detailed appearance.

CHAPTER XXIX

Silver Bullet

13 March 2023

Mayurakshi and Doctor Dutta had seen the video footage of the ghost walking in the garden of Senjuti.

"I remember Rimjhim wearing a red dress. She was a head-turner, and she used her charms on men. The ghost lady walking in Patravali's garden might be a stunner, too, if seen without that horrid sheen. She is very convincing as a ghost. How did she achieve this ghostly appearance?" Doctor Dutta looked fascinatedly at the video and commented.

"Somebody who knew about Rimjhim's beauty, her taste in clothes has created this ghost. I wonder how Jhimli would look now? She must be around thirty-three or four. Patravali suspected Jhimli of dressing up as the ghost, and Ayah knows it. We have to read Patravali's will to know what she thought." Observed Mayurakshi.

Suddenly, the bell rang, and Doctor Dutta said concernedly, "Mou, I suggest you put everything out of sight. Patravali's materials are pieces of evidence and may help in finding her killer."

Mayurakshi agreed, and the Doctor continued, "Patravali knew she was in danger, yet she never told me about her suspicions. Timir was my best friend, and they were there for me when Sujata died. I should've been there for Patravali too. I didn't know anything that was happening to Patravali." Doctor Dutta lamented as they were putting the things in Mayurakshi's bedroom.

Mayurakshi patted the doctor kindly and said sadly, "She worried about your health, Doctor Dutta. She was strong in mind, and she took care of things intelligently. She thought she could protect herself from whatever was coming. She knew about the vigilance and the fake ghost. I also feel lousy because I forgot to return her missed calls, as my phone had no charge when she called.

I feel like a selfish, irresponsible, and uncaring person. But is it the correct time to play the 'blame' game? Let's read her will and the journals and try to find the culprit. I am sure she knew something that would help us unmask the murderer. I am certain that the guilty is hiding in plain sight."

Dipto Bhanu awaited them when Mayurakshi and Doctor Dutta returned to the living room. After the introduction, Dipto Bhanu said, "You are the writer, Mayurakshi Bose, and my mother is a big fan of your books. She would be thrilled to know that I have met you. Recently, my parents shifted to Kalimpong. I think your mother and my mother are friends."

Mayurakshi said surprisedly, "Is your mother, Mrs Sushmita Chowdhury? My mother, Basundhara Guha, told me about her friend's son, Dipto Bhanu, being a police detective. And I was going to contact your mother for your number..."

"It is a small world, after all," Laughed Doctor Dutta.

Mayurakshi became serious and asked about Senjuti and its new owner. Dipto Bhanu said, "I saw the papers related to the sale and purchase of the property. Everything looks okay, but... still, I will arrange to send them for scrutiny by our legal experts. According to the documents, the sale happened just the day before she was seen going away with the man."

"But he was an imposter! I have read the news of the murder of the real Professor Ahmed. I am sure the imposter was connected to the vehicle thieves, Rakesh and Jaipal. Is it not possible to make fake documents?" Asked Mayurakshi.

"Having all the correct stamps and signatures is difficult, but nothing is impossible. Someone may have pretended to be Patravali when the sale deed was made. I know about the death of the Professor and the imposter who lived here as Professor Ahmed. Your friend's murder may be connected with Rakesh or Jaipal. They were responsible for killing the real Professor Faisal Ahmed. May I see the letter that made you suspicious?" Dipto Bhanu answered.

Mayurakshi gave him the letter and contemplated showing the contents of the steel safe to the detective. Dipto Bhanu read the letter carefully and asked about the photograph.

"That is Jhimli's photograph when she was about fifteen, some eighteen years ago... now she...," Mayurakshi could not finish her statement as Dipto Bhanu looked excited and asked, "Did you say Jhimli? How is Jhimli related to Patravali Chatterjee?"

"Jhimli is her stepdaughter. Timir Babu's daughter from his first marriage with Rimjhim... Patravali has mentioned Rimjhim's ghost in the letter. She is the rightful heir after Patravali."

Dipto Bhanu looked excited and became completely quiet. It was evident that he was having a brainstorm.

Mayurakshi and Doctor Dutta waited for some time before Dipto Bhanu decided and said, "We are also looking for a Jhimli as she had provided an alibi for a suspected murderer. She has been missing for twelve years. At least, the police do not have any records of Jhimli since 2011. There is no trace of her in West Bengal. And the once murder suspect, Neelesh, has also vanished."

Mayurakshi and Doctor Dutta looked questioning at each other. Mayurakshi broke the silence and declared, "We have recovered some important documents and legal papers of Patravali, which she left for me... I can share them with you, detective, but do not take them elsewhere... at least till we have been able to go through them."

"When did Patravali leave you the documents? Did she post them?" asked Dipto Bhanu interestedly.

"She did not post them to me, but I trespassed into her property to get hold of it. I read all the clues correctly as she wrote in the letter. I suppose I might land in trouble for it..."

"Mou was so brave in doing the whole thing alone... I am sure you will overlook the means of getting the important documents...there was no other option as the property now has a new owner until they are proven otherwise," Doctor Dutta commented.

"Okay, I promise to turn a blind eye to the means, but I need to know the contents of the documents. After all, Patravali Chatterjee's murder might have been pre-planned," said Dipto

Bhanu.

"I do not doubt her murder was preplanned because the murderer had got the staff involved. I have every reason to believe that Jhimli was pretending to be the ghost. Ayah was spying on Patravali. She had brought up Jhimli like her daughter and knew about the ghostly visits, too." Mayurakshi stopped speaking as Dipto Bhanu looked upset and cursed under his breath. He wrote some notes in his little diary and phoned his office. He repeated on the phone what Mayurakshi had told him about Jhimli and Ayah.

After what seemed like a lifetime of waiting, Dipto Bhanu turned to the puzzled duo and said, "Dhaniram is missing, and Ayah was found on the verge of collapse. Her pulse was very low, and her body temperature was considerably lower than healthy. She is now admitted to the hospital. I have very little hope of her surviving the crisis."

"Ayah has collapsed! Was she poisoned? If she were instrumental in the manifestation of the ghost, then the ghost would want her to disappear now, as Ayah knows the identity of the person who dressed up as the ghost... If I were writing this story, then Ayah and Dhaniram would have been murdered by now. They have served their purposes. What did I see..." Mayurakshi did not finish her sentence and became thoughtful.

"Let me look at the documents that you brought by trespassing. I want everything," Dipto Bhanu said authoritatively.

Mayurakshi brought the steel safe and showed each of the documents. Dipto Bhanu photographed all the things and made a list. He leafed through the journals first, then started looking into the envelopes. After a while, he handed a journal to each of them. Dipto Bhanu found a copy of the will and was reading it when Doctor Dutta asked, "What is this cheque for? Do you know anyone named Nirmala? A payment was made to Nirmala by Timir Chatterjee," Doctor Dutta held a photocopy of a cheque.

"Nirmala?!" Dipto Bhanu almost jumped at the name.

"Why are you so excited, Detective? Do you know anything about Nirmala?" Asked Doctor Dutta.

Mayurakshi became thoughtful and muttered, "Nir...Nirma... Nar..."

Doctor Dutta said excitedly, "Those were the last words uttered by Timir. Patravali was also puzzled at the time."

"Who is Nirmala?" Asked Mayurakshi.

"One of the vehicles' thieves, Jaipal, had hidden a video of Nirmala's statement. I retrieved it from a dancer's dressing room who was murdered recently. Nirmala was talking about a murder case in the video. She had provided the alibi for a suspected murder," elaborated Dipto Bhanu.

"Jhimli also provided an alibi for a murderer! Can Jhimli and Nirmala be the same person? Where is she now? Did Nirmala give her statement in the same case?" Mayurakshi asked.

"How much is the cheque worth?" Asked Dipto Bhanu.

"Five crores," informed the Doctor.

Dipto Bhanu noted, "There are too many similarities and common factors. Firstly, why was Nirmala given the money? Secondly, Is Jhimli and Nirmala Devi, the proprietor of Tezz, the same person?"

"We have to read through the journals to know about Nirmala. Timir must have known Nirmala quite well to give her such a big amount of money." Doctor Dutta said thoughtfully.

"Five crore is not a small amount, and Patravali must have known about Nirmala. Where is Nirmala now? I am sure that Jhimli's new name is Nirmala. And she should be found and interviewed as soon as possible. There are too many coincidences and similarities. Detective, please give us the details of the murder case where Jhimli had provided an alibi. Who was the suspect, and where is he now?" Mayurakshi asked.

"Our team is still working on the details of that case. It happened about fourteen years ago in Kolkata. There were two accused of the murder of Sajal Haldar. One was Prakash Sur, and the other was Neelesh. Jhimli provided an alibi for Neelesh, who got away scot-free because her statement cleared his name while the other suspect, Prakash Sur, was sentenced. There is no record of Neelesh and Jhimli's existence after the verdict was announced. They seem to have ceased living. Nirmala Devi is the proprietor of a car rental and garage in Kolkata. My team is looking into Nirmala Devi's details. She might be the same person as in the video." Dipto Bhanu elaborated.

"There are so many missing links... first of all, I find it improbable that this new owner of Senjuti is telling the truth. I don't believe it! Patravali made a new will to save Senjuti. Then, how is the sale deed genuine? Either they have successfully deceived you, Detective or else they, themselves, have been cheated successfully. I have to rethink my theory. In my opinion, Jhimli was the ghost and is pretending to be Mrs Lahiri, the present owner of Senjuti. She tried to scare Patravali away from the property or perhaps wanted to prove Patravali mad. Ayah was helping her as she was like a daughter. Ayah was blinded by love," Mayurakshi commented.

"Mrs Patravali Chatterjee's new will states that Jhimli's daughter would inherit everything. There is no mention of Jhimli or her husband. It is quite possible that Mrs Chatterjee found out Jhimli's details before making the new will. Inspecting all the legalities of the new owner's documents would take some time. But first of all, Dhaniram has to be found before someone harms him." Dipto Bhanu got busy with his phone. Mr Jana had returned to the police station before Dipto Bhanu came, and he assured the detective that he was looking for Dhaniram and his family.

"Perhaps Jhimli's grandmother can lead us to Jhimli," said Doctor Dutta.

"Patravali did not meet the grandmother. She mentioned that the grandmother's house was locked up, and she was not there. Mrs Sneha Mitra, her neighbour, may help us find Jhimli and her grandmother. Patravali had talked to the lady when she went to Kolkata to talk to Jhimli's grandmother. Detective, can you arrange a meeting with the lady? We can speak via Google Meet," Mayurakshi.

"I would also like to hear what Mrs Mitra has to say. But before talking to her, I must arrange a visit to the grandmother's house,"

Dipto Bhanu said. Mayurakshi found the address written neatly in the back of one of the journals.

Detective Dipto Bhanu got busy with his phone after getting the address while Mayurakshi and The Doctor read the journals. They were all busy when Dipto Bhanu received the news of Ayah's death. He shared it with Mayurakshi and Doctor Dutta.

"Have you seen Mrs Lahiri?" Asked Mayurakshi.

Dipto Bhanu described the morning visit to Senjuti and assured that he had checked their identities.

"What surprises me is that no one had heard any bullet sound, or did they?" Mused Dipto Bhanu.

"I also wondered and asked Dhaniram about the noise. He said that there was thunder and it was raining too. Perhaps the sound of the bullet was drowned in the sound of the thunder. I hope that Dhaniram is safe. He had seen a woman getting in the car with the imposter professor. I thought that Dhaniram was confused about her identity. Maybe, now, Dhaniram has realised that the person he thought to be Patravali might have been somebody else pretending to be her. Umanath ji also saw them going, but he too was confused about her identity. Dhaniram was getting paid from somewhere else, too. Maybe for keeping his mouth shut about the ghostly appearance. So, he is one of the witnesses. I would like to know who started the whispers of the love affair and why. Gossip can be a useful strategy to gain selfish interests," Commented Mayurakshi.

"Yes, gossiping can become dangerous if used to achieve someone's downfall," Doctor Dutta supported Mayurakshi.

"I forgot to mention something significant. I had seen a car leave Senjuti when I was returning home. It was nearly four in the morning. I cannot confirm the colour or make of the car. Neither can I confirm the driver's identity." Mayurakshi said thoughtfully.

"A car! That opens several other possibilities." Dipto Bhanu said thoughtfully.

The phone ringtone broke the spell, and Dipto Bhanu took the call. He heard only for a few seconds and retorted, "The dead body of a man has been found near the side tracks between Simlipur station and Madhupur station. He was partly concealed in the shrubs. I am sure his death is not accidental or suicide."

Mayurakshi and Doctor Dutta exchanged tensed looks. Both of them had the same fear. "Is Dhaniram dead, too?"

CHAPTER XXX

An Evening of Rememberance

20 March 2023, A Week Later

The Gazebo at Senjuti was adorned with white drapes. The big cemented tubs were full of lilies in bloom. Candles were lighting the Gazebo pleasantly, making the atmosphere serene and poetic.

A big framed photograph of Patravali was placed on a coffee table adorned with scented candles and white flowers. A bunch of incense sticks were burning at the side of the table. Seating arrangements were made around the smiling, lively photograph of Patravali. The arrangement seemed like one of Patravali's soirees.

There was still time for the day to end. The sky looked blue with a mellowed sun. Many guests were already seated, and they were waiting for Mayurakshi. Doctor Dilip Dutta, Mr Ashok Trivedi, Sri Umanath Ji, Mrs Rosie Alvarez, Mr Sayantan Mukherjee, the train ticket collector, Mr Sujit Dhar, the manager of the factory, Mr Phagun Das, the Club Manager, Mr Raha, and Indu Raha sat quietly. Indu Raha had many questions but was silenced by her husband whenever she tried to speak. Nimmo came in with coffee and snacks for the guests. Mr Sanjay Lahiri and his wife came in after Nimmo. Everyone looked at the couple with interest. This was their first social interaction. Mrs Lahiri wore tight jeans with a pale orange T-shirt, enhancing her dark complexion. She had bob hair, which showed off her several earrings. Her short hair framed her face. She could have been beautiful save for the dark patches with acne marks on her facial skin. There was something very unusual about her mouth, too. Mr Lahiri was looking handsome despite his high teeth. He was wearing a white kurta pyjama. Just then, Mr Das, the Club Manager, also joined them. He asked, "Where is Mrs. Bose?"

Doctor Dutta replied, "She is on her way and will be here any minute... here she comes." Doctor Dutta smiled as Mayurakshi came in with a lady. She apologised for being late. She introduced the lady, Ms Angana Deb, as a friend.

Mayurakshi greeted everyone present there and thanked Mr Lahiri for agreeing to organise the Remembrance Wake for Patravali at her beloved Gazebo. He looked humble and ready to help.

Mayurakshi began, "Today, we have come together to remember our friend Patravali. At this Gazebo, she organised many cultural evenings filled with music, poetry, and excellent food. She was a wonderful hostess and always entertained her guests creatively. And she was a loving, faithful wife. She deeply mourned her husband's death." Mayurakshi stopped and looked around at all the present guests before concentrating on the Lahiri couple and started speaking again. "And today, we have organised this meeting to remember her. She was a loving, faithful widow until she met a handsome man suitable to her age. He was well-read and an enchanter. No doubt, she fell for his charms. Many of you would swear she was in love with the charming professor."

Mayurakshi deliberately paused and looked at the expressions of the guests present. Mr. Ashok Trivedi looked uncomfortable, while Sri Umanath Ji looked sad and nodded in disagreement. Indu was excited and said, "When I caught her with the Professor, she blushed like a bride. I congratulated her for finding a replacement for Timir Babu within a year of his death. The dear Professor was so delightful. They made a wonderful couple. Then, I did not know that she would be murdered and he would vanish."

Mr. Raha did not like his wife's loose talk and big mouth. He persuaded her to sit quietly.

Mayurakshi nodded in agreement and turned to the club manager, "Mr Das, I think you introduced the charming Professor to the Club. What documents did he produce as his identification to be allowed into the club?"

Mr Das hesitated for a few minutes, then replied, "He gave me a Xerox copy of his driver's license and Adhaar card. I am not responsible for introducing him to the club. He walked into the club as we are open to everyone with proper Identification documents. He was a very nice gentleman. He was always polite and paid his bills on time. As a club manager, I must see the club's profit."

Mayurakshi nodded in agreement. She turned towards Sri Umanath Ji and said respectfully, "That other day, you told me about Patravali's visit to the temple. She had asked your opinion about a certain gentleman. Can you please repeat what she had asked?"

Sri Umanath Ji bowed his white-haired head and kept silent. He looked distraught. "Please, Umanath Ji, tell us about her visit. We are not judging her but want to know if she was in love..." Mayurakshi coaxed him.

"Uh... She... came to offer her puja and stayed back until most of the devotees had left. I was cleaning up after the puja when she asked my opinion about Professor Ahmed. As I didn't know the gentleman, I couldn't give my opinion of him. She looked a little upset and said that the gentleman claimed to be Timir's acquaintance, and they had worked together on several occasions. She told me that the gentleman was visiting her frequently, and she wanted to know more about him. I told her that the staff at Timir's workplaces would know better, but she said they didn't know the gentleman." Umanath Ji looked more embarrassed.

"Is that true, Mr Sujit Dhar?" Mayurakshi looked pointedly at the quiet man. He was the manager of Timir's factory. He knew all the business deals and associated people.

Mr Sujit Dhar answered straightforwardly, "I had never heard of Professor Faisal Ahmed before Mrs Patravali Chatterjee mentioned his name. She came to the factory in January to sort out some papers. In the last week of January, she called me to find out about Professor Ahmed. I regret that I did not try to find anything about the gentleman. This tragedy could have been prevented if I had checked the gentleman's background."

Mayurakshi nodded her agreement. She smiled sadly as she thought about her regrets. But her guilt and sadness all would have to take a back seat now. She had a more important mission to accomplish.

"Mr Trivedi, please tell us about Patravali and the Professor. I believe that you saw them together. What did you think of them as a couple?" Mou looked at Mr Trivedi and waited for his answer.

"I –I have seen them together at the party. She was... seemed to be flirting with him. She was happy to be the centre of attraction, and the Professor doted on her. You can also check the video footage. Timir died last year, and she fell in love with Professor Ahmed. That was no crime," Mr. Trivedi spoke hesitantly.

Mayurakshi changed the subject of Patravali's love affair and asked, "Mr Trivedi, did you ever deliver a cheque to a person on behalf of Timir Chatterjee? Please think before you answer because I already know the details."

Mr Trivedi became thoughtful at the sudden direction of the question. He seemed tensed as he answered, "I was a close friend of Timir, and he had asked me to deliver the cheque to this person, and I followed his instructions. There was nothing illegal about it."

"Did you go alone to deliver the cheque, or did Mr Timir Chatterjee go along?" Mayurakshi asked very conversationally.

Mr. Ashok Trivedi looked angry now. He rudely said, "I refuse to say another word about the incident. Why am I being interrogated like a suspect?"

Mayurakshi was expecting some opposition from him and said soothingly, "Patravali was murdered, and we all need to know who committed such a horrible crime. I am just trying to find out more about her affairs. But if you have something to hide, then..."

Mr. Ashok Trivedi was irritated and said roughly, "Timir had asked me to be his messenger, and I followed his instructions. I did not ask for details about the lady. I did not see the amount either."

"So, the person was a lady... does she have a name? Or any description to help us find her. Or any other small thing that you might have remembered," Mayurakshi said and waited for his response.

"There is nothing more to the story. I do not remember the date or place of the meeting or the face of the lady," Ashok Trivedi almost barked in reply.

"Is she present here today? Was that the only time that you met her?" Mayurakshi asked and looked at the guests.

"I-I did not know her. She is not present here today. I can only say that I acted as the messenger and have not kept in touch with the lady." Mr Trivedi looked angry.

Mayurakshi looked at her watch thoughtfully. It was nearly in the evening. She was expecting them to join at any moment now.

"Can I ask you something, Indu?" Mayurakshi looked at Mrs. Raha inquiringly. Indu Raha rejoiced at the chance to speak. She nodded happily.

"Did you see Patravali often with Professor Ahmed? Socially, were they acting as a couple?"

"I have been thinking since Patravali was found. I did not know Professor Ahmed, but I met him for the first time in the last week of January on the club premises. He was having coffee with Patravali. He was a charmer, and I thought they were cautious about their relationship. I was surprised at first that Patravali found a person to love even before a year passed after her husband's death. But then, she was still young, and he was handsome. I saw him coming and going from Senjuti several times. When I went to invite Patravali to the party, he was also present, and I invited him along. He hinted at their love. After the professor left, I asked her about her plans regarding the Professor, and she became angry but couldn't deny that the Professor was in love with her. I was certain that she would ultimately agree to his proposal. But her death news was so shocking... I felt cheated because I was certain about their love," Indu said hesitatingly.

"And you told all your friends and acquaintances about their relationship. You took the responsibility to spread the word. Correct?" Mayurakshi observed.

It took several minutes for Indu to understand the implications. Mayurakshi was accusing her of spreading rumours! She became indignant and said rather hotly, "Patravali Chatterjee was a Brahmin widow and did not hesitate to romance a Muslim gentleman. Then why should I have kept my mouth shut and not spoken about it? She was no saint. We all know who she was before Timir Babu married her out of pity. She married him for his money; he was twenty years her senior. At the first chance, she drove Jhimli away from Senjuti. Timir Babu died last year, and Patravali Chatterjee became a free bird with all the money that Timir Babu had made. She was sitting on a golden throne like a queen and..."

Mayurakshi interrupted her and said accusingly, "I believe you were interested in buying Senjuti. You are looking at properties to make a resort. Patravali refused to sell Senjuti. Is that the reason for you to spread the rumours of her affair? Indu, I thought you were a friend."

Indu was angry and answered rudely, "Yes, we were looking at Senjuti because it is just the right property for building a small, cosy resort. But our looking for a property doesn't change the fact. I didn't say anything wrong. Patravali was coveting the handsome and charming Professor. Age-wise, he was more suitable for her. Ayah and Bindi also confirmed that the Professor visited her every day and stayed till late. You can also ask Mrs Mishra and Mrs Sharma. And you saw the video footage. He was being so attentive..."

"STOP it!" Mr. Raha exploded, making everyone stare at the quiet gentleman. He looked at his wife threateningly and said in a repentant manner, "I am sorry for what my wife said. Patravali Chatterjee was a gem of a person. She never took advantage of anyone, and I have never seen her flirting with anybody. I think she was just polite to the Professor. Her friendship was broadly social. I do not know if there was any love or sex angle to her friendship. Timir Babu and Patravali shared an extraordinary bond that could be seen without them exerting their love. She became shy when all of us implied a love relationship. I deeply regret taking part in spreading the whispers of her affair. Now, I have understood the meaning of her silence. For her, the rumours of the affair were not important."

Mayurakshi smiled sadly and said, "The whispers of her romance helped the murderer to execute his plan smoothly. The killer knew that gossip, in its rawest form, can be used as a strategy to further his selfish interests."

Everyone looked surprised. Mr Trivedi was the first to break the silence, saying, "How could the rumours help the murderer?

Mayurakshi scanned all the faces of the guests and said slowly, pronouncing each word distinctly, "We are talking about a brilliant but ruthless criminal who always does his homework. He is smart, charming, well-read, and understands the psychology of common people. This is not his first crime. He is experienced in committing evil. He might be one of our neighbours or acquaintances. He knew people in a small town like Simlipur would talk and relish if someone made a different decision. Patravali, as Indu pointed out, was a Brahmin widow. When Professor Ahmed came onto the scene, people started talking. The murderer's plan worked perfectly. First, he established a loving relationship with Patravali in a publicised manner. Then he killed her and took her body away. He spread the news of their elopement very cleverly and tactfully. He even confirmed it by speaking to Mrs Indu Raha and Dhaniram. Almost everyone believed the elopement story because the murderer had prepared well and played his part accordingly. The plan would have been completely successful if I had not been interested in her elopement."

Mr Trivedi asked in amazement, "Do you mean that the Professor and the killer are the same one and only person? How did he convince Ayah, Bindi, and Dhaniram? They knew Patravali too well. They knew Timir also. And when did she sell her Senjuti?"

Mayurakshi replied, "Yes, that is the most interesting question. Mr. Lahiri, how did you buy Senjuti when Patravali was already dead?"

Mr Lahiri looked uncomfortable and answered apologetically, "It is my misfortune that I bought this property through an agent. I knew nothing about it except that it was a good investment. But I did not know the details."

"But there has to be a meeting between the buyer and the seller to register the deed. If the seller or buyer is absent, your document can be contested. So, when did you meet her?" Ms Angana Deb asked authoritatively.

"On the 26th of February at the court premises. Detective Dipto Bhanu has seen our papers," Answered Mr Sanjay Lahiri confidently.

Mayurakshi looked at Mrs Lahiri for a moment. She seemed to be a timid person. She lowered her eyes often as Mayurakshi continued her scrutiny. Mayurakshi asked, "Mrs. Lahiri, how are you adjusting here now that you know about Patravali's murder? Ayah also died mysteriously, and Dhaniram's death is yet to be categorised as suicide or accidental or murder."

Mrs Lahiri looked unflinchingly at Mayurakshi for a second. There was a spark of anger before she controlled herself and said politely, "I find this whole thing very annoying and disturbing. We looked forward to starting a family and living peacefully in this small town. We agreed to this Wake for the late Mrs Chatterjee, but now you are insulting us."

"I apologise for your inconvenience, Mr and Mrs Lahiri, but I have to satisfy my... curiosity. When did you come to Senjuti? How did you come? I mean, what was the means of transportation?"

"Why do you ask? Our coming here is nothing illegal. We do not want to sit here and be insulted. You may finish the Wake. We would excuse ourselves." Mr Sanjay Lahiri seemed angry.

He stood up from his seat and started walking out, followed by his wife. He limped slightly, and only Mayurakshi noticed it because she was looking for it.

"How did you get hurt, Mr Lahiri?" Asked Mayurakshi.

"Oh, you mean my limping? That is due to a bike accident," replied Sanjay Lahiri.

"Where were you going on the night of Ayah's death? I saw you leaving that night," Mayurakshi said matter-of-factly.

Sanjay Lahiri looked furious momentarily, but he controlled his emotions and said plainly, "You are mistaken. I was sleeping in my bedroom."

"I am so sorry Mr Lahiri. I am still puzzled by the incident. A fellow passenger had shoved a canvas bag under the berth on the train. Later, she was not found. And neither the other person who had boarded the train at Durgapur. And I think Mr Sanjay Lahiri is the same person who boarded the train at Durgapur station. Police officers were searching for a fugitive criminal, and he was hurt in the leg. You were in disguise. You had shoulder-length hair and a moustache. Your wife or partner had shoved your bag under the berth on the train. You were limping. Would you show us your bike wound?" Mayurakshi finished speaking and stood in front of the couple.

"You are mistaken and do not have any proof of your accusation." Sanjay Lahiri looked around at the spellbound spectators. He stepped a few steps back, and in one swift movement, he started on his feet. Suddenly, Police officers surrounded the area, and Dipto Bhanu ran to Sanjay Lahiri and took hold of him. Several police officers followed him. There were two men with the other police officers. Mayurakshi recognised one of the two men. He was none other than Harman Handa. The other man looked frail.

Dipto commanded, "Sit down, Mr Lahiri." He pointed towards the weak-looking man and said, "I believe that about fourteen years ago, you two were friends. Let me introduce him once more. He is Prakash Sur. He was released from jail after ten years of imprisonment. Do you have anything to say, Prakash?"

The man named Prakash nodded his head. He looked outraged and upset but addressed Mr Lahiri in a controlled manner, "Neelesh, don't you recognise me? Now, I know why you were not charged with murder. You took shelter under Jhimli's skirt. Do you remember how Sajal Haldar was murdered? Where is Jhimli now? She saved you with her statement, but now she must tell the truth. Were you really with her that monsoon night? Did you seduce the poor girl to save yourself? I have told the Police about Jhimli's boyfriend, Rakesh Gupta. I think he can remember how

Jhimli saved you. And someone named Zinnia was trying to contact me. I am sure that she has some evidence..."

The man named Sanjay Lahiri looked a little frightened, and he denied knowing Prakash Sur. He denied knowing Sajal Haldar. Suddenly, in one lithe movement, he took out a small pistol and aimed at all the guests present. He ran towards the low wall of the Gazebo, followed by his female companion. Dipto Bhanu also jumped, and at the same time, Sri Umanath Ji suddenly hit Neelesh with his coffee mug as Neelesh and his wife passed him. Neelesh lost control for a moment, and he fired. The bullet grazed the old priest's left hand, and he cried out in pain. Dipto Bhanu was close behind him, and he pounced on him like a cheetah and caught hold of Sanjay Lahiri. Dipto Bhanu handcuffed him efficiently, and the woman named Mrs Lahiri was also handcuffed. The next few moments were chaotic. Sri Umanath Ji's hand was bleeding. Doctor Dutta attended to his wound. Umanath Ji was taken to the hospital. Everyone present at the Gazebo was stunned and open-mouthed. Mrs Raha looked scared and had nothing to say for the first time.

"Sit down, Mr Lahiri, or shall I call you Rakesh Nag, or how about Neelesh? We have a video statement of Nirmala. She has said everything clearly. You killed Zinnia, too, for the video. By the way, your friend Jaipal has regained consciousness and gave his statement. Now, we also know that Jhimli changed her name and became Nirmala. Tell us how you convinced Jhimli to change her name to Nirmala. How did Jhimli's grandmother die?" Dipto asked sarcastically. Neelesh glared at the detective in answer. His hands were tied back in handcuffs.

"Well, we know how you staged her grandmother's accidental death. And regarding Nirmala, we have other witnesses, such as the resort manager at Mandarmani, to testify against you. We know that you pushed your wife Nirmala into the sea." Dipto Bhanu continued, "You cannot escape. The police of many states want you. Your friend, Harman Handa, has already testified against you. He is now our State Witness. A waiter named Vivek Malakar returned to give his statement against you. You are charged with the murder of

Sajal Haldar. The murder of Jhimli. The murder of Zinnia and the murder of the original Professor Ahmed. You are also charged with the robbery of many vehicles across the country. Your associates are being caught at this moment." Said Dipto Bhanu.

Ms Angana Deb, who had been watching everything quietly until now, said, "I can prove that Mrs Patravali Chatterjee's Senjuti could not be sold because I have her new will. According to her will, this property, Senjuti, and all her money belong to Jhimli's thirteen-year-old daughter. So, Mr. Lahiri, whatever documents you have produced are fake and invalid."

Dipto Bhanu said, "Yes, I forgot to mention your daughter. Where is she now? It must have been Jhimli's decision to send her to the boarding school. She did not take your money for her schooling. Your daughter will tell us how you treated Jhimli or Nirmala."

Dipto Bhanu and his team were preparing to leave when Mayurakshi came forward with Nimmo. She was holding a big basket.

"Please, may I show something? It will take only a few minutes." Mayurakshi asked, and as Dipto Bhanu nodded in agreement, she bent down in front of Mrs Lahiri. Mayurakshi took out a big, wet-looking sponge and started wiping the lady's face. Mrs Lahiri protested as best as possible with her hands tied at the back, but it proved futile. Everyone was amazed to see the dark, patchy skin colour change to a smooth, fair one. Nimmo pulled her hair from behind, revealing long tresses from under the short wig.

"She is the one who stayed with the man who claimed himself as Professor Ahmed." It was Mrs Rosie Alvarez who pointed out at the lady.

Mayurakshi said, "Open your false teeth. I know you are not what you are portraying yourself as. Let us all see your real beauty, Madame Ghost of Rimjhim Chatterjee."

Mrs Raha gasped loudly, and everyone stared as a lady constable, and Nimmo forced her to spit out the rubber in her mouth.

Mayurakshi said satisfyingly, "You are the ghost of Rimjhim Chatterjee. And you are the same person Dhaniram had mistaken for Patravali but later realised you were not Patravali. Umanath Ji saw you leaving with the Professor, and he was confused. Your face is the same as that of Rimjhim's ghostly face. Thanks to Patravali, we have proof of your ghostly appearances. Did you pretend to be Jhimli and convince Ayah to help you?"

The woman glared with intense hatred.

Mayurakshi turned to the man in handcuffs and said, "You made a brilliant plan, but a simple handwritten letter ruined all your hard work. You underestimated the power of the pen and forgot that crime cannot remain hidden. You cannot hope to finish victoriously when you start the journey with lies. Right Neelesh?"

The man could only scowl furiously at Mayurakshi.

Dipto Bhanu and his team took the couple away.

CHAPTER XXXI

An Evening of Stories

23 March 2023

The sun had just gone to see the other part of the world. The living room at Suprabhat was lighted with candles and soft yellow lights. Umanath Ji was in better spirits and sported the wounded arm proudly. The spacious living room at Suprabhat was lively with all the guests who had been present at Patravali's wake. The accused couple were missing. Everybody had adjusted to the arrest of the criminal couple. Now, the guests wanted to know the details of the crime and Patravali's role in the story.

Mayurakshi looked at the lively photograph of Patravali placed among the seats. She felt sad but, at the same time, a little triumphant as she was able to avenge Patravali's murder.

Indu Raha had recovered from the shock of the incident and said in her usual delightful manner, "I couldn't understand all that happened. Doctor Dutta, you knew all these! I am still in the dark and cannot understand why Jhimli's husband came here with his lady love. Mou, when did you know that foul play was going on?"

Mayurakshi replied, "Patravali wrote me a letter which contradicted everyone's viewpoint about her love affair. Indu, do you remember how you called me and insisted that Patravali was in love with the Professor? You were so convinced that they were in love and had eloped. Patravali emphasised her concern about Senjuti in the letter. She was afraid that someone was keeping a constant watch over her. Someone was going through her documents. She mentioned Rimjhim's ghost walking in her garden in her famed red dress. The ghostly appearance was seen only by Patravali, and there was no witness. Her first impression was that Rimjhim's ghost was a real apparition because she had a sort of unhealthy sheen, and instead of walking, she seemed to be floating. Patravali was frightened, but she did not give up. After watching the ghost for several days, she realised that the floating-like walking was achieved with some technical help. And in her letter, she mentioned technological evilness. I thought someone was trying to scare her so she would readily sell her property or perhaps was trying to prove her mentally incompetent to look after her property. But she never wanted to sell Senjuti. She alluded to the protection of Senjuti, Rimjhim's ghost, secretly being watched, new will, journals, and evil schemes, but there was no reference to any new man in her life. The man was not important to her as she was troubled by many other things."

"That means she was intrigued by the appearance of the ghost. What did she do to find out more about the appearance? Did she know the identity of the fake ghost?" Ms Angana Deb asked.

"I don't think that she knew the true identity of the fake ghost, but she was trying to find all the missing pieces of the big puzzle. She filmed the ghost walking in her garden, removed the memory disk from the camera and kept it safe. Then, she started sorting out her documents and made a new will. Her journal was updated with all the major happenings since she came to Senjuti as a bride. Patravali knew that her staff..."

Indu Raha interrupted Mayurakshi in the middle of her sentence and said in a complaining note, "Mou, please will you tell the story from the beginning. I am unable to follow the whole thing. Why should Mrs Lahiri dress up as a ghost and scare Patravali? How did you find out so much? You should tell the story from the beginning."

Doctor Dutta smiled at Indu's reaction and said appreciatively, "Our Mayurakshi has proved herself to be an expert in not only cooking up stories but also revealing other people's secrets. Now, please tell us the story from the beginning."

Mayurakshi began her narration, "I am forever indebted to Patravali for her meticulous documentation of facts. Patravali has helped me to solve the mystery. She wrote about her fears, her findings, and her suspicions. It all began with ego and selfishness. Jhimli was only fifteen when Timir Babu married Patravali. Jhimli could not accept Patravali as her father's new wife because his time, money, and resources were now divided. Jhimli had been neglected by her biological mother, Rimjhim, and was compensated for the loss by her father's affection. Jhimli became unsure of herself as she had grown up knowing her mother's neglect. The sense of abandonment by her mother made her selfish and uncaring, too. Jhimli was studying at a boarding school at the age of fifteen. In the summer break of 2005, she visited Senjuti for the last time. It was the same summer when Patravali had set foot as a new bride at Senjuti for the first time. Jhimli stayed in Kolkata with her grandparents for the following summer holidays. She received a good amount of pocket money and pampering from her grandparents. Her grandmother, Narmada, supported Jhimli in every manner. But despite all the money and the love from grandparents, maybe she suffered from jealousy and restlessness. She was displeased easily. She was known for breaking the hearts of young men. At the time, she had a boyfriend named Rakesh Gupta, but Jhimli fell in love with Neelesh. He was like a magician with girls. The boys were his fans, too. They all obeyed his rules and let him use them mercilessly. He could charm anyone. He was doing a diploma in engineering at the time. He did not come from a wealthy family but had expensive tastes. He got into lousy debt, but his rich friends always saved him. He was not serious about Jhimli until he needed her to be his alibi. Neelesh and his friend Prakash Sur committed the heinous crime of killing a fellow friend, Sajal Haldar. Neelesh and Prakash had hidden Sajal Haldar's dead body. The same night, he went to Jhimli's room and spent the night with her. Jhimli didn't know anything about the murder. She was happy to be Neelesh's girl at last. A few weeks later, Sajal Haldar's dead body was found, and Neelesh had an alibi for the night of the crime. He told the Police that he was with Jhimli at the time of the crime. Jhimli was summoned to give her statement as a witness. She readily issued her statement and gave evidence to the police of Neelesh's stay with her on the night of the murder. Neelesh was set free based on her evidence. Neelesh's partner, Prakash Sur, was arrested for the murder of Sajal Haldar. Jhimli's father and grandfather were against the relationship of Jhimli and Neelesh. Timir Babu and Patravali went to Kolkata to stop the imminent wedding. But Jhimli and Neelesh eloped and married secretly.

Neelesh and Jhimli changed their names soon after their wedding. I think they did that to evade the law. Neelesh became Rakesh Nag, and Jhimli became Nirmala Nag. Jhimli was pregnant was pregnant at the time and gave birth to a daughter. Jhimli gave him all her mother's jewellery and all the bonds in her mother's name. She helped him financially to open his garage and car rental company called Tezz. However, on paper, Nirmala Nag was the owner of the company. Patravali knew about the financial help because Jhimli's grandfather had communicated it to Timir Babu, and she had mentioned it in her journal. Neelesh and Jhimli became cautious in their ways as the daughter grew. When the daughter was about eight years old, Jhimli decided to remove her daughter from Neelesh's crime-filled life. He was already stealing cars and other vehicles at the time. Jhimli contacted her father and asked him to support her daughter's education. Timir Babu readily agreed and wanted to rekindle the broken ties. Jhimli took his money, which Timir Babu paid to her by cheque. Mr Ashok Trivedi was asked to act as the messenger and handed the cheque to her."

"Jhimli had particularly asked me to be the messenger. She did not want to meet her father. She told me that it would not be safe if they met. Timir did not know that she had changed her name. I know this because she had asked him to keep the name blank in the cheque," Ashok Trivedi explained.

Mayurakshi nodded her agreement and continued, "Perhaps she was frightened of Neelesh. We would not know for certain why she refused to meet Timir Babu. About five years ago, Neelesh met automobile insurance agent Harman Handa. They both hatched a brilliant and devious plan of stealing expensive cars. Neelesh and Harman meticulously removed the new cars' chassis numbers and replaced them with old discarded scraps. They did a fine job selling the stolen cars across the border, and the Police could do nothing. They also made a nexus with Jaipal Bajwa, and the three became the most dangerous car thieves. Rakesh, that is, Neelesh, became an expert with practice. He was the mastermind behind the teamwork. They had several drivers, mechanics, and informers working for them. Neelesh had firearms and was involved in several other crimes. Sometime last year, Jaipal Bajwa became estranged from Neelesh while they operated together as a team. Neelesh and Harman Handa were making separate plans."

Everyone was absorbed in the story, but Mr. Ashok Trivedi interrupted and asked, "What does all this have to do with Patravali? How did she become involved? Why was the ghost needed to scare Patravali?"

"Have patience, my dear Lawful. Mou is coming to that, but first listen to the background." Doctor Dutta said.

Mayurakshi smiled and continued, "Jhimli had matured with age and experience. She understood that her father was right to disapprove of her marriage to Neelesh. I cannot tell exactly when that happened, but the realisation started a mental process within Jhimli. She began asking many questions, and Neelesh did not like it. He had been controlling her since the day she got involved with him. But now, Jhimli started resisting and often did not comply with his demands. Jhimli traced back all his ex-friends and started gathering details about his criminal activities, which he took great care to keep hidden. Neelesh's close associate in crime was Jaipal Bajwa, and Jhimli made friends with Jaipal, perhaps to feel secure. Neelesh sensed that Jhimli was changing, and he threatened her. Last year, during this phase in their relationship, they went to Mandarmani. Jaipal and his girlfriend, Zinnia, also went with them. Jhimli gave a video statement to Zinnia, which alluded to the murder of Sajal Haldar. At Mandarmani, Jaipal and Zinnia were busy with themselves, and sometime during the evening, Jhimli drowned. Jaipal and Zinnia were suspicious of the drowning incident. Jhimli's body has not been found till today. In Kolkata, Jhimli's grandmother became anxious and started questioning when Jhimli did not answer her calls. She became desperate and came to know about Jhimli's death. I assume Jaipal gave her the news as Jhimli had befriended him. Last year, on May 28, Jhimli's grandmother called Timir Babu and gave him the news of Jhimli's death. The news of Jhimli's death appeared in a local newspaper, where her name was Nirmala Nag. Timir Babu never recovered from the shock and suffered a heart attack. He died on the same night. His last words were, 'Nir, Nirma, Nir' and Patravali or Doctor Dutta could not understand the implication. At the time, Patravali was shocked and did not know about the phone call. Some months later, she started investigating the phone call. She found out the last call that Timir Babu had received was from Jhimli's grandmother. Her name was Narmada, and Patravali thought Timir Babu was referring to her at the time of his death as Nirma and Narmada are close in pronunciation except for the ii and a sound. Patravali had never met Jhimli's grandmother in person as the grandmother had an aversion to meeting her. She knew about the money given to Jhimli, but then she did not know about the change in her name. Last year in December, she went to Kolkata to meet Jhimli's grandmother and talk about the phone call. She found the house, which was built in a posh locality. The house was locked up, but the little garden didn't look abandoned. She waited for some time, but the house remained closed. Patravali couldn't return without any news of the grandmother, so she went to the next-door neighbour. Mr and Mrs Sneha Mitra lived in the next house. Mrs Sneha Mitra told Patravali that she hadn't seen the grandmother after their return from Bengaluru. They had been visiting their daughter in Bengaluru from April and returned before the Durga Puja in October. She also said that Jhimli's husband had informed the maid that Grandmother Narmada had a fatal accident while she was visiting Jhimli. Patravali became suspicious and wanted to know more about Jhimli and her grandmother. Mrs Sneha Mitra told about Jhimli's daughter and couldn't say much else about her, but whatever she said was enough to make Patravali cautious. In January, she started making new documents for the factory, which she wanted to sell, and for that, she was away from Senjuti when

Neelesh came to visit her in disguise as the professor. He did not waste time; he met Ayah, Dhaniram, and Bindi and planned to use them. He brought his girlfriend, Layla, into the plan. Layla convinced Ayah that she was Jhimli and wanted to scare Patravali for revenge. Ayah agreed readily because Jhimli was like an angel to her. She had brought her up as a daughter. Love can be the most dangerous weapon when used for manipulation. Neelesh, dressed as Professor Faisal Ahmed, came to Simlipur in the last week of January when Patravali was home. She had returned from her visit to the factory. He introduced himself as a friend of Timir Babu. Professor Ahmed, that is, Neelesh, very cunningly narrated true incidents that Patravali could relate to. I surmise that Jhimli had told him of her childhood incidents, which he used in his way. Neelesh knew about Ayah, Bindi, and Dhaniram. He portrayed himself as a learned teacher. He made sure that everyone witnessed his lover-like attention. People like Indu were convinced easily that he was in love with Patravali. He wanted to create the impression that being a Hindu widow, Patravali would be shy to get married to a Muslim gentleman, and so they would elope. His devious plan worked smoothly. Indu, Mrs. Sharma, Mr. Trivedi, and many others believed Patravali had found love again."

Mr. Ashok Trivedi looked stunned and said demurely, "I had no idea about Jhimli's death. I thought Jhimli was somehow responsible for the ghost and the vigilance. I tried to protect her. I did not want Patravali to die in that horrible manner. I never dreamed of Patravali being harmed."

Indu Raha commented sarcastically, "Your affection for Jhimli is quite understandable, Trivedi Ji. She must have looked a lot like her mother." Everyone understood her indication of the love affair that happened a long time ago between Rimjhim and Mr Trivedi.

Mayurakshi observed, "Layla started walking in the garden of Senjuti dressed up as Rimjhim's ghost in a red flowing dress to scare Patravali. Ayah, Bindi and Dhaniram kept their mouth shut. On the other hand, Neelesh professed his love to Patravali in his disguise as the learned professor. And many of the neighbours and friends of

Patravali helped Neelesh establish a loving bond."

Indu was indignant and rude. "How was I to know he was the devil incarnated? I thought she was looking for a man close to her age, and I was helping them come together."

Mr Trivedi said gruffly, "The whole town whispered about the love affair. Their affair was a sensation. If Patravali had not written the letter, no one would have known she was dead. Killed mercilessly. I blame myself for being such a blind..."

Mayurakshi looked sadly at Mr Trivedi. His remorse was genuine. She said, "Yes, the devil's plan was based on the psychology of common people. He knew that people in small towns would love a clandestine love affair and would not think of ulterior motives. If Patravali had not written that letter to me, I would have no choice but to believe her elopement with the learned Professor. You know, whispering lies repeatedly can be dangerous. In this case, it ended with murder. The letter made me look into the matter thoroughly. Layla approached Ayah, Bindi, and Dhaniram. She introduced herself as Jhimli, and they believed her. She narrated Jhimli's childhood memories to convince them of her credibility. Ayah was the easiest to convince. Neelesh wanted to prove that Patravali was insane and could not make any new will. He also wanted to make Simlipur his base. He was starting something big with Harman Handa, and the Club Manager, Mr Das, was also involved. Patravali was fleeing from the attention at the party and went to the first-floor bathroom. Accidentally, she heard some of the secret meeting conversations and recorded it on her mobile. The same night, she was killed. I think Layla was called to pretend as Patravali when Neelesh was taking her body for disposal. But when I came into the scene and asked about Patravali's disappearance, Dhaniram became suspicious. He started gathering evidence of Patravali's disappearance and, in the process, was killed. They could not let Ayah live as she knew Layla as Jhimli. She was the prime witness and would know Mrs Lahiri was the ghost. So, she also had to go. All these would have been very difficult to prove, but Jaipal became estranged from Neelesh. Jaipal wanted to avenge his girlfriend's murder, whom Neelesh had killed recently at the Durgapur Club. Jaipal has given detailed evidence against Neelesh. Patravali has also left enough documents and notes about Jhimli. And Police Detective Dipto Bhanu efficiently gathered other minute details necessary to imprison Neelesh."

Doctor Dutta commented, "In today's digital media, it was surprising that Jhimli or her grandmother had no social accounts. Neelesh controlled them in all aspects. They did not have friends or family, maybe because he threatened to harm their near and dear ones. Jhimli approached Ashok to act as the messenger because she feared for her father's safety. She did not want to harm Patravali either."

Ashok Trivedi nodded in consent.

Everyone became silent and thoughtful. Nimmo brought another round of tea and snacks to liven up the mood. Ms Angana Deb said, "Now that the criminal is behind bars, I must see Patravali's will is honoured. Mayurakshi Bose is the executor of the will, and with Doctor Dutta, she has to take care of Jhimli's daughter. She is at her boarding school in Darjeeling."

All the guests looked sadly at Patravali's photograph and saluted Patravali's courage.

Mayurakshi said gently, "Let me conclude today's meeting by reading a few lines from Patravali's journal as a remembrance."

Indu interrupted and asked, "One last question: how did you know that Mr. Lahiri and The Professor are the same person? And that person is none other than Jhimli's husband?"

Ashok Trivedi said, "And also, tell us about the train passenger's bag you referred to."

Mayurakshi told about the train journey and the hunt for a wounded criminal. She smiled and continued, "As a writer, I often see incidents that can be used in my novels. I saw an interesting episode with the bag during my train journey to Simlipur. I wondered who would gain Patravali's property after Patravali and Jhimli. I did not know about Jhimli's daughter. The only person to gain was Jhimli's husband. Mrs Rosie Alavarez told us about the professor and his lady love. I showed her the photographs taken at Indu's party and the video of Layla dressed as Rimjhim's ghost, and she confirmed. I had seen a cut mark in the train passenger's hand and the same mark in Mr Sanjay Lahiri's hand, too. I wondered about the lady's ghostly appearance and had the idea of disguise. Neelesh had an aversion to being photographed, and there were no photographs of him to compare with. So, it was easy for Neelesh to disguise himself as the Professor and later as Mr Lahiri. Dipto and his team did the rest of the background check for Mr. Sanjay Lahiri and found the deception. After reading Patravali's journal, I could join the dots and complete the picture. I could compare the photographs of Jhimli taken at the resort at Mandarmani with the images of Rimjhim's ghost taken from the video filmed by Patravali. I understood that the ghost and Jhimli were not the same person. Jaipal also gave enough evidence, which Detective Dipto Bhanu shared with me."

Everyone had become quiet and thoughtful.

Mayurakshi said, "Let us remember Patravali by reading one of her journal entries addressed to her husband."

'I pass by that house every day,
It reminds me of a life I once lived.
All my pages were empty until you walked in on a wet July day.
And the monsoon drew your wet footprints on my heart.
At dusk, the trees whisper of beautiful days of spring
when the rosebud had bloomed and filled every corner with
The fragrance of love.'